KATHERINE BELLE

Havenwood

First edition

Proofreading by Ashley Bell
Proofreading by Katelynn Oldham

This book was professionally typeset on Reedsy.
Find out more at reedsy.com

Disclaimer

The fictional town of "Havenwood" is a made-up New England town based North of Boston, Massachusetts. This book makes reference to the "Havenwood Historical Center", "Salem Historical Guild" and the "Massachusetts State Historical Conservancy Foundation". All of these are works of fiction and are not based on or related to real, existing organizations.

Dedication

To my husband, who reminds me every single day why I am a hopeless romantic.

Prologue: Courtney

I kick my wedge-clad foot below the table, allowing it to swing back and forth as I wait anxiously.

It's twenty minutes past our planned meet-up time, and Carter has yet to arrive. I decide to go ahead and order my coffee without him, hoping to avoid any accusations of loitering from the sharp-featured barista who has spent the last agonizing twenty minutes staring me down.

"Hi," I greet her with a smile that is only returned with a look of boredom.

"May I please have an iced chai latte with oat milk?"

"Name?" Is her only uninterested response.

"Courtney."

"$7.75." I retrieve my card from my purse, tapping the rectangular piece of plastic to the reader. The barista's judgmental gaze flickers between me and the "APPROVED" message on the screen, as if surprised the transaction went through.

"You can pick it up at the end of the bar," she informs me with her top lip curled back ever so slightly.

"Thank you," I barely get out before she walks away from me, tugging on her green apron as she goes.

"For $7.75 you'd think the drink came with customer service," I whisper to myself, not appreciating her demeaning air one bit. Her attitude is literally the epitome of Los Angeles culture, and I remind myself that I can't blame my dislike of it on her. Yet when an iced chai latte with oat milk is called for "Whitney" a few minutes later, that sentiment is a bit harder to remember.

I count the seconds as they pass by, watching the ice cubes slowly melt inside my plastic cup, watering down an already weak chai, and Carter is still nowhere to be found. I pull out my cell, noting that he's now thirty minutes late without so much as a text. I debate calling him, but before I decide, Carter enters through the swinging glass door of the cafe, combing back a strand of blond that has dared to move from its gelled position.

My face lights up at the sight of him. Part of me is relieved that he didn't forget about our date entirely. Carter and I have been dating casually for the last six months, and on several occasions, I've had to eat alone at nice restaurants because he forgot about our plans. *Busy men have a lot on their plates*; I try to remind myself each time it happens. At least being stood up at this coffee chain would've been less painful than the time Carter forgot about our date at Flemings.

"Hey!" I wave him down. He cringes slightly as his grayish-blue eyes scan the other faces in the sleek cafe.

"Not so loud, Court." He reminds me in a low voice as he pecks my cheek and takes the seat across the table from me.

"Right, sorry." I giggle. Carter and I aren't *technically* dating, but for good reason. Carter is trying to make it big as an actor, and as such, he can't be seen as someone who is "tied down already." He's worried that he will be typecast as the attractive boyfriend and can't risk that limitation at such an early point in his career. Initially, I didn't understand his reasoning, and admittedly, it stung when he told me we should be seen together as little as possible in public and avoid titles.

Personally, I don't think dating a screenwriter like myself would stunt his career as badly as he seems to think it will. But, as always, it's Carter's way or no way. I suppose I've become desensitized to it all, just glad to have his company whenever he's able to give it. Carter's uncle is a big-name director who constantly has Carter auditioning for roles or making connections, leaving little time for us besides late at night.

"How are you?" I ask, mindlessly rubbing condensation from my cup. Carter crosses his leg over the opposite knee, looking confident in himself as he always does yet weary of our surroundings. I wonder what exactly about the coffee shop has him on edge. Is it the risk of people seeing us?

I look him over, admiring the way he looks so put together. Carter is conventionally attractive, sporting a chiseled jawline and butterscotch blond hair that he always keeps gelled back. His expensive, blue-tailored suit makes his eyes pop against his sun-kissed skin. Anyone can see that he is out of my league, and that is probably why I haven't pressed him to elaborate on the current situationship we had going on, although the question burned inside me daily.

Despite my unrest about our unlabeled status, I have a feeling that today is the day Carter will officially ask me to be his girlfriend. I mean, he probably won't say it like *that*, he'll phrase it more maturely. He'll probably ask me to be *exclusive*, a word thrown around constantly in LA. And of course, I'll say yes.

Why else would he ask me to meet him at this ridiculously overpriced coffee chain at 11 a.m. on a Tuesday when this is normally his sacred gym time?

"Sorry, I waited for you but figured I should probably buy something if I were hanging out here." I signal to my chai. In return, Carter offers me a tight-lipped smile, his eyes squinting despite the smile not reaching them. I can tell it's disingenuous. *Is he upset I ordered my drink without him?*

"I can wait in line with you if-," He cuts me off with a raised index finger, his way of commanding silence when he wants to speak. It always feels extremely degrading when he does that, but I figure that is just one of those things that make Carter *Carter*. I close my open mouth, a questioning look overtaking my face as the words die on my tongue.

"I just had a meeting with my uncle," a proud smirk teases at his oval lips.

"That's exciting, good news?" I raise an eyebrow that follows the pitch of my voice.

"He thinks he'll be able to get me the leading role in his next project." As he tells me this, his smirk turns into a full-fledged grin, putting Carter's pristine veneers on display. "Wow, Carter, congrats." I breathe excitedly, reaching across the table and cupping his hand with my own. He looks down at our hands with an expression I can't quite place. Carter awkwardly pats my hand with his free one, a gesture that is meant to appear endearing but instead feels hollow. His body language reads as a mix of discomfort and disgust, as if I'm a filthy peasant daring to touch a king, not a woman he'd hooked up with a dozen times. He pulls his hands away, folding them together over the table a safe distance away from my own.

"Listen, Court, that's why we're meeting today."

My stomach flips as I note the patronizing tone in his voice.

I pull my hands back cautiously, tucking them into my lap. *Where the hell is this going?*

"What's going on?" I question warily.

"I hate to do this, but you understand." He offers me a look of faux sympathy, and, for being an actor, he isn't very good at pretending to be remorseful. I knit my eyebrows together in response, not trusting my voice enough to ask him straight up what he means by that statement.

He sighs as if I'm making his life more difficult by being unable to read between his very confusing lines. Reality comes crashing down on me as I put together the meaning of his words, hitting me over the head like a rock. He didn't come here to ask me to be his girlfriend at all.

"Are you breaking up with me?"

"Come on, Court. We were never *together,* so I can't break up with you. I just think it's best if we go our separate ways." He gives me a bored shrug. I scoff in disbelief, double-checking my hearing in the process. There had been no prior indication that Carter wanted to go separate ways. He had never expressed being unhappy with me before, and I had abided by every ridiculous rule he had laid before me.

"Can I ask where this is coming from?" I'm too stunned to be emotional or else I might have shed a tear over our relationship ending so abruptly like this. Or maybe I would've kicked him in the balls, but instead, I sit there with my mouth hanging open in disbelief.

"I don't know how much more obvious I can be." Now he sounds flat-out annoyed with me, the way he does when an unhoused person *dares* to ask him for spare change.

"I am going to be a movie star, I'm getting my big break. You are a low-level screenwriter who hasn't worked on anything big in months."

"Carter, there's been a writing strike. " I remind him. He knows that my union and I are advocating for higher pay since the cost of living has skyrocketed, and it's almost impossible for any of us screenwriters to survive in Los Angeles. Many of us are forced to live in cheaper, less safe outer skirts of the city and commute to work. I'm privileged enough to stay within city limits, but my budget is dominated by rent and never allows for much else, a fact that always pisses Carter off.

"Excuses." He rolls his dull blue eyes, the same ones that I had found so attractive not long ago. Now I see them for what they are: cold and unfeeling, even a bit manipulative. He checks his boujee watch, a displeased hum coming from his throat as he notes the time.

"This is taking too long, I'm going to be late for the gym. Look, Court," he repeats the nickname I hate.

"It was fun; we had some good times; now it's time to end things gracefully. I can't date a *nobody*. Please don't embarrass yourself."

He rises from his seat and hesitantly pats me on the shoulder. His look of faux sympathy sliding off his face by the second, only to be replaced with one of relief as he adorns his luxury brand sunglasses and walks out the door.

I stare at him in bewilderment as he goes, finally able to see him for what he is. The gaslighting, calculating, awful side of him is finally shining past the rose-tinted lenses I always regarded him through, and I feel sick to my stomach. *God*, I feel so stupid and so naive for not seeing the signs sooner. Carter Forbes is an awful person, why had I made so many excuses for him?

My cheeks burn with embarrassment, and my throat stings from holding back angry tears, I wish I were anywhere but in public right now. I scuttle out of the overpriced coffee shop, ordering an Uber from my phone as I do.

* * *

Once I'm through the front door of my apartment I head straight for my ratty, old couch. I pull my beat-up laptop into my lap and pop it open, staring at the blank screen before me. Whenever I find myself going through something as emotionally tumultuous as a break up I like to write about it. I prefer to get my thoughts down on paper to help work through them, I like to feel my pain so that I can heal from it. But I don't feel much of anything right now, it's all still so fresh.

I'm out of a boyfriend, out of a job (temporarily), and almost out of money. Luckily, I have a large savings that I spent years building, out of fear of a strike like this lasting as long as it has. However, I don't want to dip into it until necessary, and as of late, it's getting necessary.

I click out of my blank document and look down at the red bubble lingering above my email's spam folder. I drag my mouse to it, drawing the little digital hand in circles over the folder before caving and double-clicking it open.

There they were—the weird, slightly ominous, and random emails from an unknown sender. There are three of them, and they all contain the same content: a listing for a rental home in Havenwood, Massachusetts. The house is a beautiful two-story Cape Cod-style home listed for a criminally cheap price, even for New England's standard.

The emails never surrender any other details, just the picture, stats of the house, and the number to call. I bite my bottom lip, twirling the ring around my thumb as I contemplate my options.

This could be a great start to a temporary hiatus, in which I won't have to think about the strike or bills or how much I hate snobby L.A. culture or men—especially not two-faced, gorgeous, golden boys who drop you like trash when you're no longer useful to them. Before I can talk myself out of it or consider any logistics, I swipe my phone off its charger, nimbly punching in the digits on the screen in front of me.

This will be good for me, I convince myself as the dial tone rings in my ear. No drama, no relationships, no boys. I'll find the first sex shop in Havenwood and buy a top-of-the-line vibrator if that's what it will take.

"Hello? Hi, my name is Courtney. I'm calling about the rental on Queens Avenue in Havenwood, Massachusetts."

Prologue: Finn

Four Months Prior

I rarely acquiesce to Milo's begging to go out to the bars, but it's a Friday night, and I need a distraction. Things within the mayor's office are seemingly going from bad to worse, and despite my best efforts, nothing is stopping the decline or even slowing it down. Don't get me wrong, I love my job; to be the mayor of my hometown of Havenwood, USA, is beyond an honor. However, Havenwood is struggling to keep its head above water, and it isn't easy to see a place you love falling off the map, completely forgotten and overlooked all because a God damn highway was built that bypasses us completely. But I'm looking for a new way, any way, to revive the town and breathe new life into it.

With the weight of the situation on my shoulders, I conceded to driving a few towns over and having a beer with my brother, seeing as Havenwood had no bars. However, upon entering The Grumpy Lobster I immediately regretted my decision. The place is dimly lit with artificial lanterns that cast the place in glowing orange light. Even from my spot in the doorway, I can tell that the bar itself is sticky, which I assume might be part of the "charm" Milo mentioned on the way here. Worst of all, my current situationship, Starr Iglesias, whom I am actively trying to break things off with is seated comfortably on a nearby bar stool. Her dark eyes lock on me as soon as I enter the janky bar, and something within me tells me she is going to be especially hard to shake tonight, the alcohol in her system motivating her efforts.

"Let's order a round before Starr tries to drag you into the bathroom." Milo teases, letting me know he's also noticed her presence here.

"This is exactly why I do not like going out," I remind him as we take two empty seats at the sticky counter. I keep my hands in my lap, unsure what diseases are caked into the bar's wood. We order our beer from the friendly bartender and tip him generously when the pints arrive.

"I had to get you out of that office somehow," Milo says, taking a sip of his beer. His hazel eyes study me as I rotate my pint glass in small circles.

"I haven't seen you this spun up since being elected. What's got your boxers in a bunch?"

I sigh, lifting my gaze from my beer and up to my brother's concerned face. Milo is not the kind of man to let a topic go so easily. Once when we were eight, I had a crush on our classmate Sally, and he bugged me for over two weeks straight until I finally caved in and revealed who my crush was. He didn't go and tell Sally or anyone; he just wanted to know so that he could be in the loop regarding the latest gossip. Not much has changed about Milo's personality since then; he always has to know everything and doesn't stop until he does. It's what makes him such a great historian.

"We all know Havenwood is treading water, it has been since Jerry left office, but things are getting bad, Milo. Really bad. If I don't find a solution soon," I shake my head, once again returning to nervously twisting the beer in front of me.

"Havenwood is done for."

"Okay," Milo nods deeply, processing my words as he crosses one leg over another.

"Then we find a solution," he says matter-of-factly, shrugging his thin shoulders as if the answer were that simple. I let out a dry laugh and run a hand down my face.

"Normally, I appreciate your carefree attitude, brother, but this is serious."

"So am I, deadly so." I quirk an eyebrow at him and notice he's wearing one of those expressions that tells me he has a trick up his sleeve. I groan, anticipating whatever mania he has in mind. Milo is a genius, and he solves any problem you put before him, but he doesn't always play by the rules, nor does he often care about the consequences of his actions and how they affect others.

"Fine," I grumble in desperation, unable to think of anything I have to lose.

"I'll hear you out." I take a hefty swig of my beer, deciding I need at least a little alcohol in my system to consider whatever craziness he's concocted.

Milo clears his throat, giving me a knowing smile before laying out his master plan. "Those remains we found last week," he raises a manicured eyebrow, reminding me of our discovery.

Not even a week prior I had agreed to help Milo search for the burial sight of Martha A. B. Brant, an infamous woman who was tried and killed in the 1690's witch trials and a Havenwood legend. Surprisingly, we had been successful in locating her thanks to new documents Milo had discovered that described her place of burial. Seeing as she was accused of witchcraft she wasn't allowed a church burial and was not afforded a headstone, making her initially difficult to find.

"What about them?" I prompt. My brother is an anthropologist before anything else, and the historian in charge of Havenwood's historic center, so I shouldn't be surprised that he would seek solutions through methods relating to his field of work.

"The tourists are flocking to Salem, completely skipping over Havenwood because of the highway, we can bring them back using the witch's remains."

I rub my chin through my short goatee, contemplating the crazy idea put before me.

"We do need the tourists to rebuild our economy," I acknowledge, Milo nods.

"And Martha is part of Massachusetts' witch history. If we market her story as a missing piece of the trials, the tourists would flock, not wanting to miss out." Milo nods again, more enthusiastically, as I catch on to his plan. Just as I'm beginning to see hope, I remember a fundamental piece of information, causing me to frown.

"Wait, but you told me that Salem's historical guild is trying to claim the remains for themselves; if we lose those remains, we lose this plan."

Milo holds up a thin finger, pausing my line of thought and offering reassurance.

"You are correct. However, I reached out to the Massachusetts Historical Conservancy Foundation to play moderator. They told me that if we're able to locate a blood relative of Martha Brant and get that relative to sign the remains over to Havenwood, she's ours—permanently."

I eye my brother, noting the hopeful expression on his face. I know Milo doesn't want to see Havenwood die. I also know he's worried his career will be over if Salem snatches those remains from under him, so he has a strong reason to want to help.

"How would we even find a living relative of Martha Brant?" I decide to humor his idea, curious about what solution he can find. With a smug smirk, he retrieves his cell phone, padding away at the screen as blue light reflects on his features. Admittedly, I have no idea what he is doing. I still carry a Jitterbug Flip and have no interest in giving in to modern technology, but I wait patiently.

"Boom," Milo exclaims and turns the screen towards my face, the light temporarily blinding me due to the dimness of the bar. I squint my eyes, and a minimalist sketch of a family tree comes into the frame; I scan it until I find the final name on the furthest branch.

"Courtney Berrycloth?" I read aloud just before Milo pockets the device once again.

"People really should be more aware when sending their DNA off to these companies," he remarks, mostly to himself. I make a mental note never to freely give away any DNA.

"Does it say how old this *Courtney* is? She's the last branch of the tree, what if she's a baby?"

"It doesn't say, but that's unlikely. To be added to your family tree, you have to consent by being over eighteen years old. My guess? Ms. Courtney Berrycloth is some lonely old lady with no kids and no spouse, which works in our favor."

"How exactly?" I ask, attempting to absorb all the necessary information despite Milo's rapid speech. He rubs his temple in annoyance as if the answer should be obvious.

"We lure her here and let Havenwood win her over. It won't be hard, considering half the population is over 60, like Courtney likely is. Then we get her to sign on the remains."

Milo's hazel eyes dart past my head, registering motion behind me.

"We'll work out details later."

I crease my brow, opening my mouth to ask my brother what paused him when I feel a familiar hand on my shoulder.

"You boys sure are scheming over here," a very drunk Starr says as she uses her grip on my shoulder for support.

"Hey, Starr." Milo greets, cocking his head, an annoying grin plastered on his lips.

She returns the grin before turning her full attention to me.

"Let's get out of here, Finn." It's not an offer, it's a demand, very uncharacteristic for the most sexually submissive woman I have ever met. Alcohol must really affect her.

"No thanks, Starr. Remember what we talked about? Getting some space?" I gently remind her of our previous conversations, attempting to pluck her fingers off of me.

"Nope," she pops the P sarcastically and grabs my hand, pulling me aggressively from my chair.

"See you later, Finn." Milo wiggles his fingers at me in a mocking wave as Starr drags me towards the door. My eyes are full of pleading for my brother to get me out of this situation, but he ignores me with a laugh.

As we exit the stuffy bar, I sigh in defeat. Starr is already half-naked before even reaching her car.

Fine. One more hookup wouldn't hurt.

1

Welcome to New England

Courtney

Aweek after my *not*-break up with Carter I'm 3,000 miles from my life in California and only minutes from my new, temporary one in Havenwood, Massachusetts. After making the phone call to inquire about the rental house that had been mysteriously flooding my inbox for weeks I was sold within minutes. The kind, older voice on the other end of the phone introduced herself as Agnes Booker and confirmed the rent was, in fact, as ridiculously low as advertised. It only took one look at my dwindling bank account to make the irrational decision to move here. Temporarily.

As I travel down the lightly used back roads of New England I can't bring myself to regret leaving city life behind, even if it is just for a little while. Robust oak, maple, and sassafras trees line the old, winding roads that only sport one lane in either direction. I can't remember the last time I had seen such lush and dense forest cover. Being so caught up in my scenery, I almost miss my turn; if it weren't for a rickety wooden

1

sign reminding me of my destination, I would have missed it completely.

I crank my wheel to the left, taking the unsuspecting exit straight into the sleepy little town of Havenwood.

The woods clear about a mile down the road and cobble-stone streets replace the worn dirt below my tires. The sight of a two-story building retrofitted with a 1980s clock tower welcomes me to town. After passing a few more, equally as old, buildings I approach my first sight of the locals. A handful of gray-haired citizens are completing laps around a large patch of manicured grass, an area I assume to be the park, their heads turning to drink me in as I slowly roll by.

A few of them unabashedly gawk in shock at my presence, but to my surprise, many of them wave. This is my first hint that little Havenwood hasn't seen any outsiders in quite a while. Besides the seniors, the place appears void of life, except for the vivacious foliage that sprouts readily in most places.

I continue through the small downtown scene, reading each business name aloud as I head for the more residential side of town. I'm able to locate Queens Avenue fairly easily due to the town's grid-like build. House 2213, thankfully, actually exists and looks just like the photo on the listing. I hop out of the car and approach the house with a reinvigorated excitement, taking in the details of the property as I do. It appears as if a new layer of white paint has been added within the last decade, which is only noticeable when comparing the house to its neighbors. The grass out front is extremely healthy and trimmed, the owner of the house has clearly taken good care of it.

I step onto the porch and lean against the glass of the kitchen window, cupping my hands around my eyes in an attempt to

2

see into my new rental.

"Good evenin'," a velvety voice greets from behind me, catching me completely off guard. I whirl around and find a woman whom I hadn't noticed before tending to a hedge in the front yard of the neighboring house. Her graying curly hair is cut into a short pixie, and her old, dark skin contrasts the gloomy gray sky above us. She studies me with thoughtful pitch-black eyes that are encased with laugh lines.

"Hi," I greet back, realizing that I totally look like a home invader scoping out her neighbor's house.

"I'm renting this place," I gesture back to the house, awkwardly.

"You must be Courtney? I'm Agnes Booker, we spoke on the phone. Welcome to Havenwood." Her welcome is genuine and warm, just like her smile which reminds me of eating fresh muffins on a cold day.

"Thank you, Agnes." I look over at the house that she stands in front of; it is similar in style to mine, only sporting a much older coat of blue paint. I guess that the big house was her own, internally speculating on whether she has children or maybe a partner to share all that space with.

"Not much going on around here, huh?" I note, resting my hands on my hips as I nod in the direction of downtown, recalling the unimpressive workout scene in the park.

Agnes chuckles at my observation before nodding, unable to deny evident facts. "Havenwood is a dying town, it has been for a good while. We used to be a popular tourist stop on the way to Salem but then they built that freeway," Agnes sighs, pursing her lips as she shakes her head in disapproval. She digs a hand into the pocket of her khakis, pulling out a bronze key with a circular bow.

3

"I lived here my whole 64 years, and I never thought it would get this bad, but you're here, so maybe our luck is changing around."

I give her a shy smile; I'm honored that she sees possibility in my arrival, even if it is short-lived. From Agnes' friendly demeanor and the waves I received on my way into town, I get the sneaking suspicion that people in this part of the U.S. are much kinder to strangers than we are in California. Agnes crosses the driveway, meeting me on the porch and inserting the key into the front door's lock.

"Is there any effort being made to revitalize the town?" I ask out of curiosity, watching the older woman momentarily struggle with the stubborn lock before it relents and clicks open.

"Sure," she straightens, absent-mindedly playing with the pendant on her necklace. "F- the mayor," she corrects herself.

"Does all he can to help this little place, I'm pretty sure it's his life's mission. Bless his heart." She gives me a sad smile.

"But we can hardly pull any of the tourist economy back from Salem and there's not much he can do about that highway. Luckily for me, I run a little bakery that ships statewide, so I stay afloat just fine, I can't say the same for my community. Seems everyone is struggling these days. We need new blood in here, that's what we need." Agnes remarks to herself, nodding decidedly.

The house being listed for so cheap makes more sense now as I listen to Agnes' story. I look over the house, longing to see the inside of my new, temporary home. I sigh happily as I take in its antiquated features and picture myself riding out the writer's strike here in comfy, New England paradise.

"I won't keep you any longer, darling," Agnes announces

making her way down the steps and heading back to her own house. "Enjoy your new home -oh! And close all your windows before night time or else you'll have to listen to the witch crying."

"The witch..?" I crinkle my brow as I process her warning, turning around in search of clarification, but when I do, the old woman is nowhere to be seen. I barely see her front door close, hinting at where she disappeared.

"She moves fast," I note to myself before heading inside.

I enter the house and take in the cozy architecture. As soon as you step inside you're deposited into the main entry room that leads straight into the living room which boasts a gorgeous, red brick fireplace. I can easily envision myself curled up next to the lit fireplace, reading or writing. To my left is a spacious kitchen and to my right is a bathroom as well as the staircase to the second floor.

Like a little kid entering a shopping mall for the first time, I take off running, enamored by the freedom of so much space. I head up the stairs eagerly, making a B line for the biggest bedroom upstairs, mentally claiming it as my own despite not having anyone to compete with.

The primary bedroom is carpeted in beige with modern white walls and two windows that allow for ample natural light to soak in. Another doorway on the right wall leads to the attached bathroom. I allow myself a small shriek of excitement as I take in just how much space I am getting and for such a low price! Something like this in southern California would easily cost $5,000 a month or more and there's no way I could afford that on my salary.

I peek into the two additional bedrooms, both of which are sizable but less updated with floral wallpaper and wooden floors. As I explore the upstairs an inconspicuous door at the end of the hall catches my attention. I swing it open on its creaky hinges and find a second, thinner staircase.

I take only a second to contemplate before hesitantly climbing the stairs which groan offensively under my weight as I ascend. They lead me to a stereotypically dark and dusty attic, the room barely illuminated by a single window that has been left cracked open, allowing a cool daft to drift through. I examine the creepy space, turning my head slowly to scan the A-framed room. An unexpected squeak from above startles me so badly that I let out a screech of my own in response.

"Holy shit!"

A little bat flaps above me, rejoicing in the terror it caused me. Her little peeps of laughter letting me know that she found my fear hilarious.

"You scared the crap out of me," I reprimand the small creature, scolding her like a displeased mother. As my heart slows to its normal rhythm, I inspect the open window that I assume the critter must've entered through.

"Get out of here, shoo! Go back the way you came!" I attempt to coax the bat back out but quickly realize my efforts are fruitless; the rodent clearly has no plans on relocating. It hangs from the rafters, completely uninfluenced, as it watches me through curious black eyes.

"Fine," I relent, too exhausted from my long car ride to fight with a fruit bat. Remembering Agnes' warning regarding witches and closing windows I reach up and do exactly that.

"As long as you promise to eat all the spiders we'll be roommates. For now."

The bat offers me a squeak in response, as if agreeing to my terms. Admittedly, I'm a sucker for animals, even the rabies-carrying ones so I don't entirely mind the bat crashing in my attic. Not that I thought I'd have much choice in the matter. I'd have to think of a name for my little roommate later.

I descend from the attic, closing the small door behind me so the bat doesn't decide to expand her territory into the house. I doubt you can potty train a bat and the last thing I need in my new rental is the lingering smell of guano.

With nightfall approaching sooner than expected, I decide it's time to untie my mattress from the roof of my car and find a way to lug it up the staircase.

That night, after struggling and surprisingly succeeding in getting my mattress up to my bedroom, I slept with only a blanket and throw pillow, too exhausted after driving all day to bother unpacking my entire bedspread.

I lay awake briefly before sleep can overtake me, I replay my day in my head. Aside from the lack of a population under fifty years old Havenwood seems like the perfect spot to lay low until the strike is over and an even better place to hide from romance. Then why does something feel *off*? Something, a thought or a feeling prods at my intuition. It's a hint of familiarity mixed with the feeling of experiencing something entirely new for the first time. It's a feeling that is almost impossible to describe, but regardless, it keeps me awake, staring at the ceiling until my eyelids grow too heavy to hold open.

Finn

The atmosphere shifted this afternoon. The air feels silkier, the early autumn leaves appear more vivid, and a strange buzzing in my chest refuses to cease. It's as if Havenwood is a photo, and someone has amplified its vibrancy, myself, along

7

with it. I sit at my desk inside my office at city hall, and even though I'm currently reviewing the town's dwindling budget, I feel a weird sense of euphoria, a calm that one shouldn't feel when the fate of an entire town rests on one's shoulders. Yet here I am, as content as could be without any indication as to why.

The hum of an engine outside the window piques my interest and I rise from my chair to investigate. Not many Havenwoodians choose to drive, saving their gas for when they have to make the rare trip out of town. You can leisurely walk from one side of town to the other in under thirty minutes, so I doubt the sound is a local. I peek out the glass and sure enough, an unknown SUV is rolling past city hall. I'm unable to see into the vehicle or identify the driver due to my high vantage point on the second story but I am thoroughly interested. Is it a tourist, perhaps? I can only hope.

I pluck my coat from its hanger, intent on following the car from a not-creepy distance to find out who exactly is inside. My cell phone buzzes from within the pocket of my coat, I reach in and flip it open, answering the call.

"Hello?" I trap the device between my shoulder and my cheek as I push my arm through the sleeve of my coat.

"She's here." Milo's voice sounds uncharacteristically serious over the phone. I stiffen, knowing exactly who he meant. A wave of adrenaline flashes down my spine as I comprehend the gravity of his words. The plan worked, it *is* working, stage one of it anyway. I run a hand into my dark hair, taking the time to process.

"If you see her before I do, make sure you send her to the historic center. We want her to get comfortable with Havenwood's plight as soon as possible and history can help us with that."

I nod, even though he can't see it.

"How do you know it's her?"

"Mom just called. It's her." Relief floods me as I accept, for the first time, that Havenwood might have a chance. I might be able to save this town, the only remnant of my parents.

"Finn, one more thing. She isn't exactly what we expected."

2

Oat Milk Latte

Courtney

Sunlight flows in from the windows on either side of my mattress, warming my body in the spots where it touches and bathing my new bedroom in soft morning light. I take in an annoyed grumble of a breath; it can't be later than 7 a.m., but the room's brightness refuses to let me fall back asleep. After several days of traveling, waking up early wasn't exactly in my plans for today but it seems I have little choice in the matter. Curtains will need to be purchased ASAP, as well as a bed frame and all the other furnishing that make a house a home, even if it is temporary.

I hold up a hand to block the sun from burning my eyes as I sit up on my mattress. Despite the rude awakening, I want to make the most of my day, and if the day has to start at 6:35 a.m., then so be it. Today marks day one of my new interim life here in Havenwood, and I'm keen to explore the charming town —and see if anyone below 40 years old exists here.

Back home, I always started my mornings waiting for a turn to use one of the rundown treadmills my apartment complex offered in their quickly deteriorating gym. The complex's gym was small and stuffy, and most of the machinery didn't work properly, but it was a lot safer to work out there than to risk the streets of L.A. in the dark early hours of the morning. That is one of my many qualms with Los Angeles, and city life in general, but something tells me I won't have to worry about my safety in little Havenwood. *If one of the residents attacks me, I can just kick their cane.* I laugh to myself, envisioning one of the old folks I'd seen in the park attempting to mug me.

I dig through one of the many suitcases that I'd managed to lug up the staircase last night, searching for a cute but casual outfit to jog in. After I find a suitable one, consisting of a matching cobalt-colored legging and crop top set, I layer it with a puffer jacket. Despite it being early September, New England is proving to be chilly compared to the California autumns I'm used to, where the lows rarely dip below 45°.

I trot down my new staircase, the patter of my footsteps against the wood sounding almost musical as I go. Everything about this house feels like a benison, a reprieve from the stress and struggles of my chaotic life. I step out onto the front porch, the gelid air reddening my cheeks. The same feeling of relief moves with me and extends past the walls of 2213 Queens Avenue, the solace I feel engulfing the entire town.

I jog blissfully along the cobblestone street that feeds into downtown, lost in my own head as I relish in the historic ambiance, reminiscing on a time when pilgrims might've made their way down these very same corridors. The same richly colored leaves that had welcomed me to town yesterday are sprinkled along my path, a sense of acquaintanceship with them causing me to smile. I can see why people romanticize living in small towns like this, the first hints of a New England autumn filling my chest with a gooey feeling of excitement.

I slow my pace as I retrace my steps back to the park and once again see the senior crowd completing laps around the green grass. I watch them as they orbit, something has most of their attention drawn to the one edge of the field. I follow their lines of sight and notice a pair of women, both of which stick out like sore thumbs among the older crowd. Both women are clad in black and moody red clothing with fishnets incorporated into their tops and worn below their ripped jeans.

Living in LA, you see all kinds of people, so the women don't immediately strike me as out of place, despite their traditional setting. I watch them staple a poster to a tree, the details of which I can't make out for certain due to being so far away. However, even from this distance, I can see that the older folks are not thrilled with the women's presence.

As I focus my eyes, attempting to read the print on their poster, one of the two women turns around, whipping her oxblood red hair over her pasty shoulder. Her dark, juniper green eyes lock on me right away as if she sensed me watching them. I almost jump at how deliberately her gaze lands on me. She gives me a once over before her eyes narrow and her upper lip raises ever so slightly, snarling at the sight of me. Then she once again gives me her back, returning her attention to fiddling with the poster.

"Yikes," I mumble to myself, severely weirded out by the unpleasant interaction. I decide it's best to keep moving. Clearly, I'm not going to make any friends at the park so I continue, following the route I had entered through town. I know I passed a coffee shop yesterday, and a hot caramel latte with oat milk is calling my name.

I locate the shop with ease. The dated diner-themed sign above the front door reads **Mystic Brew—Coffee House**. I note how faded the large lettering looks, it's rustic charm is a stark contrast to the pristine signs of L.A. coffee chains. A small bell attached to the door frame alerts the single worker to my arrival.

"Hi, welcome in!" The young woman at the front counter gives me a pleasant smile, her existence proving that there is at least one Havenwoodian under thirty.

"Thanks," I respond shortly, a bit intimidated by her overeager eye contact. I've never seen a barista excited to see a customer; baristas at large coffee chains act like ordering a coffee from them is a personal inconvenience. This positivity is definitely a refreshing change but one I will need to adjust to.

I take a few steps into the shop, making my way to the register and admiring the inside decor as I go. Contradictory to the white walls of most minimalist L.A. coffee shops, this place is moody with stained wood walls that host copious amounts of photos, kitschy antiques, and quirky signs in various colors. Intricately designed black tables and chairs are scattered throughout the small space, adding a welcoming vibe that encourages you to sit and enjoy your coffee here.

"May I please have a hot caramel latte with oat milk?" I ask once I reach the front counter, briefly studying the woman standing behind it. She looks to be in her early twenties, a few years younger than myself with freckles dusting her round face, arms, and likely, the rest of her. Her ginger hair is weaved into a loose braid on her shoulder and a pair of green glasses frame her small brown eyes and thick black lashes.

"Oh wow, let me double-check. I have oat milk," she

exclaims, seemingly surprised by my choice of alternative milk. She ducks down to check inside a mini fridge before bouncing back.

"Sure do," the barista confirms, checking the expiration date on the side of the jug. "Alright. That will be $4.50."

"$4.50?" I raise a suspicious eyebrow. She nods, her braid bouncing as she does, that overly joyous smile still plastered on her thin lips.

"It's normally $4, but oat milk is a fifty-cent upcharge - inflation, ya know?"

I hand her a five-dollar bill from my pocket, still confused over the cheap cost of my coffee. How can a business profit at such a cheap price? When she hands me my change back I deposit it into the tip jar resting between us.

"Do you need my name?" I offer.

"Oh," She giggles, pushing her glasses up her nose.

"Of course, what's your name?"

"Courtney," I tell her, expecting her to write it down on a plastic cup instead, she extends her hand.

"Nice to meet you, Courtney. I'm Elsie," I look around to ensure no cameras are set up for a hidden prank show. After a thorough search, I laugh softly at myself and shake the girl's hand.

"Nice to meet you, Elsie. Do you own this place?"

She appears to be the only person on staff, which seems odd for a coffee house at 7:30 in the morning, but what do I know? Maybe she is a one-woman show.

"Not exactly," she sighs, smoothing a nonexistent wrinkle on her walnut-colored apron.

"My grandmother is the owner but I'm our only employee." The corner of her mouth tips as she finishes her sentence, signaling that she doesn't mind that fact.

"I'll get your latte made," she beams at me before whipping around and busying herself grinding espresso.

I take a seat at one of the many open tables, still slightly baffled by the young barista's enthusiasm and kindness. *I wish she were my barista the day that Carter-* a buzz from my pocket prevents me from finishing that thought. I fish my cell phone out of my pocket, the notification on my screen alerting me that I have a text from Kashvi, my coworker and best friend. She was the hardest thing to leave behind in California.

Kashvi: Negotiations not going good :(strike may be lasting a while. How's New England? Any hot warlocks?

Her message causes me to exhale through my nostrils, the only thing that would make this little furlough better was if she was here with me. But Kashvi's parents were very family-oriented, bordering on strict, and wouldn't approve of her moving states. Even though it was temporary, and she's an adult, I wouldn't hold it against her. I'd just have to make some new friends while I'm here, given how friendly most everyone is it doesn't seem like it will be too difficult.

The door of the shop opens and dings once again.

"Hi Fred, hi mayor," Elsie calls out casually.

I raise my eyes from my phone screen to examine the two men who have entered the shop. One is in his fifties with graying hair and a rounded belly; the other is closer to my age, in his late twenties or early thirties. He's undeniably handsome with sharp cheekbones and raven-colored hair that matches his well-manicured goatee. Both men laugh together as the older one, presumably the mayor, insists that coffee is on him this time.

The younger one's eyes are still squinted with laughter when they land on me. The second they do, I watch them round at the edges, putting his gorgeous blue irises on display. That weird gooey feeling from earlier rises in me with a vengeance. *Get it together, Courtney!*

The older gentleman orders his drink from Elsie and then turns back to his stunned colleague.

"What're you having, mayor?"

Mayor? So the young, attractive guy is the mayor and the older man is Fred? I couldn't have pinned them more wrong. I had assumed that a sleepy town like Havenwood would have an old man for a mayor, not a tall, dark, and handsome one with amazing arms...

"Oh," He blinks rapidly, turning his attention to the counter.

"Latte please, Elsie. Thank you, Fred." Then his attention is back on me and I feel like I'm sitting under a heat lamp and a spotlight simultaneously. My palms go clammy as I become hyper-aware of my breathing, *is it too loud? Is it too fast? Oh shit, he's walking over here.*

"Hello. I'm Finn Abernathy. You must be Courtney?" He greets me, sliding one hand into his pocket and extending the other to me. After a prolonged beat, I accept his hand, the feel of his smooth palm against mine doing weird things to my vagina.

"Uh, yeah, how'd you know?" I raise an eyebrow at him as he politely shakes my hand.

"I'm the mayor; it's my job to know every resident of Havenwood." He flashes me a beautifully imperfect and timid smile. If I didn't know any better, I would've guessed that Mayor Finn Abernathy was nervous to talk to me.

"Plus," he adds with a knowing shrug.

"Agnes is my mom."

I nod slowly. Recalling the image of my landlady and comparing it to the very pale man in front of me, my eyebrows knitting in confusion.

"*Adopted* mom," he clarifies with a chuckle. I offer him an uncomfortable, small laugh, realizing how insensitive it is of me to question their relationship. Luckily the friendly barista interrupts us, setting my coffee down in front of me and saving me the embarrassment of explaining myself.

"Enjoy!" She remarks before toddling off to make Fred's coffee. I look down and am surprised to see a cream-colored ceramic mug in front of me instead of a disposable cup with a cardboard sleeve. I smile a little at it, deciding this is another thing I like about the way things are done here.

"Well, you already found the best coffee shop in town," the mayor says, pocketing his other hand and nodding toward Elsie.

"The only coffee shop in town," Fred whoops from behind us as he pays for the lattes. "He's not wrong," the young mayor relents, chuckling as he scratches his dark brow. So this was the man Agnes had talked about, her son, the mayor who is doing all he can to save the town of Havenwood. To my dismay, knowing the nobility of his actions makes him even more attractive. I will need a literal ice bath to wash the image of Finn Abernathy from my mind.

"When you get a chance, you should check out our historical center. We poured a lot of resources into upgrading it. Milo, our historian, will be thrilled to give you some Havenwood history—if you're interested."

I shoot him a soft smile. This guy is *cute*, in like a Clark Kent kind of way and I am infuriatingly eating it up. What happened to my no-boys rule? I convince myself that I should

17

shake him now so I'm not tempted during the rest of my stay.

"Thanks for the suggestion," my words come out sounding more uncomfortable than cold as I had intended, causing him to bow his head slightly. *Did I embarrass him? Shit, that's the last thing I wanted to do.*

"I am! I am interested. I'm on a tour of town so I'll probably stop there next. Thank you." I word vomit, unable to stand the sight of him looking even the slightest bit dejected.

His blue eyes meet mine again, a bashful smile crawling onto his face. I take solace in the fact that at least he doesn't look like a kicked puppy anymore, but now I notice the little gold flex in his eyes, and I physically have to pry my attention off of him. I redirect it down to my caramel latte which has exceeded all my expectations, much like the mayor has.

"I've taken up enough of your time, enjoy your day, Court-ney. It was a pleasure to meet you." Why did he have to say it like that? In his deep, sexy voice? As if meeting me truly was a highlight of his day? Pull it together, Courtney. *It was a pleasure to meet you too.*

I only nod in response, resting my eyes back on the light brown liquid in front of me. The two men exit the coffee house, the bell above the door signaling their departure. Before I can pull out my cell again to text Kashvi back the red-headed barista is sitting across from me, her jaw dropped in a cartoonish fashion.

"Oh. My. Gosh. Finn was totally into you!" Elsie gawks, her hands splayed on the table in front of her.

"What? No. Can you keep your voice down?" There's no one else in here, but I don't want to risk someone overhearing her—or, worse yet, the mayor hearing her.

"He totally is," she whisper-yells, which is not really an

improvement.

"I think you're mistaken. He was just welcoming me to town. That's what mayors do." My eyes fly to the window, desperate for another glimpse of him. My words are anything but convincing. I don't even believe myself, but I haul my mug up to my lips to relieve myself from having to say anything more.

"Nuh-uh," Elsie persists.

"I haven't seen him this goo-goo since he went around with Starr. He didn't even seem half as interested in her as he seemed in you!"

Who's Starr and why do I suddenly care? I set my mug down, forcing a polite smile.

"Elsie, I did not come to Havenwood to date. I came for peace, quiet, and quality *me* time." I hint to her, raising an eyebrow. She picks up my meaning and rolls her eyes with a smile.

"Okay, be stubborn, but I watch a lot of RomComs, and this is the start of one. Mark my words." She gets up and resumes her position behind the counter. I laugh to myself once she can no longer see me, Elsie reminds me a lot of Kashvi but in a different sort of way that comes with adolescence.

I pull out my cell and ramble off a text.

Me to Kashvi: Nope. Just me, myself & I

3

Witch Trial

Courtney

I watch the brown acorns crunch between the soles of my shoes and the cobblestone street I find myself traveling down. I could walk on the paved sidewalk like a normal person, but the lack of traffic makes the historic roads too tempting not to utilize.

I follow the instructions the barista gave me as I make my way to the Havenwood Historic Center. She said to take a left at the split oak tree and then a right at the house with three chimneys. It isn't the type of directions I'm used to, but they make as much sense as they need to, and after turning right upon spotting a house with three chimneys, I actually end up in the right place.

A freshly assembled metal sign hangs from a post outside the historic center announcing it as such. I turn my attention from the sign to the building itself, the structure resembles a newly renovated version of a 17th-century church, virtually preserved in every way aside from a new coat of paint and gold placards spotted along its front. I eye the tower decorating the top of the building, wondering if an old-fashioned bell resides inside of it. *Why had the mayor suggested I visit this place?*

He mentioned that the historic center was newly remodeled, and maybe he simply wanted to show it off, but that explanation feels hollow. There must be another reason why Finn Abernathy wants me to see this place. My desire to decode his motivations is the sole reason I ascend the narrow walkway leading to the historic center's front door.

As I approach, I take in the rows of arched windows lining the center's facade, rapping a timid beat against the door when I reach it. I half expect a colonial-era priest to answer based on the design of the establishment but I'm pleasantly surprised when a very modern, yet very confused-looking man answers instead.

"Hi," I greet, feeling the need to look as harmless as I am under his scrutinizing gaze. The unwelcoming way he fills the doorway tells me he's attempting to determine the reason for my visit.

Despite his unfriendly demeanor, it's easy to see he is good-looking. He is approximately 6 feet 2 inches tall and lanky, with short black hair that tapers the closer it comes to his ears. His sepia-brown skin is complimented by his periwinkle blazer, the matching suspenders he wears underneath speak to his impeccable style and manicured look.

"I'm Courtney. I just moved here, and Mayor Abernathy told me I should check this place out, so... that's why I'm here." I finish with a less-than-confident smile, rocking anxiously on the heels of my sneakers. I look down at the scuffed-up workout shoes, suddenly feeling like a fashion flop in his well-tailored presence.

I watch a metaphorical cog turn into place somewhere inside his head right before his confusion melts away, quickly replaced with surprised excitement.

"Holy shit," he exclaims, his expletive very much contrasting his setting. He smacks a palm to his forehead in disbelief of himself.

"Come in, immediately." He hooks an arm around my shoulders, pulling me into the naturally lit main room of the historical center. Once I'm whisked inside with the door closed behind us, he strolls past me further into the wide room, and I immediately begin to reprimand myself for letting a stranger lure me into a building by myself. I look around the large room, noting the rows of pews before us, an homage to the building's former identity as a church.

"I apologize for my coldness. We have another historical guild breathing down our neck right now. Seeing as I didn't recognize you, I knew you weren't a local, and I figured you were one of *them* coming to harass me." He throws his hands expressively as he speaks, extending one out to me before I can respond.

"I'm Milo Booker, anthropologist, historian, and head of the Havenwood Historical Center." I admire his coral nail polish as I take his hand and give him a polite shake.

"Booker? Is everyone in this town related to Ms. Agnes?" I raise a brow. Surely Finn didn't send me here just to meet his relative, but it is an interesting coincidence—another piece of a confusing puzzle.

Milo gives me a full-lipped smile. He removes his thin-framed glasses from their resting place high up on his nose and confidently swipes any smudges from the lenses.

"Agnes is my mother. That mayor you referenced? He's

my adopted brother and best friend." The well-decorated historian does a visual scan of me from head to foot and then back up again, searching for an answer to a silent question.

"What brings you to Havenwood, Courtney?" Milo ticks his head to one side, leaning against one of the replica pews as I formulate a short versioned answer. For some reason that I can't explain, it feels like he's anticipating my answer before I even begin.

"I'm actually a screenwriter from California but we're on strike right now, so I figured now was the perfect time to take an extended vacation." I omit any mentions of a breakup with a D-list actor that had contributed to my decision to move here. My "no boys" rule also extends to discussing my breakup, the last thing I want for this trip is to dwell in my heartbreak. I want to take all the pain and anger and simply compartmentalize it away until I hop back into my car and drive back to LA.

"I saw an advertisement for your mom's rental and it just felt like a sign," I raise my eyes to the high ceilings of the former church.

"Or, er, divine intervention?" Milo's light eyes flash with a flare of knowing before it's quickly extinguished.

"I hope Havenwood will be the resolution you're looking for." He says distantly, picking himself off the wooden pew and strolling down the center of the room.

"Follow me, I have lots of fascinating history to show you!" He calls, obviously expecting me to fall in line and keep pace. I laugh a little as I obey, so far thoroughly enjoying all the personalities Havenwood has to offer but not so much its secrets.

Milo embarks us on a brief tour of the historic center, the

antique pews take up a majority of the first floor but the remaining space hosts a small display dedicated to Havenwood's roots. The second floor consists of a storage room filled with records, artifacts, ecofacts, and anything else deemed too precious to be kept in the display on the main floor. The rest of the second story hosts Milo's office, which doubles as a library; the entire wall behind his desk is dedicated to bookshelves filled with historical texts.

I do a lap in the small office, discretely eyeing the papers that clutter the lamp-lit desk.

"Milo, you mentioned another historical guild is breathing down your neck? What do they want?"

The tall historian shifts his weight as he considers his answer.

"I'm sure you've noticed Havenwood isn't exactly New England's number one tourist spot?" I nod, recalling the town's languid feel and Agnes' story about the town's decline after the freeway was built.

"Tourists used to flock here, they would stop on their way to Salem to see the sights and hear about the witch trials- trials that Havenwood was heavily involved in."

I swallow hard, only now considering the fact that this side of the United States has a lot of dark history that California was too young to have ever known. A shiver flies down my spine as I acknowledge my temporary home having ties to the infamous 17th-century witch trials.

"Nobody stops here anymore, they bypass us and go straight to the tourist traps in Salem. Havenwood is dying because of it as I'm sure you've learned by now." I offer another nod, confirming I've heard the town's plight.

"With the new freeway built, there's no draw to loop back

and see Havenwood." I acknowledge.

"We *had* no draw BUT we uncovered something big recently and Salem wants it. But they're gonna have to pry it from my cold, dead hands." He flexes his long fingers to emphasize his point, his excited demeanor returning at the mention of this secret weapon meant to boost Havenwood back to its former glory.

"What did you find?" I ask curiously, finding myself more invested than I originally thought.

"That's for another time," Milo gives me a smirk before shooing me out of his office.

"Let's go, Hollywood. I've got some work to do now."

I feel disappointment sink in as I follow Milo's lanky frame down the spiral stairs and towards the front door. *How can he reveal that he has a secret weapon up his sleeve that might save the town but refuse to share it?* I justify that he might not want to tell me because I'm an outsider, unsure if I'm someone he can trust. Regardless, I'm already mentally making plans to return and get some more local history from him and hopefully, more answers to my questions. As we pass the display on the first floor something about it catches my eye.

"Who is that?"

Milo turns his head, his eyes slightly rounding at the corners before a collected expression washes over him. He takes a few steps towards the portrait that caught my attention, staring up into the warm brown eyes of the woman portrayed in the painting.

"That is Martha A. B. Brant. A Havenwoodian woman who was accused of witchcraft in the 1692 trials and was burned for it at the stake. A lot of modern historians ignore her story but she's a major part of our history here and our urban legends."

Milo lifts his eyebrows at me, invoking a grin.

"Local lore says she was innocent, wrongly accused, and wanders the streets of Havenwood crying and seeking justice."

I rub my arm, fending away goosebumps, this must be the witch Agnes warned me about. I've never been one for ghost stories but something about this one fascinates me. I thank Milo for his time and prepare to retrace my steps home when he calls out to me from the front porch of the historical center.

"Hey, California. You should take a peak at the apothecary."

"What did you just say to me?" A smile pushes his sharp cheekbones skyward, enjoying my immature sense of humor.

"Apothecary, you know, a store where people sold medicine before insurance companies ruined the world? My friend Micah runs the place for his mom. Check it out, thank me later."

The anthropologist provides me with more unofficial directions involving taking a hard left at the turkey pen. I give him a final nod and set out to find the apothecary.

Finn

I stand on the short side of the metal restaurant-grade table watching Agnes tuck and fold a piece of dough into itself over and over again. The repetitive motion reminding me of the acrobatics my stomach has been engaging in since the moment I met our new transplant, Miss Courtney Berrycloth.

"She is very pretty," Agnes points out the obvious, attempting to add a glimmer of positivity to my negative mood. She had clued into the root of my uneasy energy the moment Milo and I entered the bakery. I watch her soft hands knead the dough until it hits the perfect consistency.

I take a deep inhale, a failed attempt at collecting my stray thoughts. The warm, buttery, sweet smell of the bakery fills my lungs with a false comfort. It has a way of providing a level of calm even when one isn't present, the same magic is soaked into Agnes through her hair, clothes, and probably even her soul. It is a lovely fragrance that follows her, one she can't shake, not that she would ever want to.

"She wasn't supposed to be... *her*. I thought she'd be an old woman, I thought she'd be-"

"Someone you'd be okay with manipulating?" Agnes raises a dark eyebrow, not bothering to look at me as she separates the dough mound into smaller clumps. I deflate at her words, simply because they are true.

I had sent those enticing emails promising a cheap rental envisioning the ideal candidate on the receiving end. Someone old, without much family or commitments, who needed a cheap place. Someone who would be willing to sign on the dotted line when Havenwood eventually worked its way into their heart, as it did with anyone who stayed here long enough. It was supposed to be someone I wouldn't have any deeper connection with. Courtney is someone I definitely want to pursue a deeper connection with but how can I, now that our meeting is based on lies?

"Milo told me she'd be someone with no friends or family who would love the opportunity to move to a community-oriented town like Havenwood. He said she'd be an old lady, and instead, she's the reincarnate of Elizabeth Taylor!" Only Courtney is far more beautiful than Elizabeth Taylor, more beautiful than any Hollywood woman who had come before her. But they do bear some resemblance in their vixen brown hair and entrancing eyes.

"I think you're overthinking it," Milo inputs from his seat

beside me, his cupped palm full of dark chocolate chips. He pops a few into his mouth.

"This girl is our ticket to saving Havenwood and yeah, *she's cute*. I'll give you that but you're losing a battle to your dick on this one."

"Milo, language." Agnes pins him with a motherly glare. Milo raises his hands defensively.

"I'm sorry, Ma. Just saying it how it is." Milo's deep hazel eyes turn back to me, his face settling back into one of disagreement.

"We need her," he reminds me, stressing his point.

"If we don't get those remains signed over to us by Halloween, we're going to lose them to Salem. I am going to be out of the best anthropological discovery of my life. You are going to be out of a tourist cash cow, and Havenwood is going to be off the map entirely."

I rub at the dark facial hair on my chin, a bad stress habit I'd developed. I force my hand away as Milo continues his scolding.

"We were lucky I was able to track Martha's bloodline down to Courtney. We were even luckier that you were able to lure her here with discount real estate. Everything lined up perfectly to bring her here. There's a reason for that, and we can't fumble now."

As much as I hate to admit it I know he's right. Every star has aligned perfectly to get Courtney to Havenwood and we can't lose this chance, a chance for Havenwood. Now that we led the horse to water we'd have to force it to drink and subsequently drown any chance of me having an honest relationship with Courtney.

"Maybe you should call up Starr for a quick fuck so that

post-nut clarity will remind you of what's at stake here." Milo huffs, crossing his long arms across his chest.

"Milo David Booker." Agnes slams her flour-covered hands on the table, causing us both to shrink into ourselves.

"I do not want to hear any of that about my sons." She swats his words out of the air with a disgusted look.

"Yes, Ma," Milo responds, much less confident now, aware of the fact that he'll get smacked with the rolling pin if he crosses the line again.

"I hate this." I sigh and drag a hand down my face, resting it on my chin where I once again begin to rub.

Agnes' eyes shift from scolding Milo to comforting me, a waft of sympathy overcoming her brown orbs. My adoptive mother hates lying and dishonesty more than just about anything, this plan of ours has ground against her morals since the moment Milo and I concocted it. It took two weeks and multiple sessions of convincing to get her to allow us to use the rental on Queens Avenue as our bait. But now, she says nothing in the way of disapproval. Proving to me just how dire Havenwood's situation is for a strong woman like Agnes to accept resorting to deception.

"Very well," I say, lowering my hand and slapping it against my thigh as it drops.

"The plan continues as originally intended."

4

The Apothecary

Courtney

The apothecary shop is easy enough to spot, a giant sign hangs above the structure reading, *HERBAL HEALTH & HEALING*.

This shop is situated in a much more humble building than the historic center. The structure consists of only one medium-sized room lined floor to ceiling with shelves so densely packed with yellowing jars that sunlight has to fight to make its way into the cramped space. The apothecary has a distinct smell of dust and aging wood, but it only adds to the shop's classic charm. I keep myself busy by reading the jars' labels while waiting for this Micah person to appear.

"Hey gorgeous, you lost?" A deep voice calls from the back of the store.

I peek my head around a cluttered set of shelves and spot a particularly muscular cashier standing at the register, a suave smolder on his face.

"Hi, I didn't see you there. You must be Micah, Milo's friend?" I greet him, tucking a brown strand behind my ear to distract from the faint blush unfurling on my cheeks. I take a few steps closer to the man, each wooden floorboard letting out a noticeable groan of protest as I move, hinting at how old this place is.

"I'm Micah, everyone's friend," His amber eyes indiscreetly slide down my torso, lingering momentarily on my chest and then back up to my eyes. I clear my throat, pretending I don't notice the liberties he is taking while looking at me.

"Including yours. You must be Courtney?"

I raise an eyebrow, noticing once again that I've let myself wander into a tight space with a man I do not know. What's worse, this man mysteriously knows my name.

"How did you know my name?"

His tan skin runs pale as his facial expression morphs into wide eyes and slightly puckered lips as if he sucked on a particularly sour candy. Also known as the, *"Oh Shit I Said Something I Shouldn't Have"* face. His expression smooths out, allowing his unnecessarily attractive smolder to return.

"Lucky guess. I heard we were getting a new resident, and there's not a lot of new faces around here, especially ones as pretty as yours." He shoots me a flirtatious wink, and my blush is back in full force. *No boys, Courtney.*

"Milo said I should check this place out, he said I wouldn't regret it." I wince as the words leave my mouth, suddenly understanding Milo's meaning. The historian hadn't been referring to the antique medicines decorating the shelves or the natural remedial herbs for sale, he meant the sexy cashier in a tight-fitting shirt. I silently curse Milo for setting me up like this, he knows I just had a bad breakup, so why put this good-looking, frisky man in front of me?!

"Oh yeah?" Micah swipes his tongue over his bottom lip,

lowering his eyes to the floor as his ego is boosted.

"I bet I know why he sent you here. Wait right here." Micah palms the counter before disappearing behind an old curtain that covers a hallway to the back portion of the shop. As he pulls the curtain aside, I can see that the back half of the building is set up as a functional little apartment. I assume that must be where Micah and his mother live. He reemerges seconds later with a small plastic bag.

"Heard you're from California, here's a little present so you don't get homesick." He reaches for my hand, holding it open in his own as he places the baggie into my palm. He's so close I can feel the heat radiating off of his broad body, his warmth doing something to me it *really* shouldn't be. Suddenly, my plan of hunting down a sex shop and buying a vibrator is at the top of my to-do list.

I take an unwilling step back and clear my throat again before examining the contents of the clear bag. Inside the tiny bag sits a hefty green bud of marijuana. I laugh at the sight of it, its mossy exterior appearance and deep color telling me it came from a well-grown plant.

"That's a really nice gift, thank you." I chuckle, depositing the bud into my pocket. I have no intentions of smoking drugs a stranger gifted me, but I appreciate the gesture nonetheless. I motion to the wall nearest to me.

"This is a cool place."

"Thanks," Micah flashes me a white-toothed smile, folding his muscular across his wide chest.

"It's been passed down through the family for years. Mom owns it now, one day it'll be mine. And while I won't offer you Tulsi basil, lavender, and turmeric for your broken leg, we still stock some of those Mayflowerian herbs and remedies, now just for fun."

I smile, looking around the shelves with a new perspective.

"Do you have anything to keep men away?" I joke under my breath. Micah chuckles in response.

"I'm afraid no remedy I could sell would help you with that." He leans against the frame of the hallway, the action highlighting his swollen biceps. I almost bust out laughing at how utterly smooth that line was, almost as if he'd rehearsed it. Before that could happen, I decide to excuse myself, acknowledging the fact I'm too horny to be around someone as muscle-y as Micah right now.

"I'll see you around, Micah. Thanks for the herbal lesson."

He waves goodbye to me with a smile that tells me he's eager to see me again. However, that smile doesn't tell me how he knew my name and that I was from California.

"A group of us are going apple picking tomorrow at the orchards. You should come! We're meeting here at 8 a.m.!" he offers as a last-minute thought.

"I'll think about it," I respond over my shoulder, feigning disinterest. Apple picking honestly sounds really fun, an activity that isn't common inside the concrete jungles of Los Angeles. Besides, a niggling feeling inside of me is warning me not to ignore it. I need an answer from Micah on how he knew all these things about me, and tomorrow's activities seem like the perfect opportunity.

I make my way back onto the cobblestone street I was coming to adore, my head swimming with all the interactions today. Milo the Historian, Micah the Flirt, Elsie the Barista— I'm curious to see who is next.

I retrace my steps and easily find my way back to my rental. As I walk up my porch steps, I notice a car in Agnes' driveway that I didn't remember being there when I left earlier. As I examine the vehicle, a subtle movement from her upstairs window catches my eye, and I quickly flick my attention in its direction. Just as I register a pair of blue eyes watching me, the curtain is quickly dropped back into place, and the window is once again still. I shutter as I quickly jam my key into my house's lock and hurry inside.

More than once today I've had the feeling that Havenwood knows a lot more about me than I know of it. Tomorrow, that changes.

5

Hocus Pocus

Courtney

Admittedly, I'm not entirely sure what one wears to go apple picking, considering I've never been. I had, however, been to farmer's markets in Los Angeles, and those were usually swarmed by rich housewives who matched their Pilates pants to their Cartier bracelets, and that hardly seemed appropriate here. Not to mention I don't own a Cartier bracelet.

I check my phone for the time, panic quickening my steps when I see that the block letters read 7:45 in the morning. I need to hurry up and decide on my outfit, or I'm going to be late. I try to remind myself that this isn't a fashionable shopping outing with Kashvi in WeHo. I'm in quiet, humble Havenwood, and apple picking is like a step above gardening. *Right?*

I slip on a black body suit, dark-washed distressed jeans, and an oversized umber cardigan before rushing out of the house, not allowing myself a second glance in the mirror or an opportunity to change my decision.

The streets of Havenwood are quieter than normal at this time of day. Apart from the birds singing and the chattering of the squirrels, the only other noise is the heels of my boots clacking against the cobblestone. The town is glorious like this, bathed in the first ardent lights of the morning, alive with small critters and a crisp autumn breeze whipping around the old structures and through the leaves of the maple trees that line the road.

I close my eyes contently as I walk, the sunlight warming my skin just enough to combat the chill of the brisk air. I might not know where those emails came from or who sent them, but at this moment, I'm grateful for them. I'm grateful for the chance to escape city life and the expenses that come with it. I'm grateful to escape Carter. I'm grateful- my eyes snap open. A new sound catches my attention, one that stands out from the chatter of animals. I recognize it as the crunch of a leaf, only feet away from where I stand. I rear my head in the direction of the noise, just quick enough to see someone retreat behind a tree not even six feet away. I freeze in place, trying to process what I just saw.

From the extremely limited look I got, it looked to be a woman in a long gray dress with deep brown hair tied in a knot on top of her head. Her emanation is the most distinct thing about her, it's that of another time entirely.

"Hello?" I try cautiously, noticing that the woodland creatures have gone unnervingly silent as if hiding from whomever I had just seen.

No response comes, though I didn't expect one. I glance around my surroundings, searching for any other witnesses who might've seen the strange woman, but I am still com- pletely alone. There's nowhere she could have run without me seeing her, so she must still be hiding behind the tree.

I do *not* want to investigate. I would rather volunteer to do just about anything else, but something draws me in. I blame it on my desperation for answers, to figure out just one of Havenwood's mysteries. Wasn't it curiosity that killed the cat?

I silently gulp as I advance a few cautious steps forward, my heartbeat ringing in my ears. I almost jump out of my skin when an irksome caw rings out from above, causing my stomach to flip and my attention to jump from the tree's trunk up to its desolate branches. A crow stares down at me menacingly, his glare practically threatening me to try and retaliate against it. I sneer at the bird as choice words run through my head, I'd cuss him out for scaring me after I confront the woman. I summon my curiosity-fueled courage and continue my creep toward the tree and whoever was behind it.

"Hello?" I tried again, louder this time, but still no answer. I plant my hands against the cracked bard of the maple tree and count to three in my head, hyping myself up to confront the woman.

One… *Why had she been watching me?*

Two.. Every terrifying possibility runs through my head of what could be waiting for me behind this tree.

Three… I pop my head around the tree and find no one, nothing.

There is no woman, no gray dress; in fact, the dead leaves resting at the base of the tree seem completely undisturbed, as if she hadn't ducked behind the tree to begin with. I stand there, leaning against the dead maple, completely bewildered when a voice from behind me causes me to scream.

"I'm sorry!" The redheaded barista takes a step back, raising her palms defensively.

"Holy shit," I pant, my lungs angry from releasing the entirety of their contents into that scream. I'm now facing her; my back pressed painfully against the tree's bark as I attempt to make myself disappear into it.

"I didn't mean to scare you, I'm sorry," Elsie repeats, offering me her hand to help me stand. I glance around the tree one more time, then up at the crow before accepting her offer and rising to my feet.

"What were you looking for?" She asks curiously as we realign with the stone road, her bright brown eyes searching my face before I even have the sensibility to mask my fear.

"I thought I saw someone. She ducked behind the tree before I could get a good look, but when I checked, there was nobody there." I shake my head, realizing how crazy that sounds out loud. I wait for Elsie to mock me, but it doesn't come; her gaze bounces from the tree to me and back, quickening her step.

"That's so creepy," she shivers, pushing her glasses up her nose and wrapping her arms around her middle.

"Let's hurry up and get out of here. I can't stand this kind of stuff!"

I was happy to oblige, matching her pace as we put distance between us, the tree, and the nonexistent woman who had hidden behind it.

"I'm supposed to meet up with Micah for apple picking," I inform her, more so to figure out where she's going than anything else.

"I figured," she smiles at me, feeling more comfortable with the tree far behind us.

"We're all meeting up at his place."

I'm glad that the barista is also joining. I wasn't sure who else would be in attendance, but it's nice to know one familiar freckled face. Micah mentioning my name and where I was from without me telling him had planted a seed of mistrust in my head regarding Havenwood and its residents but Elsie had proven to be a kind and genuine person. Her inviting personality makes me question whether or not I'm being ridiculous in even questioning Micah.

As we near Herbal Health and Healing, the air gradually reignites with the chatter of small animals, and the heaviness from before melts away entirely, giving way to a much more jubilant climate. Though, admittedly, the woman in gray and that awful crow still linger in the back of my mind. Ready to take center stage of my nightmares tonight.

No sooner have Elsie and I stepped onto the dirt patch that surrounds the small shop when the barista cups her hands around her mouth and calls out.

"MICAH NAMAAS. GET YOUR BUTT OUT HERE!"

I laugh quietly to myself. Her attitude reminds me of an older sister, ready to scold her tardy little sibling. Rushed shuffling is heard from within the back portion of the building before a face and bare, muscular upper torso pop out from one of the furthest windows. "Hi, Els. Courtney! I'm glad you came!" Micah beams, his bright white teeth contrasting the soft brown of his skin, his expression just short of ecstatic. I give him a smile and a wave, too caught up in my own inner turmoil to say anything. All morning, I've debated whether I should address my suspicions of him. Today is supposed to be a fun, carefree day, and I don't want to ruin that by asking pointed questions. But on the other hand, I'm worried that if I don't ask now, there might not be a better opportunity, or Micah might have time to think of a better excuse for his foreknown knowledge. I mentally war with my options, not wanting to strain a new friendship but also not wanting to call the wrong people friends.

"I'll be out soon," he promises, once again disappearing into the old house. The sound of an electric razor buzzing through the open window hints as to why he's running late.

"Hurry up! You can barely even grow facial hair; it shouldn't take you that long to shave off peach fuzz!" Elsie calls after him, clicking her tongue impatiently as she pushes her hands inside her jacket pockets. I watch the barista with amused contentment, genuinely happy that she's coming along for the adventure today. With her here, I know I have at least one person in my corner. That's when the idea hits me. I'm worrying myself in circles, debating who I can trust and who's keeping secrets from me when I already decided I can trust Elsie.

"Havenwood is a small town, right? Everyone knows everyone... I assume news travels fast?" I prod, jumping right into my investigation, but Elsie doesn't seem to mind. She kicks a rock as she answers, peeved about Micah keeping us waiting.

"Oh yeah," she huffs as if she's experienced the effects of the grapevine firsthand. Her confirmation releases a pinch in my chest. Maybe Micah truly had heard about my arrival, and that's why he knew so much about me. That's not so ridiculous, right?

I nod, letting out a relieved breath.

"So you probably smelt me coming from a mile away? Already knew my name and zodiac sign and all that?" I laugh lightly, trying to keep the conversation casual and less like the probing that it actually is. Her tangelo brows knit together as she ponders for a moment, attempting to recall.

"Actually, no." Her words reinstate the nag of suspicion inside me, its grip much tighter than before.

"You coming here was a surprise to all of us. I only learned about you when you came into Mystic Brew for the first time."

"Ready!" Micah bellows as he jogs towards us, clearing the long dirt driveway in a few bounds. I smile tightly as he gives Elsie a hug, then myself, now ten times more skeptical of him than before. I run out of time to ponder my suspicions as the rest of our group arrives.

"The best-looking attendee has arrived," Milo's theatrical voice echoes from behind us, his words highlighted by the crunch of gravel below his feet as he approaches.

"And look, Milo's here too." Finn quips in true brotherly fashion, seeking out a reaction that his adoptive sibling gives willingly. My core instantly tightens at the sight of the mayor.

He's wearing a black shirt that molds nicely to his firm chest, and his muscular arms are covered with a vintage-looking brown bomber jacket, but his tan pants are the true star of the show. I let my gaze linger on them a bit too long, enjoying the way his thighs fill the fabric. The longer I stare, the more definition I'm able to make out of the bulge near his zipper, and *oh my-* my lungs suddenly betray me as I suck in an audible jagged breath. All while my mind is begging my abdominal muscle to relax and attempting to coerce my eyeballs to focus anywhere but on that damn bulge. What is it about Finn Abernathy that causes my body to have such a visceral reaction to just the sight of him? Sure, he's undoubtedly handsome with striking features and, from our one interaction at the coffee shop, seems like a gentleman, but that doesn't explain why I forget how to breathe in his presence or why I'm mentally undressing him right this very moment.

"Are you okay?" Micah asks, putting a steadying hand on my shoulder. *Shit, had they all heard me struggling to catch my breath?* Of course, they had; it was embarrassingly loud. I can only hope that I averted my gaze before any of them saw where I had been staring.

Finn watches me cautiously, keeping a respectful distance, but his obvious concern for my well-being only deepens my want for him. I rip my eyes off the mayor and offer Micah a placating nod.

"I'm fine. I just didn't realize so many of us were going." I make the excuse up off the top of my head, regretting it the second it leaves my mouth.

Finn's gaze drops to the ground as his tongue peeks out, rolling over his bottom lip, a subconscious expression of his discomfort. He knows I'm referring to him. Hurt is the only word to describe the emotion on his handsome face, and I hate being the cause of it; I loathe it. I open my mouth to say something, anything that might explain my cold behavior toward him. But what can I possibly say when the truth is that I want- no -need him to stay away from me so I won't develop feelings for him? Feelings that were already disobediently developing regardless of the distance I kept between us.

Milo speaks before I decide on what to say.

"The more hands involved, the more apples we can pick."

"And the more apples we pick, the more apple pies and cider Agnes can make." Micah hums as if he's already able to taste the treats on his tongue.

Micah rubs his hands together excitedly and Elsie laces her

arm through mine.

"Let's go!" She announces eagerly, and the five of us are off. I follow the group towards the open field that backdrops Herbal Heath & Healing.

"The orchards are just outside of Havenwood proper," Milo leans over to explain to me as we tromp through the tall grass.

After crossing the vast field, we enter the tree line, following a wide and well-worn path in the dirt. It's clear that this is a commonly traveled path, and Elsie later confirms my suspicion, informing me that it's a tradition among their friend group, as well as other younger locals, to visit the orchard during harvest season. A part of me feels grateful to be included in their traditions, especially since it seems I'm now inducted as an honorary member of the group, but I need to know what my new friends are keeping from me.

I stay silent for the majority of our walk, choosing instead to listen to the conversations happening around me, afraid to say anything else that might be found offensive. During a lull in the chatter, I manage to get Micah somewhat secluded from the other members, choosing now as my time to get any answers from him that I can.

"Hey Micah, how did you know my name before I told you?" I turn to my full attention to my right to look him in his amber-brown eyes. Micah is barely an inch taller than me, so I'm able to face him straight on, which makes it much easier for me to gauge his initial reaction to my blunt questioning. His eyes round ever so slightly before he quickly regains his composure, chuckling anxiously.

"I told you, lucky guess. Everyone was talking about this Courtney chick who was moving to town." His gaze flicks to Finn, who is deep in a conversation with Milo and Elsie.

I narrow my eyes on him, my suspicion rising. *Why was he looking at Finn?*

"Really? Because Elsie told me that no one knew I was coming to town."

"Uh, you look really pretty today," Micah attempts to reroute me, giving me a once-over with a sultry smirk. If I were a lesser woman, his distraction probably would have worked. I open my mouth to press him further, but Elsie shouts in excitement, cutting off my opportunity.

"There it is!"

We all turn our attention to the quaint orchard in front of us, planted peacefully in a meadow void of maple or pine trees. Elsie takes off in an enthusiastic trot towards the apple trees, taking me with her via our still interlocked arms and unintentionally ruining my plan. I scowl inwardly, still desperate for answers I didn't get.

"Whoever finds the best apple wins!" The barista giggles delightedly as we run into the first row of the orchard, the sound of her laugh killing any semblance of annoyance inside of me.

I may not have gotten any answers from Micah, but I now have confirmation that something strange is definitely going on, and I intend to find out exactly what it is.

6

Apple Cider

Courtney

The five of us disperse as soon as we reach the orchard, separated by our competitive desires to find the best apple. Sure, it's a silly little competition, but my competitive side won't let me lose. We each claim a row of apple trees to search, and it looks like I've gotten lucky with the strip I picked.

Just a few unreachable feet above my head dangles a glossy, ruby-colored orb. It's a perfect apple if I ever saw one and one that will easily win me first place. I make a reach for it, but it's clear that I'm too short to come close to nabbing it; even on my tiptoes, my fingertips are still a good foot away.

"That's a good one," a smooth, deep voice compliments from behind me. I peek my head over my shoulder to see Finn observing me from a small distance away, looking devilishly handsome as always and holding his own basket full of apples, none of which look as amazing as my ruby apple.

"Finders keepers," I retort, in an admittedly immature tone. He chuckles, taking a few apprehensive steps towards me.

45

"I wouldn't dream of stealing your apple. It would only add to your dislike of me." I trap my lower lip between my teeth, embarrassed of myself and my behavior towards him and even more embarrassed that he's calling me out on it. I'm desperate to dowse the false idea he thinks I have of him but even more desperate to protect myself.

"I don't dislike you," I say softly, barely loud enough for him to hear. I watch his reaction closely yet hesitantly, my insides already doing somersaults in his presence. He doesn't acknowledge what I said with words, but a soft smile spreads onto his full lips anyway, a sign that I had managed to extinguish some worry inside of him. He eyes the minimal ground between us, taking another step closer, testing my reaction to our proximity. More than that, he's testing my tolerance of *him*, watching to see whether or not I recoil. I lower my stare to his chest, breaking our eye contact in a vain attempt to ignore the heat that's pooling low in my stomach. As the subtle scent of his cologne wafts into my nostrils, an undeniable frenzy claws to find purchase inside of me. *When had we gotten so close?*

"I would, however, be honored to help you retrieve said apple. If you'd like," he politely offers, inclining his neck and squinting at the offending fruit. I look up at it as well, weighing how badly I want to win and comparing it to what it might cost me. I swallow the stones that have piled up in my throat.

"Okay," I relent before I can talk myself out of his help.

"Ask me nicely."

My eyes dart up to meet his icy blue ones; my brows scrunched together in shock at his audacity. Had he not just offered me his help and now commanded I beg him for it? I scoff in his face, ready to tell him exactly where to shove it, but my attitude is quickly lost when I see the carnality swirling in his irises, the desire in me recognizing the same in him. This isn't him being an entitled prick; this is a different game entirely, and I'm all too willing to play. I wet my lips and take in an unsteady breath.

"Please."

Finn takes a step into me, our eyes still locked and our bodies now inches apart, I can feel his breath fan across my face as he looks down at me. My center constricts once again as he lowers himself before me, my heart thrumming in my chest as I wonder if he'll undo my jeans and devour me right here in the middle of the orchard. *Will I let him?* Instead, he wraps his arms securely around my thighs, just under my ass, and once again rises to his full height, lifting me into the air with him.

I almost forget about the apple entirely as I stare down at him, trying to read his indecipherable expression and regulate my racing pulse at the same time. I blink repeatedly, willing my attention to the red orb in front of my face and plucking it from the safety of its branch. Before I can enjoy another second of Finn's body sealed to mine, the closeness of his mouth to my... my feet are on the ground again, and he's taking a respectful step back. *Damn him.*

"Thanks." I press my lips together in a flat line, holding up my prized apple. "Anytime," Finn's lasciviousness is locked away somewhere inside of him by the time he picks up his basket, a faux calm overtaking his handsome features that were just ablaze with lust. I open my mouth to say one of the dozens of things on my mind when Elsie rounds the corner to our private row of trees.

"Courtney, you *have* to see this apple Milo picked!"

"Okay," I smile back at the barista, giving the mayor a curt nod of gratitude and allowing Elsie to drag me away. Before we make the curve to the next row, I risk a peek over my shoulder, and sure enough, Finn's icy blue eyes are still watching me.

"Look how thick she is," Milo praises his impressively plump apple, holding it up for Elsie and I to see.

"She is thick," Elsie nods, adjusting her frames and looking at the fruit in wonder.

"I think it's safe to say you won."

"Not so fast," I challenge confidently, reaching into my basket and presenting my ruby red apple. Milo and Elsie both gasp melodramatically, Milo clutching at his imaginary pearl necklace as Elsie feigns, wiping away a tear. My apple is not only slightly larger than Milo's in circumference but a much more vibrant shade of red; with little debate, Milo and Elsie both congruently declare it as the winner.

They both applaud and remind me that my prize is bragging rights, which I accept gracefully. Our baskets are full, and Agnes will be opening the bakery soon, prompting our decision to locate Micah and Finn and head back into town.

We reconnect with the two of them a few rows to our right; both have sizable finds, but none of them hold a candle to my apple. Finn pretends to be amazed as Elsie puts my apple on display before him, even taking the bit as far as complimenting the fruit.

"It looks delicious," he says, but his eyes are on mine as he says it, causing my mouth to dry, the moisture heading south and seemingly pooling in my underwear.

The rest of the trek back to Havenwood proper was,

thankfully, uneventful for the integrity of my panties. The five of us joke and laugh and genuinely enjoy each other's company as we go. I find myself learning little details about my new friends, such as Micah having a fear of chipmunks after being bit by one as a child and Milo's celebrity crush being Charlie Hunnam. As we chat and share, I find myself growing less and less suspicious and feeling guilty for even suspecting Micah or the rest of them of any malice. People as kind as they are simply couldn't be up to anything devious.

"Thanks for the fun, gang," Finn announces as we near the town center, passing his basket to Milo and signaling his unexpected departure. We're only a block from Agnes' bakery and, therefore, only just as far from the reward of warm cider and apple pie.

"You're not coming?" Micah asks, just as confused and curious as the rest of us. "'Fraid not." The mayor answers back casually, his face giving away nothing to elude to the reasoning behind his decision.

"How come?" Elsie pushes, her eyebrow rising.

The action is almost over before I can register it; I look up in just enough time to catch Finn's blue eyes flicker to me before they retrain on the barista. His answer is clear, at least to me. I'm why Finn isn't coming to the bakery with us, because of our moment in the orchard.

I shift awkwardly, hoping no one else caught the mayor's subtle answer in his body language. Although I feel bad that Finn doesn't feel welcomed because of me, or uncomfortable, or whatever he's feeling, I completely understand why. Each interaction I've had with him has been standoffish, mixed signals, and flat-out confusing. I wish there were a way to tell him that I'm the problem, not him, my resolve is the issue between us. I try to convey the message in my stare but he doesn't risk another glance in my direction.

"Mayoral duties call," a small, polite smile tugs at one corner of his lips. This is his version of a poker face, and honestly, it isn't very convincing. I can see straight through his facade, but his response satisfies the other group members.

"We'll save you some cider," Milo asserts, reprieving his brother from any further questioning.

"No promises," Micah adds with a snorty laugh, earning him an elbow to the rib from Elsie. Finn dips his head in a general farewell nod and, without another word, turns on his heel and heads in the opposite direction. I watch him go until he rounds a corner out of sight, a handful of new emotions clogging my brain.

"Coming?" Elsie asks curiously, surveying my face in an attempt to translate the myriad of emotions that have surfaced and culminated there.

"Mhm," I nod, plastering a smile on my face that I can only hope is more convincing than Finn's had been.

* * *

Despite the full trays in her hands and the ample ingredients sprawled on the stainless steel table before her, Agnes is pleased to see us all, eagerly dropping her current tasks at the sight of our apple baskets.

"Looks like a bountiful season," she remarks pleasantly as she studies my ruby apple. Agnes whisks our baskets away and begins divvying up the apples, selecting the sweeter-looking ones for cider and the firmer ones for apple pie. As the four of us watch Agnes assemble and retrieve the necessary ingredients, we converse lightly, enthralled in watching her work her magic.

"He's not so bad," Milo remarks out of the blue, his hazel eyes trained on me. His boldness surprises me, causing me to choke on the pumpkin spice pastry Agnes provided us all with.

"S-sorry?" I sputter as cinnamon dislodges itself from my throat.

"You heard me," he smirks as he rips off a corner from his pasty elegantly, tucking it politely in his mouth.

"Finn, he isn't so bad. Sure, he snores, and he uses way too much salt when he cooks, but if you can look past that, he's a great man."

I don't know how to respond, choosing to chew on the inside of my cheek instead. But Milo's gaze is unrelenting. I sigh in defeat; knowing I'm caught, I tuck a strand of brown behind my ear.

"He seems great, trust me. It's not a him issue; it's a me issue. I've sworn off men, and I'm done with them."

"We'll see." He winks at me knowingly.

"Cider's ready!"

Finn

The walk to city hall is quick but torturous.

I had thought about Courtney Berrycloth endlessly since she had arrived in Havenwood; maybe "fantasized about" is the more correct verbiage. But to hold her in my arms, to breathe in her fresh fruity scent, to feel the heat emanating from the apex of her thighs was a completely different and euphoric experience. One that had caused my cock to thicken the instant I fastened my arms below her ass. Blood rushes back down to my groin as I remember the sight of her looking down at me, wishing I had been looking up at her from a much more compromising position.

"Finn!" A painfully familiar voice causes me to bristle, my shoulders physically rising to meet my ears in protest. The heavy doors of city hall are only a few short feet away, tempting me to ignore the call and jet inside. Unfortunately for me, I'm a better person than that.

I let out an annoyed breath, attempting to regain candid composure before turning to address her.

"Hello, Starr. Hello, Soul." I greet the pair, digging my hands into the front pockets of my pants in an attempt to hide my now-deflating erection. The two women stand side by side, Soul looking as she always does, cool on the surface with some unreadable storm crackling right below it. She's wearing blackout contacts today, adding to her unapproachable demeanor. Unlike most of the residents of Havenwood, I have no issue with their alternative style, I know it's a way for them to express themselves. Soul studies me with a blank expression that would make a lesser man squirm.

On the other hand, Starr's expression gives away her intentions almost immediately, causing me to groan internally.

"It's good to see you," She begins her routine, rocking on her heels and biting back a smile.

"It's good to see you two, as well." I choose my words carefully, not giving her any reason to hold onto false hope of us rekindling our relationship. My feelings on the matter haven't changed, especially after discovering the depth of my

52

feelings for Courtney. Starr's smile falters only momentarily before she hoists it back onto her face again.

"I was wondering if you wanted to-"

"Starr," I say sternly. I shake my head once, focusing on the cobblestone between us to avoid shining my irritated gaze directly onto her. I take a step closer to her, meeting her eyes now as I lower my voice. An attempt to not embarrass her in front of her friend.

"We cannot keep doing this. Please respect my wishes." I watch as her grasp on control falters, and she takes a heated step.

"How can you tell me you don't have feelings for me? After all the time we spent together?" Her murky green eyes dart back and forth between mine, searching for an answer that isn't there. I take in a deep breath, deflating as my anger with Starr is replaced with sympathy. I now know what it feels like to be her, to pine after someone who tries at every turn to shake you, clinging to delusional hope that *maybe* they feel the same way for you.

"I'm sorry." Is all I can think to say because I truly am, knowing nothing I can say will soothe her. Starr stares into me for a few more beats before stepping back and smoothing out the front of her black leather bodice.

"That's not why I wanted to talk to you, anyway." She turns her attention behind her, motioning Soul forward.

"Tell him." Soul takes a few platform boot-clad steps closer to us, crossing her tattooed arms across her chest. An emotion pinches her features, almost startling me, considering this is the first time I can remember seeing Soul emote anything.

"I, um," she searches for the words. I look between the two of them, my concern growing as I try to guess what could be so important that Soul is nervous to tell me about.

"Your plan with Milo?" I feel my heart skip a beat as I'm transported back to that night at the Grumpy Lobster. I assumed Starr was too drunk to remember eavesdropping on Milo and I's plan, but clearly, she wasn't and had shared the details with Soul. My eyes widen as I turn to Starr, who raises her hands in defense.

"I only told her." Her reassurances do little to calm me. Havenwood is a small town, and private news is never private for long once word gets out.

"What about it?" I try to keep my tone cool as I question Soul; she chews on her lip ring in response.

"I told Micah about it," she finally admits. My face numbs, and my tongue feels like lead in my mouth as the realization hits: The plan is out.

"I'm sorry!" Soul apologizes genuinely, sensing my shift in demeanor.

"We were hooking up one night after a few drinks, and it just slipped. He promised not to tell anyone!" She offers as if it matters. I drag a hand down my face, rubbing at my beard anxiously. The only thought on my mind is how absolutely fucked I am. Courtney already doesn't like me, and once she figures out that I lied and lured her here, she will hate me.

"The apothecarian won't say anything," Starr tries to reassure me.

"This plan will still work, and Havenwood will still be saved. And, if it does fail for some reason, I know you'll find another way. You always do." Starr places a comforting hand on my bicep, but it doesn't have the desired effect. For the first time in months, I'm not concerned about Havenwood but about ruining my chances with Courtney.

"It's not about Havenwood." I bark with disinhibition, instantly regretting my words.

"It's her, isn't it? It's fucking her!" Starr hisses, stomping her foot as she makes her accusation. Courtney is not the reason I broke things off with Starr but the way I feel about her is why there will never be a future between Starr and I.

"It is not what you think, Starr." I try to calm her, unsure what to say to ease the hurt I know she's feeling. Starr growls a guttural growl of rage, throwing her hands in the air, most likely to keep them from connecting with my face.

"Let's go," Soul says, placing a guiding hand on Starr's back, recognizing the detonation that is being narrowly avoided. Starr swats her friend's hand away but obeys, storming off, Soul close on her heels.

My head is swimming as I push myself into city hall, numbly greeting my receptionist, Cathleen, before trekking up the stairs to my office. I take a seat at my desk, letting out a deep exhale. Starr might be pissed with me, but I know she won't reveal our plan; as desperate as she is, Starr is loyal, and she'd see telling Courtney as a betrayal to me. Micah, I'm less sure about that; the man will do or say just about anything anyone wants to get his dick wet. I can only hope that he cares enough for Soul to keep the secret between them, but if he gets close enough to Courtney, he might feel obligated to tell her. I rub my temples, a headache forming at the stress of it all.

A dull ache in my scrotum reminds me that no solution will be coming from me until I release some of this pent-up stress. I unzip my pants, the thought of Courtney on my mind, as I intend to do just that.

7

Hex Girls

Courtney

The squeaks of the little bat in my attic kept me awake most of the night. I had finally succumbed to exhaustion in the early hours of the morning, but thanks to Olive, I'm again awake before 8 a.m..

I've grown used to the house's built-in alarm clock and have been using my extra morning hours to get my runs in. Something about having a pet keeps me on a routine, though I could argue that I'm Olive's pet based on the way she has me trained.

After delivering Olive a plate of sliced figs from my fruit bowl, I slip into a matching workout set and tie my brown locks into a tight runner's bun.

A week has passed since the five of us went apple picking, and I've spent almost the entirety of that time thinking about my fleeting moment with Finn, his firm body pressed against my own. Each time I recall the memory, liquid heat licks up my insides, setting gears into motion that I'm certainly not allowing myself to act on.

I keep hoping to bump into him at some small corner of this archaic town, at the grocery store, or maybe Agnes' bakery. I plan to apologize for my behavior but he's nowhere to be found. It seems as if the tall, dark mayor has simply disappeared into the crisp New England air.

I lock up my rental and head South, setting a calm pace to ease into my natural rhythm. I jog down the rows of residential streets, familiarizing myself with the quaint houses as I go until I hit the edge of an overgrown field. It isn't dissimilar to the one we encountered apple picking but far more wild and yellow. I recognize it as an indication of Havenwood's border and prepare to double back, but that's when it catches my eye. An old, colonial-style house sitting on the fringe of the pasture, backdropped by the pitch pines trees of the forest just beyond it.

I take a hesitant step towards the antiquated property, squinting my eyes for a better look at its dust-fogged windows. As my foot flattens the dry grass below, a resounding caw from behind me causes my anxiety to spike and my flight or fight to kick in, sending me into a crouched position. Whipping around to face the offensive sound, I spot the same obnoxious crow from a week ago, sitting in the mangled branches of the tree closest to me. Its beady eyes stare me down, daring me to disobey his warning call. A shiver courses up my spine as I make eye contact with the bird's endless black eyes.

"You little shit," I hiss under my breath, sick of the little terror.

"You're an asshole, you know that?" I call up to the bird in vain. My insult doesn't deter him in the slightest as he continues his surveillance of me. The ominous feeling that accompanies the creepy crow is enough to shake my interest in the mysterious house and send me back jogging toward town, desperate to have its intense gaze off of me.

I head deep into the center of the town, wanting to be as far from the crow and the house as possible. I pass the same shops and boutiques as I did on all my jogs, but this time, something is new. A storefront that has sat empty since my arrival now has a "RENT ME" poster plastered across its gorgeous bay window.

The window has been one of the highlights of all my morning runs; its design reminds me of one of my favorite bookstores I'd visited in northern California that sported a similar one. I slow my pace to look at the stores that line either side of the empty shop, noticing for the first time that Havenwood doesn't have a bookstore. I've been so caught up trying to track down Finn that I hadn't taken the time to scope one out.

A brazen thought crosses my mind, *what if I open a bookshop in this space?* Logistically, it would work; this is the ideal spot for a shop due to its proximity to the park and town square.

I pick up my pace once again, the idea still prominent in the back of my mind as I debate the rationality of opening a business in a dying town—and with my dwindling savings— but it excites me nonetheless.

I settle on Mythic Brew as the final destination of my jog, wanting to end a weird run with a familiar face. Instinctively, I break right at the end of the street to head in the direction of the coffee shop. As I lean to take the blind corner, a pair of women round the building at the worst possible time. With no time to react, I slam right into them.

"Shit," I mutter as I hold my head. It feels like I must've collided with one of their elbows with how hard it's pounding.

"I'm so sorry, I didn't know anyone was-."

"Watch it!" One of the human obstacles hisses. To my displeasure, the pair I've collided with are the two goth women I saw in the park yesterday. Based on their less-than-excited faces yesterday and my stunt today, it's safe to say they both hate my guts by now.

I ramble off another quick apology before resuming my pace and getting the hell out of there before they drink my blood or something. I peek over my shoulder as I sprint away, and sure enough, two pale faces are staring daggers at me. *What is their problem?* I silently wonder to myself. Everyone I've encountered in Havenwood seems more than delighted with my presence but these two act like I'm here to ruin their lives personally.

Thankfully I make it to the drowsy coffee shop without ruffling the feathers of any more locals. I push open the creaky front door and am immediately greeted by the smell of delicious, fresh espresso and the bell chime, alerting Elsie to my presence.

"Hi Courtney," Elsie calls over her shoulder as she pulls perfect golden brown shots. I offer a wave as I make my way to the counter, leaning against it to give my tired legs a break.

"Caramel latte with oat milk?" Elsie doesn't bother to face me as she recites my order from memory. I'd stopped by several times over the last week and hadn't strayed far from my original order but I decide to get something different today, inspired by the impending fall season.

"Actually, I'll take a hot, dirty chai latte with oat milk, please."

Elsie grins, excitedly retrieving a golden bag from the cupboard above her.

"You always order such fun drinks. It never fails to spice

59

up my day." I smile back at her, her presence brightening my mood like I knew it would.

"Hey, do you know two women who dress in dark colors and really light foundation? Lots of piercings?"

"I see you've had the misfortune of meeting Soul and Starr already." Elsie huffs as she dusts cinnamon over the top of my chai.

I raise an eyebrow. "It sounds like I'm not the only person they are unpleasant to?"

"They're brats," Elsie admits, sliding my drink across the counter where I'm still resting.

"They were always full of themselves but then they started to get some notoriety outside of Havenwood and it only fueled their egos."

"How do you mean?" I sip the perfectly brewed chai, the taste of autumn dancing across my taste buds. Elsie's drink-making game is truly magical.

"They're a band," she clarifies. "Soul plays electric guitar, and Starr sings. They started out super local and then gained some fame opening at shows. Now almost anyone in the state knows 'em. Not to say everyone likes them, especially not conservative mothers. Or me." We share a laugh as she cleans the oat milk from her steam wand.

"They've been touring Massachusetts for the last six months. They're only back in Havenwood because they're putting on a hometown show on Halloween night. Which, unfortunately for you, means you're visiting at the same time they are."

"Lucky me," I smirk over the ceramic mug at the barista.

"I may or may not have plowed into them when I was jogging here." Elsie covers her mouth as a small giggle escapes her.

"You are going to make them hate you! Especially with Finn

being into you."

She quirks an accusatory eyebrow and I feel my face numb at the mention of the mayor. The warmth of my fingers laced around my mug seems to spread throughout me as I drop my eyes to avoid Elsie's. *Am I blushing?*

"He isn't into me," I laugh dismissively, fumbling with the white mug.

"Why, um, why would Soul and Starr care if he was, though?" I pull my coffee to my lips, taking a prolonged sip to hide my expression. Elsie looks around the empty coffee shop before leaning in and whispering.

"Up until recently, Starr and the mayor were a thing." The name now rings a bell, as I recall Elsie mentioning Starr and Finn's relationship the first time I met the mayor.

"A thing?" I question, an unsolicited pang of jealousy corkscrewing through me.

She nods, taking a sip of her coffee.

"I don't know a whole lot, only what Milo tells me, but he's totally trying to break things off with her. He insists it's mutual because he's too nice. Rumor has it that's why she insisted on having their Halloween show here; Starr knows how badly Finn wants to bring money into Havenwood, and she thinks if she can do that, then maybe.." Elsie shrugs her petite shoulders, sipping again from her mug.

"Then maybe he'll get back with her?" I follow her prompt, she nods in confirmation. *See? Even if you did like him, he already has someone else chasing after him. You do not want to get in the middle of that.* The little voice in my head heeds. I ignore it as I refuse to admit to myself that I even like him in the first place.

"There's a shop for rent downtown with a big bay window.

Any idea what it used to be?" I change the subject, trying to remind myself how insufferable men are. No matter how tall, dark, handsome, or mayoral they are... but damn, I do like a man with a title.

"Oh yeah," the barista recalls the space, putting our now empty mugs into a sudsy sink.

"That was a flower shop. It didn't stay very long and didn't do too well. I wonder if anything will ever fill that space again with how things are looking here."

"You never know. What time are you off?"

"Closing time, 4 p.m., what's up?"

"Want to have dinner tonight at my place? My treat."

Her face lights up with excitement as we work out the details.

* * *

Elsie and I sit on the cherry hardwood floor of my living room, giggling over take-out containers full of the worst Chinese food I've ever had. I didn't even consider the fact that I have no furniture before inviting a guest over to my new house, but luckily, Elsie just seemed happy to be here. After we'd shared the special gift Micah had given me, she seemed *extra* happy to be here.

"Favorite color?" I ask, shoveling another clump of over-cooked sweet and sour chicken into my mouth. Elsie and I were taking turns asking each other questions to get to know each other better. So far, I learned that Elsie lives with her father and grandmother, who owns Mystic Brew, and that she hopes to inherit the place one day. I also learned that she is twenty-two and loves cats, women's basketball, and crocheting.

Elsie's brown eyes lift to the ceiling as she considers the question.

"Blue, like navy blue. Basic but true. What about you?"

"Mmm," I contemplate momentarily, enjoying the tingling sensation in my cheeks brought on by our smoking session.

"Maroon." I decide with finality.

"Good answer," Elsie nods, scooping a spoon of rice into her mouth. She tucks a strand of ginger hair behind her ear as she begins to speak, not bothering to finish her bite before beginning.

"Okay, what do you hate about Los Angeles?"

I shared basic information with her throughout our silly little meal. The fact that I'm twenty-eight, I'm a California native on break from big city living, as well as my first dog's name, but this question feels heavier. Not because of the question itself but because of my answer. I suck in my bottom lip, confessing the answer to myself before her.

"I hate the way people are there. They are insincere, image-obsessed, disingenuous liars, especially the men." I huff out a dry laugh, my attempt at lightening my answer as I stare into the fried rice.

"My final decision to take a break from the L.A. scene was getting dumped by my boyfriend. He broke up with me when he decided I wasn't good enough for his public image. He never cared about me. I see that now, but it still hurts."

While Carter and I weren't officially boyfriend and girl-friend, we were definitely dating, and I had considered ourselves to be exclusive; regardless, the lack of titles didn't relieve me of any pain. However, I must admit that the past few weeks in Havenwood have helped dull some of the aches. Hell, the attractive mayor of Havenwood has put Carter's memory on the back burner—the *far* back burner.

Before I can register what's happening, a pair of freckled arms are wrapped around me.

"Woah," I verbalize, steadying myself so I don't tip over. Elsie is hugging me tightly and genuinely, even rubbing my back as she does so—a gesture that feels way more soothing than I thought it could.

"I'm sorry, Courtney." She whispers, her thin arms still securely laced around me. I smile a little despite myself and return the embrace. Living on the West Coast, personal space was a big deal; you don't even dare to bump arms on the Metro, but Elsie seems at ease with holding me, despite hardly knowing me. An olive branch of trust that Los Angelenos don't offer, ever. I give her one more squeeze before she releases me.

"Do you ever hate Havenwood?" I return the question to her, pushing the attention off my breakup. Elsie shrugs her shoulders, pushing her glasses further up her nose.

"I'm happy here. I wish there were more people my age, but other than that, I have no qualms. As long as I can inherit the coffee house, I'll stay here forever and raise my kids here."

"You say that like you might *not* inherit it, aren't you your grandma's only grandchild?" I question, closing up the leftover food containers.

"Grandmother says I can only inherit it if I'm a *true barista*, whatever that means. I'm passionate about coffee but I have to convince her of that somehow. If not, I'll have to split the business with my dad, who doesn't care about the art of coffee at all, only profits."

64

"If she watched you work a single shift, she could see that you are a true barista." I express in confusion. Anyone could see from a mile away that Elsie loves coffee and her little coffee shop; her grandma must be blind or simply idiotic, respectfully.

Elsie flashes me an appreciative smile.

"She knows it. It has to do with family politics; she doesn't like who my mother is, and I can't change that, so she picks on me any opportunity she gets. I'll only know if she truly plans on passing me the shop when her final will and testaments are read."

Before I can think of a response, my doorbell rings. It takes me a moment to process the sound, partially because of my high and partially because it doesn't sound like the stereotypical ding-dong a doorbell makes but instead sounds like a church bell chiming. I crease my eyebrows, share a curious look with Elsie, and rise to my feet to see who could be at my door.

I open the heavy door to find my porch devoid of anyone. Instead, a small basket sits patiently on the stoop. I pick it up, inspecting the contents trapped behind the cellophane. Once I deem it safe, I bring it inside, resuming my seat on the living room floor across from Elsie.

"A gift basket, how exciting!" Her face lights up as she claps her hands together. "Who's it from?" She points to a card nestled snugly outside the plastic.

I free it from the card from its resting spot, reading the note out loud.

"Apologies for the delay. Consider this your official welcome to Havenwood. We hope you stay forever. Finn Abernathy"

8

Cream Pies

Courtney

Shortly after the gift basket arrived, Elsie and I decided to call it a night. She wanted to walk home before nightfall, citing her fear of running into "the witch." I was okay with ending our evening a bit short, considering that I now need to decode the meaning behind a certain welcome gift from a certain mayor. Is this as innocent a gift as it seems, or could this be his weird yet charming way of making a move?

Elsie had sworn up and down that the motive behind the gift was romantic in nature, his thinly veiled attempt obvious to even her. I had kept it cool, though, and argued that he was probably being overly gracious since I was the first person to move to Havenwood in over a decade.

Once Elsie is gone, I begin to unwrap the basket, my face turning crimson when I notice the potted flowers nestled amongst the other gifts. The flowers and chocolates hidden inside the basket hinted at an attempt at flirting but the "I Love Havenwood" mug is a safe scapegoat. If I were to question his motivations, he could argue that he's genuinely just welcoming a new transplant to town; the romantic gesture behind flowers and chocolates being just a coincidence. A small part of me enjoys this little game, pretending he isn't interested in me and just as I'm not interested in him. It keeps what I want a safe distance away, just out of my reach, and what I want is him.

Regardless of his true, unknown intentions, I appreciate the sentiment and I *really* like the chivalry behind giving a woman flowers and chocolates. *When was the last time Carter had hand-picked a gift for me? Why am I comparing Mayor Abernathy to Carter?* I shake my head, doing my best to fling the romantic thoughts straight out of my brain.

I end the confusing night by delivering some strawberries to the diva of a bat inhabiting my belfry, a peace offering to keep her quiet enough for me to get decent sleep tonight. However, my efforts are in vain, as I'm kept awake not by Olive but by thoughts of Finn Abernathy and his piercing blue eyes.

* * *

Still groggy and fuzzy-brained from lack of real rest, the sun streaming into my bedroom feels agonizing, refusing to let me fall back into a restless sleep. I climb out of bed, shielding my puffy eyes as I pull myself to my suitcase, fishing out a clean outfit to run in.

"This is getting ridiculous," I complain to no one but myself, referring to my lack of curtains and a dresser. Living out of a suitcase was fun in college, but at 28, it's just a reminder of my uncertainty.

I quickly dress myself and pull out my cellphone, locating

the website of a nearby home goods store and placing an expensive order: a dresser, curtains, curtain rods, kitchen table, and chairs. They don't have any attractive couches in stock, so I decide to hold off, my dwindling funds also playing a role in that decision. A couch, bed frame, and headboard will need to come next. Feeling satisfied with my purchases, I depart for my jog.

As soon as I step out onto my porch the chilly September air pinches at my skin, it carries the smell of freshly cut grass and wet pavement. It must've rained last night but the sun is out now, dutifully drying patches of light gray sidewalks. I decide that today I'm going to head towards the town square but take the long way around, approaching the shops from the opposite direction and staying far away from that creepy, old house.

I didn't consider the fact that this route led me right by Agnes' bakery; I'm only reminded when a delectable smell grabs onto my olfactory nerve with a strong grip, refusing to let go. Rather than fight to ignore the delicious aroma, I let it guide me straight to the bakery, a part of me hoping I'll find Finn inside.

A familiar face smiles at me as I pull the front door closed behind me, the warmth of the bakery feeling like a hug from a grandmother.

"Hello, Courtney," Agnes coos, removing a large tray from the oven.

"I was wondering when I'd see your pretty face in here again."

"Hi Agnes," I chirp back happily. "What're you making? It smells amazing."

"Sweet ham, jalapeno, and cream cheese danishes," she calls

as she sets the tray on the cooling rack and tucks her oven mitts into a drawer.

"Ring me up for two, please," I say, fishing my card from my bra. Agnes chuckles at the sight, smile lines deepening at the corner of her eyes.

"You California folk are interesting. Six dollars," She reads me the total before swiping my card and handing it back with a smile.

"How are you liking Havenwood?" She busies herself bagging two of the piping hot danishes, making sure to double bag them to avoid them burning me through the paper.

"I love it, I just ordered some furniture to make the rental feel more homey," I confess, tucking a flyaway brown strand behind my ear.

"I honestly can't believe more people don't move here. It's so quaint and charming."

Agnes' full lips curl into a sad smile as she slides the danishes across the counter, letting out a long breath as she leans against it.

"Most folks want to move to Salem for its morbid history or Nantucket for the beaches. Havenwood needs some sort of notoriety, something to pull people here." She says distantly, a sad tone to her voice.

"It's a hard thing to watch a place you've known and loved for so long slowly fizzle out of existence. Time is not forgiving."

I nod in understanding, looking down at the counter, its top randomly decorated with speckles of flour. Havenwood needs a change, I can agree. My idea from earlier drifts across my mind as I regard the sweet old baker.

"There's an empty store for rent a block from here. Elsie

said it used to be a floral shop?" Agnes nods in recognition, eyeing me for a further explanation.

"I was thinking, maybe, just for the time being, while I'm here, I could rent the space out. I noticed Havenwood doesn't have a bookstore. It's always been a small dream of mine to own a bookstore." Agnes' dark eyes light up with amusement.

"That'd be something," She says noncommittally, not seeming to believe I'll carry out my vision fully.

"How long do you plan to stay in town? Opening a business is no small feat, believe me." She raises her arm, the loose skin on her biceps jiggling as she gestures to the walls around us.

Before I get a chance to answer, the glass door to the shop opens, and we both turn to face the noise. Standing right in front of me is Finn, his blue eyes scanning my face as a look of surprise overtakes his sharp features. Sweat has glued his raven black hair to his forehead, causing it to look disheveled, a stark difference from the well-tamed vision it normally is. His pale cheeks are flush with swirls of crimson, and his built chest rises and falls in rhythm as he catches his breath; it appears that I'm not the only one out for a morning run.

"Courtney, hi." He greats me breathlessly, running a hand into his hair in an attempt to style the wet strands. I give him a half smile and a wave. *Don't get too close*, a voice inside me warns. Hadn't I come here hoping to see him? I'm giving myself whiplash attempting to listen to the two warring halves inside of me. I ignore my inconsistencies and inwardly fawn over how attractive the mayor looks, soaked in sweat and out of breath. I wonder what it would look like to have him over me, breathing that hard, getting that sweaty...

"I haven't seen you around. Thank you for the welcome basket, I hope you pay your secretary extra for after-hour errands." I attempt to keep my tone casual, not wanting him to see how excited I am to see him. A confused look overtakes Finn's face, his dark brows creasing as his icy eyes search mine.

"I don't have a secretary?" He cocks his head slightly, attempting to understand. I open my mouth to question him but then it dawns on me that Finn must have hand-delivered that basket last night himself.

Shit, the realization sets a thousand butterflies loose in my stomach, all of which flutter up towards my throat, attempting to avoid the heat settling low in there with them. A smile almost bubbles to my surface but I quickly tamp it back down before it dares to show on my face. I need to get out of here. Seeing him is a mistake; each time I do it becomes more and more difficult for me to deny my attraction to him.

"Thank you for the danishes, Agnes. It was nice to see you, mayor." I rattle off quickly, excusing myself from the counter stool I had perched myself on and B-lining for the exit. Finn doesn't move as I near the door, forcing me to come face-to-face with him. As I near him, I can feel the heat from his body radiating on my skin, and suddenly, he is the sun pulling me into his orbit. For a beat I stand completely still, soaking in his warmth and the faint smell of cedar mixed in with sweat emanating from his pale skin.

"Elsie mentioned you have a leak under your kitchen sink. I could stop by later today and take a look at it for you." Finn offers before I can remember how to form words and ask him to move. I give him a bewildered look as multiple questions fight for dominance in my head. *What leak? How would Elsie even know if I have a leak? Do you want me on my knees or my back?*

71

Noting my confused expression, he holds up a to-go coffee cup that I only just noticed he's carrying. That explains when he spoke to Elsie but still leaves open the question of how she would even know about a leak. *I* don't even know of any leaks; she certainly shouldn't. Why wouldn't she have disclosed it to me instead of Finn if she had discovered one? It makes no sense.

"I don't have a leak," I state firmly, squirming my way past him, out of the shop and onto the sidewalk outside. Thank God I'm wearing athletic wear because before I know it, I'm running away, my legs carrying me down the block and back towards my house without my brain telling them to do so. My legs might know what's best for me but my vagina sure doesn't, if I let her have her way Finn would've been receiving an invite back to my house to fix a different kind of leak.

Within minutes I'm through my front door and heading straight back to the kitchen. I toss Anges' pastries onto the counter as I squat down to face the cabinet under the sink. My hands hesitate on the knobs, despite my brain demanding them to open it. After a brief second of conflict, I will them to move, throwing the small doors open. My eyes zone in on a small conjunction of water pooling on the trap pipe; once enough volume gathers, the water droplets dive off the pipe, splattering into a small puddle below it. A leak.

My jaw hangs open in disbelief. Is Finn some sort of witch? A wizard? Warlock? Whatever the hell you call them, somehow, this man knew about a leak inside a house he'd never been in! The nagging suspicion I dismissed last week begins to rebuild inside me. As I try to rationalize Finn's knowledge of the leak, my phone begins to buzz in my sports bra. I pull it out, half expecting the screen to read Finn's name despite me never giving him my number. Instead, Kashvi's name and picture stare back at me.

"Hello?" I answer the call, still muddled from my discovery.

"Hey girl," Kashvi's valley girl accent brings a subconscious smile to my face. Only now, as I hear her voice, do I realize how much I miss my friend.

"How're the cream pies?"

"I haven't made it to Boston yet," I inform her, running a hand into my hair.

"Not what I meant." Kashvi giggles evilly. I scoff and attempt to think of a smart-ass response but fail to come up with one before she speaks again.

"This strike thing needs to end like yesterday. My bank account is looking rough."

"You should try New England, it's a lot more affordable. You could sublease one of my three bedrooms." I tease, my eyes scanning the parts of the house I can see from my resting position against the kitchen counter. It all still seems too good to be true, which means it probably is.

"I wish," she sighs. "I also wish I was smart like you and had a savings to fall on. Oh well, it looks like I'll be groveling to Daddy for October's rent."

I laugh as I absentmindedly play with my hair. Kashvi comes from a wealthy family, and despite being strong and independent, she knows they will happily support her if she asks.

"Oh, by the way," her voice drops to a more serious octave.

"Rumor is that Carter's trying to wiggle his tight blond ass into a movie deal. A big one."

I feel my lower eyelid twitch at the mention of his name, a reaction I'm not proud of but we just broke up a month ago for shit's sake, of course, every little thing he does is still going to piss me off.

Even though I'd already heard about this movie role first-hand from the prick himself, hearing Kashvi mention it meant that production is moving along, and sooner than later, Carter will have his face on the big screen. Just like he always wanted. The thought of him being rewarded for his shitty behavior causes my knuckles to whiten around my phone.

My doorbell rings and I'm grateful for the excuse to stop this conversation about Carter.

"Hey Kashvi, someone's at my door. I'll talk to you later, okay?"

"So about those cream pies.."

I pad the red button to end our call before she can finish and make my way to the door. Instinctively I check the peephole, my heart jumping into my throat as I recognize the man on the other end. I sigh in defeat before I answer the door.

Finn Abernathy is standing on my porch, holding a tool kit and a small grin on his handsome face. I force my heart to give up its seat on my vocal cords long enough for me to speak.

"Mayor?" The one word comes out sounding a lot more sultry than intended and I'm suddenly aware of how this exact scenario has definitely played out on more than one porn website.

"I came to fix that leak," he offers, motioning to his tool chest, his prop for gaining entry to my house. I take a deep breath, contemplating whether or not to let this man in. If I do, I'm resigning myself to admit I want him. If I don't, I'll be up all night regretting it.

"Come in."

9

Bewitched

Courtney

I watch Finn reach for a wrench before his head disappears once again under the sink. Even from my position a few feet away from him, I can see his back muscles through the casual tee he has on. I grumble to myself in annoyance, even when fixing a sink Finn Abernathy dares to be so unfortunately attractive. I check his backside, but of course, there's not even a damn plumber's crack. Just a perfectly tight ass.

However, It's not him I'm truly annoyed with; it's myself for even letting him inside the house in the first place. In doing so, I solidified something inside myself that I secretly knew was there all along— genuine feelings for Finn. I can't hide from them anymore and it infuriates me. I came to Havenwood with one rule: no boys, and not even a month in I've ruined my chances. But even still, I can hardly blame myself; beyond his striking looks, his stoic and reserved personality is all but irresistible. He's the complete opposite of Carter in every sense.

Where Carter is self-obsessed and egotistical, Finn is considerate and thoughtful. No man had ever given me a gift basket or willingly fixed my sink without taking no for an answer. Why does he have to be so perfect? Finn's lack of undeniability is aggravating.

Yet lurking below the mayor's chivalrous surface is something sexy, depraved, and needy. I had seen it in the orchard when he demanded I ask him nicely for his help. I had only caught a glimpse of it, and I'm itching to explore further..

"I'm glad you let me take a look at this," Finn's deep voice echoes from the cabinet. "It's not a bad crack; just needed some plumber's putty, but these things can lead to more damage. Worst case scenario is a sinkhole," he jokes.

"It's not often a man tries so hard to get a look at my leaks." I freeze the instant the words leave my mouth, realizing just how unhinged and horny that sounded. I cough into my fist to irradicate some of the tension caused by my statement, I decide that now is a great opportunity to excuse myself. I try to silently tip-toe out of the room but Finn's head emerges from the cabinet.

"Your leaks are great but I'm curious to get to know you better, Courtney." His icy blue eyes lock on me and I stiffen, any thoughts of escape turning to sand in my palms as he pins me with his stare.

Does he mean that as suggestively as it sounds? No, of course not. His words unintentionally came out that way, just as mine had. He's just being friendly. Regardless of his meaning, I'm burnt out from regurgitating my lackluster life story. With an internal grimace, I stare down at my nails.

"I was born and raised in Northern California and moved to L.A. for college. Once I got my B.A., I stayed down there permanently since I knew I wanted to be a screenwriter, and Hollywood was the place to do it. But now the writers are on strike, money's tight, and I needed a change." I give my temporary handyman an open palmed shrug, indicating I have nothing else to say.

"Don't worry, mayor, I'm not here to infiltrate your town and make everyone drink oat milk."

I register the look on Finn's face before he even says anything. He looks offended, and his words confirm it.

"I didn't mean to pry. I would never disrespect you by assuming you came to Havenwood for any nefarious reasons. I just wanted to get to know you."

My stomach twists with guilt. For the second time today I've been an absolute ass to Finn, a mayor just doing his best to get to know the newest member of town. Instead of being kind, or at least polite, I've stomped all over his kind gestures because I can't keep my feelings for him in my pants. Have I even thanked him for fixing the pipe?

"Finn, I'm sorry. I've been awful and it has nothing to do with you." I admit, shaking my head in disappointment of myself. I want to make it up to him and the best way I can think to do it is with food.

"Can I please order us some dinner and we can start over?"

A warm smile brightens his pale face and I feel some of the heavy guilt lift from my shoulders.

"You don't have to apologize for anything, Courtney and I definitely don't want to start over." Heat swirls in my cheeks as I mentally recount our experience in the orchard. *Okay, maybe I didn't want to start over either.*

"Dinner sounds great, though. How about we try a local spot? Do you like Italian?"

I contemplate the idea for a beat, only for appearances, knowing deep down that I would accept even if he suggested that we get fast food. But I can't let him see my eagerness, not yet.

"Sure," I offer a soft smile, not allowing my excitement to bubble to the surface. I don't love the idea of going out to eat in public view but I owe him for being so standoffish, even if it's a vain attempt to protect myself from falling for him.

Besides, it wouldn't be so bad to be spotted at dinner with the handsome mayor of Havenwood.

He returns my smile, his baby blues drifting down to the humble watch on his wrist. "Let me just wash up at home quickly and I'll pick you up. How's 6 p.m.?"

"I'll be here," I assure, nibbling nervously on the inside of my cheek.

"Great," he says, sounding pleasantly surprised at my approval of his plan, as if he half expected me to say no.

I watch as he presses his lips together, trying to suppress the excitement evident in his eyes. As I map his expression, I try to remember the last time Carter was this happy to spend time with me. I rack my brain, trying to recall a time. Had he ever been *excited* to spend time with me? The answer causes a little pain but also relief knowing that I'm over 3,000 miles from Carter, and Finn is right in front of me.

An altruistic, sexy, genuine man is right in front of me, so why am I not reaching out to snatch him up? Partially because I'm not 100% sure that that's what Finn even wants, he could just be chivalrous by nature and be acting as the good mayor he is. The other, more pressing, reason is that I'm scared. I don't want to be burned again, and though I doubt Finn Abernathy has a manipulative bone in his tight body, I can't allow myself to give in to him fully. Not yet. But tonight is a great place to start, to let him get to know the real Courtney, the unguarded Courtney.

A warm resinous scent sweeps by me as Finn passes to get to the front door, the appetizing smell bringing me back to the present moment. I realize that I'm now the one blocking his exit.

His warm breath fans across my forehead as he squeezes by, his proximity doing funny things to my pussy. I tip my chin up towards him, practically inviting him to take my lips in his, and for a second, it looks like he's contemplating doing so. He reaches his hand up to my face, his thumb skimming over my bottom lip, his icy eyes locked on the movement.

"See you soon," he promises softly, stealing a final glance into my eyes before heading out the front door.

"What the hell was that?!" I groan once the door shuts behind him and I've managed to regain control of most of my senses. I shake my head in disbelief, physically trying to soothe the emotions stirred in me by our almost-kiss. Finn Abernathy wanted to kiss me; he almost had!

I roll my eyes, trying hard to convince myself that that is *not* what just happened. Finn does *not* have feelings for me; he can't. Can he? If it were possible to feel the electrical currents in your body, I would argue that that is exactly what I had just felt; even Finn, barely touching my lip, had sent every receptor in my body on high alert, each of them thirsting for more of him.

I only have about an hour until the mayor is back on my doorstep, ready to whisk me away to dinner, so I need to make the most of my time. Not only do I need to get myself ready for my *not*-date, but I also need to make a phone call.

I grab my cell phone from its resting spot on the kitchen counter and dial. It rings a few times before a husky, older voice rattles out a rough "Hello?" in a Boston accent.

"Hi, my name is Courtney Berrycloth and I saw your storefront for rent.."

* * *

My phone call with the storefront's owner, a man named Mr. Gable, went better than I could've hoped for. We ended the call with his promise to give me a start date for the lease as soon as possible.

After the call, it was just my luck that my furniture order arrived while I was supposed to be getting ready for dinner. The delivery driver had left the cardboard boxes on my front porch, forcing me to drag the large boxes of unassembled furniture to their respective locations. I don't bother to begin construction now, as only thirty minutes separate me from my dinner with the mayor.

When the boxes are all dragged to their respective locations, I raid my suitcase, searching for something acceptable to wear, and settle on a burnt orange dress. It's not a date, but for some reason, I still contemplate shaving my legs. *I'm not putting out*, I remind myself, *so why shave them?* Yet somehow, I end up with the razor in my hand anyway. *Things happen*, I tell myself; *better safe than sorry*.

Midway through my rushed shower, I hear a faint, obnoxious screeching coming from above me. Olive. She's probably made her way through the strawberries I'd given her and is now demanding more like the little princess she thinks she is.

I wrap up my shower and change into my pre-selected outfit, I give it a once-over of approval in the mirror before heading to the kitchen to appease the rodent. I pick up a banana and peel it on my way up the attic steps.

I search the tall rafters, finding Olive tucked into a corner, her pitch-black eyes watching me. I set the peeled banana on the table below her, offering her a curtsy.

"You're welcome." I turn to leave the dusty attic when something catches my eye from the corner of the room. The moonlight shining in from the window highlights the edges of what looks to be a trunk, its design as archaic as the town of Havenwood itself.

I take a step towards it, curiosity winning me over despite the countless horror movies I've written exactly like this.

As I close in on the mystery box, the loud echo of church bells freezes me in my tracks. The doorbell. Finn must be here. I cast the trunk a final look before abandoning it and heading down the stairs, not wanting to keep the mayor waiting.

I place a hand on the doorknob and allow myself a steadying breath. *It's just dinner*, I remind myself and my over-eager vagina.

I pull the door open to find the mayor standing on my stoop, his raven hair combed neatly back and wearing a delicious maroon button-up. The sleeves are rolled up to his elbows, and he has a few casual buttons undone. My eyes immediately gravitate to the open space, his light dusting of chest hair threatening to peak out from the relaxed collar, sending my pulse into orbit.

"You look beautiful," he compliments, smiling at the sight of me.

"I brought these for you," he says, handing me a gorgeous

bouquet of blue hydrangeas that threatens to break my resolve entirely. Instead of admiring the flowers, I admire how his veins pop from his exposed forearms.

"Thank you," I say after finally remembering the proper words. I accept his flowers graciously, seconds away from pulling him inside the house.

"Let's get out of here. Now. Please?"

10

Black Cat Fight

Courtney

We sit in silence inside his well-kept sedan. I recognize it as the same car that I had seen parked in Agnes' driveway weeks prior and I question if his eyes were the ones I had seen watching me from her window. A part of me knows it must have been him but why had he been watching me? Did it have to do with how he knew about the leak? Or how Micah knew about me before meeting me? Are we ever going to discuss our moment in the orchard? I have so many questions that I'm dying to berate Finn with, the silence between us is now grinding against my will to stay quiet.

The fact that Havenwood is a comparatively microscopic town works in my favor, the drive from my house to the restaurant clocks in in under seven minutes. I manage to keep all my probing questions inside my head until we arrive at the restaurant. My rampant thoughts had kept me preoccupied during the short ride but why had Finn been so silent? Is he nervous about this not-date, or is he trying to prevent himself

83

from saying something he shouldn't?

"This place is locally owned, just like most businesses in Havenwood," Finn remarks as we pull into a parking spot beside the restaurant. I glance up at the sleek sign adorning the building, the stylish writing reading, *La Trattoria*.

"The owners are close friends."

I nod in response as I take note of the several other cars parked out front, silently cursing Havenwood for its lack of inconspicuous chain restaurants. God, I would kill for a desolate McDonald's right now, where I wouldn't run the risk of running into the town's entire population. Like I said before, being seen at dinner with Finn definitely isn't the worst thing in the world, but knowing how rumors swell in small towns like this, I don't want any witness rewriting tonight's narrative. This is a not-date and I don't want anyone thinking differently.

Finn steps out first, making sure to open the passenger door for me just as he had when we entered the SUV. The more time I spend with Finn Abernathy, the more I learn that chivalry is a turn-on for me, or maybe *he's* just a turn-on for me. Finn holds open the door to the restaurant and we enter the establishment as a pair, immediately earning me a look from the blonde hostess. Envy flashes across her thin face before she corrects it, greeting Finn with a toothy smile.

"Mayor, it's so great to see you." The slender hostess steps out from behind her stand, placing a slow kiss on either of Finn's sharp cheeks in a traditional la bise, her eyes remain fixed on me as she does. Her stare sends jealousy rising inside me like bile.

"Hi, Danielle. This is Courtney, Havenwood's newest transplant." A small blush has risen to the surface of Finn's pale face, a blush I selfishly want as my own. *Why hadn't I taken the opportunity to kiss his cheek when he brought me those flowers?*

"Temporary transplant," I correct, smiling politely at him. Danielle gives me a curt nod before flicking her warm honey-colored eyes back to my not-date.

"How's your little one?" Finn asks her, a genuine smile gracing his lips as he buries his hands in his pockets. How did he personally know everyone in this town and how did they know him? Hell, I can't even tell you what gender the mayor of Los Angeles is.

"He's great." Danielle coos as she gathers two menus. "I'm giving you our best table, as always." She shoots him a flirtatious wink before beckoning us to follow her. I do so with an eye roll as we are led to the back of the restaurant to a secluded table beside the glowing fireplace. The flames lick up the sides of the stone hearth, casting a romantic light onto the space. We take our seats on either side of the table's corner, and I waste no time perusing the menu, mostly in an attempt to keep my eyes off Finn. He already looks delicious but bathed in the fire's light he looks next to Godly. So I force my eyes to blaze through the menu instead of him.

"Enjoy," Danielle remarks coquettishly before making herself scarce.

"So you're a screenwriter? Admittedly, I don't know much about that." Finn lowers his dark eyebrows as he asks, his long fingers fidgeting with the precursory glass of water left atop the moody golden tablecloth. I observe the motion, wondering how a man can be so gentle and sensitive yet secretly so sexy and domineering.

"Well, I wrote-" I pause, mentally slapping myself on

the wrist. "I *write* scripts for television shows mostly but occasionally movies or podcasts," I explain. I am *still* a screenwriter. Carter might have driven me out of L.A. and shattered my confidence, but he can't take that from me.

"That's extraordinary," Finn regards me with a look of newfound admiration as if I'd just told him I'd discovered the cure for cancer or something.

"You can work and write remotely from here?"

I shake my head, tucking a strand of brown behind my ear. Why's it so difficult to get my words out around him? It's probably because I hand-select each one before letting it pass my lips, afraid to somehow ruin this moment with him.

"As I mentioned earlier, my writing guild is on strike right now due to conflicts over our pay, so I'm not working right now, unfortunately." Finn's eyes reflect sympathy as he studies me for a beat.

"I'm sorry to hear that. Writing is an art and deserves to be paid justly. Are you doing okay without a source of income?"

"Well, actually," I didn't plan on revealing my next move yet, certainly not to Finn, but I'm so excited I can't keep it in. "I'm going to be temporarily opening up a bookshop in Havenwood. So that will be my job until our union can negotiate a fair deal. I noticed an empty storefront downtown and called the owner; he was willing to rent it to me on a short-term lease." Finn beams as I tell him the news, excitement evident in his expression just as I'm sure it is evident in mine.

"The old flower shop? That's amazing, I'm so happy for you." His hand darts out, eclipsing my own as he rests his on top. I instantly love the sensation of his warm, inviting touch on my skin. Realizing his forwardness he pulls his hand back, an apologetic and shocked look on his face. I say nothing, afraid to encourage him yet also afraid to discourage him; I attempt to keep my face as neutral as possible. A waiter passes by our table and Finn politely flags him down.

"May we please order a bottle of the French Chestnut Wine?" he requests. The young waiter nods, scampering off to retrieve the bottle. Finn turns his attention back to me, nervously kneading his hands. "I-".

"Did you just order nut wine?" I change the subject and interrupt the unnecessary apology he's about to give me. I want to tell him that I love how his touch feels and that he certainly does not need to apologize for it but of course, I say nothing.

He sputters out a laugh, running a large hand through his dark locks.

"I suppose I did but don't knock it until you've tried it," he chuckles, pointing a warning finger jokingly.

"Yes, Mr. Mayor." I giggle back, taking a sip from my glass of water. Our eyes meet over the brim, and for a moment, I swear I can see that same fiery desire gleaming below his icy pools. Just as I think nothing can ruin this blissful moment between us, clouds of thunder and lightning settle in above us or, should I say, beside us.

I track Finn's eyes as they drift beside me, a displeased look spanning his face before he quickly neutralizes it. I turn and find Soul and Starr standing beside us, the fire's light reflected in their glare. Soul tosses a strand of dark purple hair over her shoulder, not blinking once as she attempts to intimidate me.

"Hi Finn, I haven't seen you in a while," Starr greets in a luscious voice, shooting Finn the most sarcastic smile I'd ever seen. "When was the last time? Hmm, let me think... after apple picking, right?"

Was that why he had left so abruptly, not bothering to join the rest of us at the bakery? I feel my blood boil, but I know that's exactly what Starr wants. Instead of giving her the satisfaction of a reaction, I sit up straight and veer onto the high road.

"Hi Starr, great to officially meet you. I'm Courtney, I'm sorry I ran into the two of you the other day." I ignore Finn as he turns a questioning glance at me, keeping my eyes set on Starr's, unwilling to be the first to look away. I don't bother offering her my hand to shake, and it's a good thing I don't because based on the look of pure disgust she's giving me right now, she would have reacted to my hand as if it were a viper showing its teeth. Though I think we're both well aware of who the snake is in this situation.

"Aw," Starr tisks, reverting her gaze to Finn. Her eyes soften from the daggers they were only seconds ago as she looks at him. She twirls a strand of inky reddish black hair around her finger.

"Finn, you're so sweet to feed the unemployed town newbie."

That's it, I'm done playing nice. I've been in one too many catfights in seedy Hollywood bars with women a lot more intimidating than her to deal with her level of disrespect. As if sensing that I'm about to do something irrational, Finn places a steadying hand on my shoulder. My head snaps to him as soon as I feel his calming touch, his blue eyes already pinning me with a warning look. He's right; there are two vampires and only one of me; it wouldn't end in my favor. This is a battle that needs to be fought with words, not claws.

I let out a shrill laugh, allowing my shoulders to bounce with faux mirth.

"That's so funny! I thought wannabe musicians were the unemployed ones but you go, girl boss." I smirk, knowing I left no crumbs. Both women clench their fists, experiencing the same rage they instilled in me and not appreciating the taste. I enjoy my victory, sipping casually on my water as if nothing is amiss. A warm sensation on my thigh causes my eyes to saucer. Finn gives my leg an approving squeeze and then the feeling is gone, taking the warmth with it. Did he approve of me sassing Starr? And he showed his approval by touching my thigh?

Before Starr can quip back Finn cuts her off, a gentle smile tugging at the corner of his lips

"Courtney just informed me she's opening a bookstore downtown. Seeing as Havenwood lacks proper entertainment, I'm sure she'll be richer than all of us pretty soon."

The waiter drops off the bottle of wine at our table, cutting the palpable tension as he comes between us and the musicians.

Starr's sour smile returns to her face as she places a hand on the table, leaning over slightly so her cleavage is visible. I scoff at the desperate move. I make her nervous, I can see that and leopards like Starr don't like it when you can see their spots.

"Totally, Finn, Havenwood needs more entertainment since Soul and I started touring." Her dark eyes find mine, attempting to throw that fact in my face. It has no effect, as I know, just as anyone in Showbiz knows that touring does not equate to being successful.

"But we're so excited to perform for you on Halloween. Who knows, maybe I'll finally be able to convince you to come on tour with me. The nights have been long and lonely." She flicks her tongue across her lips and winks directly at me. "But not as long as they used to be."

Finn offers her a tight-lipped smile as the waiter finishes pouring our glasses full of reddish-brown wine.

"Havenwood is my home, Starr, you know that. I'll never leave." His voice lowers an octave, "and we've already had this discussion."

"Things change." Soul speaks for the first time, allowing me a look at her bifurcated tongue. The sight of her body modification is ominous, causing me to feel a little queasy.

"I'll be seeing you later, Finn." Starr removes her palm from the table and stands to her full height.

"Nice meeting you, Chelsea." She wiggles her thin fingers at me in a mocking wave, their tips topped with sharp nails that resemble claws. *How fitting.* The two depart the restaurant, their absence soaking Finn and I into an awkward silence.

My blood boiling at the possibility of him and Starr still messing around.

11

Chestnut Wine

Finn

"How do you know Elvira?" Courtney nods her head towards the now-exiting pair. Her words are playful but her tone harbors the slightest bit of jealousy that she attempts to hide behind a tight-lipped smile. Her jealousy is hot; I like when a woman is protective of what she wants. Admittedly, I don't know if Courtney wants me or if she simply wanted to win that catfight. Either way, I'm grateful that she was able to put Starr in her place, a task I'm far too polite to do. I gently swirl my wine glass, staring into the dark liquid before answering her question.

"She was born and raised here just like me. We went to school together from elementary to high school."

"She's certainly a fan of yours," Courtney remarks, her bark brown eyes watching my response closely. I offer her a small smirk, her bratty tone causing my cock to jerk in my pants.

"She's always been fond of me." I immaturely play into her envy, curious as to how far she'll push to find out more about Starr and I. I shouldn't do this, I shouldn't allow myself to sink

91

to this level of juvenility. It isn't very demure of me, a quality I strive to embody each day but there is always a man in every gentleman and the man in me is desperate to know how badly Courtney Berrycloth wants me. I want her to admit it, to tell me that her feelings for me are as undeniable as mine are for her. They're right there, rippling below her guarded facade, ready to break the surface tension and driving me crazy.

"How about the other shining twin?" She sips her wine, changing the subject in an attempt to hide behind another topic.

"Soul isn't originally from Havenwood. Starr met her on a weekend trip to Salem; they started making music together, and the rest is history." The same waiter returns for our food order, and I have to force my eyes off Courtney's beautiful face.

"What can I get for you, sir?" He asks politely, poising his pen to his paper pad, eager to jot down my order.

"May I please have the fettuccine Alfredo with a side salad?" I order my typical, safe option with a healthy side. I never stray much from regularity or routine; it's made my life quite predictable, but the woman sitting across from me is anything but predicted. I'm unable to look into her warm brown eyes without feeling a twist of guilt and the pain intensifies each second that I spend in her presence without being truthful with her. I grit my teeth, worried the immense turmoil I feel for secretly luring her here will become unbearable and break me, forcing me to confess and reveal our entire plot to her. I keep myself silent, remembering what is at stake if she doesn't sign over those remains, and for the moment, it's enough to muzzle me.

"Very good and for you, miss?"

"I'll take the eggplant rollatini, please; thank you." We hand back our menus, and Courtney's focus is on me once again. My cheeks heat under her gaze as if she can read my mind.

"Your turn," She nibbles on a piece of warm bread that the waiter had dropped off at our table. I cock my head at her questioningly.

"Tell me how Finn Abernathy became the beloved mayor he is today." She clarifies, throwing her compliment in so casually as if it's simply a fact that I'm beloved. My dark eyebrows knit together and I try to pick out the important details before I decide on the best synopsis of my life.

"I was born and raised in Havenwood, like my great-great grandparents before me. My parents passed when I was eleven." Guilt flashes across her features as her plump lips part. I shy away from her gaze, not wanting to see the all-too-familiar pity in her eyes.

"Finn, I'm so sorry," Courtney's words are soft and comforting like a silk blanket but I don't want her to see me as wounded or damaged because of my unhappy past.

"It's okay, I promise." My tone is reassuring, and I try to keep it strong, but some of the pain bleeds through like it always does when I talk about my parents.

"It's part of my history and it's no secret. It still hurts and I miss them but I think they'd be proud if they knew what I was doing for the town they loved so much." I admit, offering her a half smile.

"I know they would," this time, Courtney reaches her hand across the table, placing it on top of mine. I stare at it for a beat, marveling at how small her palm is compared to my own. I take in a small breath and continue, not wanting to deter her.

"Agnes took me in without a second thought. Milo and I were best friends from school and practically brothers anyway, so it was an easy choice. So she says." I tilt my head and chuckle, raising an unsure eyebrow. I was always a tame child, just as I am a tame man now, but I always canonize Agnes and Phil for taking in a traumatized orphan.

My joke draws a giggle out of Courtney, the joyous and enticing sound reminding me of wind chimes tinkling in a warm summer breeze. It's a noise so genuine and loving you almost can't help but smile.

"College was a requirement for Milo and I, so he commuted to Boston University, and I took my classes online. You're looking at a man holding his B.S. in Political Science, you know," I joke, taking a sip of the wine. Courtney smirks back at me, loading her metaphorical gun.

"And you're looking at a woman with her M.A. in creative writing."

I scoff playfully and grasp my chest.

"You've outdone me; that hurts my manhood." She giggles, releasing that precious sound once again. I wrap up my life story, boring even myself.

"From there, it's not very interesting, not that the first bit was. I shook hands and kissed babies, and when elections came, I did pretty well. I won't lie. It helped that our last mayor completely squandered the town's funds, so his reelection was off the table. "

I know I won the election because of my organic efforts. Many people told me they would have voted for me regardless of Jerry's slip-up, but I'm not one for boasting, especially not to my dates. I know my accomplishments, and that is enough.

"Havenwood is the last piece of my parents I have left. Being its mayor is a privilege that I don't take for granted." My blue eyes drop down to the golden tablecloth, I study its embroidery to distract from the truth of my words. "I'll do whatever I have to to save it."

That's the most honest and unguarded thing I've said to Courtney all night, only it isn't just a figure of speech it's a promise. One I know I have to fulfill, for my parents, for the residents of Havenwood, and once upon a time, for me. But now there is something else, someone else, I want more than I want Havenwood to survive. My motives for getting close to Courtney all stemmed from a place of genuine attraction but she will never believe me once she knows what I've done, and I couldn't blame her for it.

My spiraling thoughts are interrupted by the waiter placing our steaming entrees in front of us respectively and offering a quick *"Enjoy!"* before dashing off to his next table.

"This looks amazing," I admire, looking over my pasta. I keep my attitude light, attempting to move on from our previously heavy conversation despite the pieces of my mind still linger there unwillingly.

"It does." She responds with a delicate smile, I see the cogs and wheels rolling behind her eyes as she thinks hard on something.

"Cheers," She offers, holding up her wine glass. I smile at her uncertainly but click my glass to hers anyway, the sound reverberating between us.

"What are we toasting?" I ask curiously as I raise the rim of my glass to my lips, Courtney closely tracking the motion.

"You," Her doe eyes are half-lidded as she raises her glass, tipping her head back and letting the wine trickle down her throat. I watch intently as her head reclines, exposing more of her long neck, the tan skin practically begging to be kissed. I clear my throat, fixing a smile on my face and shoving down my desire before she looks at me once again.

The rest of the dinner was amazing despite its rough beginnings. At one point, the restaurant owner, Amir, came out from the back to greet us and introduce himself to Courtney. Amir is a kind man in his mid-forties with olive skin, a thick Italian accent, and a plump belly, one I imagined I would also have if I had constant access to this amazing food.

After finishing our meals, we drive back to her house in the same silence we arrived in; this time, the quiet is much more comfortable, with both our stomachs full and lingering smiles on our faces. A sufficient end to one of the best nights I'd had in a while.

As we pull into her driveway beside Agnes' house, I hesitate, unwilling to say goodbye so soon. I feel like I've just started to get to know the real Courtney and crave more of her.

"Oh, hey, I think I left my wrench inside. Could I grab it?" I wait for her permission. I'm not entirely sure if I left the wrench or not, but I want more time with her, regardless.

"Yes," she answers quickly, her cheeks flushing as she turns away from me. I grin as slip from my seat and loop around the vehicle to open her door.

We approach the wooden front door together and I watch with adoration as Courtney anxiously fumbles with her keys. I wait patiently behind her in no rush at all, keeping my hands shoved deep into my front pockets, hiding the erection mounting in my jeans from being so close to her. She locates the correct key and lets us inside.

Within seconds of us stepping inside, thunder cracks loudly from the heavens, and a downpour ensues immediately after, as if by divine intervention.

"Shit," Courtney jumps at the sound, watching the buckets pour from the safety of the entryway. I chuckle softly at her jumpiness, reminding myself Californians probably forget what weather even is. The wrench truly was left on her counter after all and I snatch it up, heading back to the entryway to make my unavoidable exit.

Courtney turns back to face me as she closes the heavy door; a look of surprise overtakes her when she notices the tool in my hand.

"You're leaving?" she asks as her head swivels to her left, looking out the window at the rain.

"Yes, thank you for an amazing night, Courtney." We stand a mere few feet apart, her sweet fruity aroma drifting directly into my nose and sending my pheromones blazing. "I enjoyed getting to know you."

I drink in the vision of her before making my way for the door, attempting to excuse myself as soon as politely possible. My erection is still very much present and more blood is flowing south by the second with her sweet scent tempting me. I need to get home and relieve myself of the ache building in my base.

"Woah," she says, holding her hand haltingly against my chest, the contact sending my emotions into overdrive.

"Did I... say something wrong?" I ask her in confusion, replaying my last few sentences in my head.

"No, that's not—you're sweet," she reassures, causing a heated blush to spread onto my high cheekbones. She jabs a thumb behind her, showcasing the blinding rainfall happening outside. "You can't drive in this; it's raining like crazy."

I can't help but laugh, not at her but at the concern of a New

Englander driving in the rain. A puzzled expression overtakes her face, so I clarify.

"I really appreciate your concern but this is normal here." I try to reassure her, biting back the desire to reach out and stroke her cheek with the back of my hand. I want to feel her skin on mine, to break my resolve and just tell her how badly I want her and that I don't care if that makes me crazy. Another crack of thunder and flash of lightning has her wide eyes flying to the window.

"Nuh-uh, no way," she shakes her head, firm in her decision. "I can't let you drive in this. Will Agnes let you stay over?" She twists the nob of the front door, poking her head out and searching the house next door for any lights. I know she won't find any, my adoptive mom prides herself on going to bed on a strict schedule.

"No chance, Agnes would kill me if I dared to wake her up right now. Ma likes her beauty sleep." I shiver as I recount a memory of when I had dared to wake a sleeping Agnes. I watch Courtney bite her bottom lip, contemplating how to proceed.

"You can stay here," she announces, nervously tucking a strand of caramel behind her ear.

"Courtney, I promise—" I begin to comfort her, but she cuts me off.

"Please?" Her eyes stare up at me pleadingly. A part of me wonders if she wants me to stay, not because of my safety but simply because she wants me here. I open my mouth to argue again, but the words die on my exhale as I search her beautiful, hopeful face.

"Okay." I relent, raising my hands in surrender.

Courtney's face lights up in a smile then quickly drops as

she remembers.

"I only have one bed."

12

Ghost Story

Courtney

I grab a blanket for each of us and quickly boil some oat milk to make chai teas, doing my best to be an amiable host.

"I appreciate your hospitality but I don't want to impose." Finn protests again as I pour steaming milk over the chai mix.

"I can't let you leave in good conscience. Hasn't anyone told you about the dangers of sinkholes?" I offer him a simper as I hand him his mug. Ardor twinkles in his icy irises as he accepts his drink. He returns my smirk but says nothing as he follows me into the living room.

"Right," I remark in a whisper as I scan the vacant room. "No couch."

"The floor is perfect." Warm breath tickles the back of my neck, causing every hair on my body to stand at attention. Finn's closeness overwhelms me; every cell in my body is on high alert, hyper-aware of his presence behind me. The electric current between the two of us flows freely, pulsing and rushing and dizzying my head. I want to turn around and climb him like a damn tree; he's so fucking intoxicating. I want to show him just how perfect the floor can be when we put it to good use.

A soft hand on my lower back calls me to action. I jolt forward and take a seat on the cold hardwood. Finn follows suit, taking a seat across from me just as the rain outside picks up its intensity. *Focus on the rain, nympho.* I try to redirect my thoughts, choosing to pay attention to the downpour outside of my window as opposed to the one in my underwear.

I've never seen such crazy rain in my entire life, which solidifies my decision not to let the mayor drive in it. Besides, I've never been completely alone with Finn before, without any friends or audiences nearby, and this is my chance. For what exactly? I didn't know.

Now that I had allowed some of my emotional walls to crumble, I had spent the entirety of dinner wondering what it would be like to be with Finn in every regard. His confidant, his lover, his friend, his girlfriend, is any of that even possible? I'd admitted my feelings to myself but could I admit them to him without knowing how he felt about me in return?

Only now, entirely alone and confined inside together by the storm, can I feel the full force of the undeniable electrical hum between us. Only now, without my attention being divided by the prying eyes of the public, can I properly hear our energy crackling and popping dangerously loud, just like the fierce lightning outside my windows. I allow my gaze to rake down his toned form, with his full lips and firm body so close to me the temptation I'm feeling is practically a physical being between us.

My hand juts out as I pass the mayor his chai. The movement is choppy and robotic from nerves, almost causing the tea to slosh over the edge of the mug. Finn gives me a wary look but accepts the drink with a polite *"thank you."* The instant the steaming cup is secure in his grip I pull away, doing my best to ignore the way his healthy veins rope along the back of his hand.

I clear my throat, the taste of French nut wine still prevalent on my breath as I pull my blanket tighter around myself. The very same infernal wine that had convinced me that Finn staying over would be a grand idea despite having literally no furniture and no way to entertain him. Each second that ticks by has me simultaneously rethinking my hospitality and fighting the urge to plant myself in Finn's lap.

"Are you alright?" Finn's pale blue eyes study me, his words guiding me out of the fog of my conflicting thoughts. His posture is rigid as he watches for my reaction, intuitively sensing and bracing for the battle happening within me.

"Yeah," I respond a bit too overzealously, shaking the haze from my head as I attempt to appear casual.

Finn had warned that the storm would likely tamper with the power, so we had lit the fireplace as a precautionary measure, but the sight of him once again bathed in beautiful firelight did little to silence my desires. The flames cast half of his handsome face into shadows, highlighting his sharp brow and the high ridge of his nose, my mind straying to how he might look wearing nothing but firelight.

"Know any ghost stories?" I quirk a brow at him, eager to offer myself a distraction. Finn's concerned expression deepens into one of confusion as he tries to follow my train of thought. Before he can verbalize his confusion, I speak again. "Crazy storm, warm fire, seems like the perfect setting to tell one," I explain, shrugging my shoulders to release some of my pent-up energy.

Finn tips his chin towards me, his perfect lips molding into a knowing grin, seemingly placated by my explanation.

"A few," he admits, his voice much too baritone for his own good. "I'd love to hear yours first."

"Well, the scariest thing I've seen in Havenwood so far," I drop my voice to a serious tone, "is the lack of alternative milk." Finn releases a booming laugh that originates in his belly, the pleasant resonate draws an unconscious smile to my face as I relish in its sound.

"I would argue that your inability to process dairy is equally as frightening." Finn flattens his tone back to a falsely serious one, causing me to giggle. He sips from his mug, his mirthful eyes remaining on me.

"Lactose intolerance, it's a thing. Google it. Do you have Google here?" I tease, ticking my head to one side in playful curiosity.

"You'll have to educate me on that later." His devilish smile melts, giving way to a more somber expression, piquing my interest. "I could tell you about this one time.."

"Do it," I insist, tightening my grip on my chai and scooching closer to the tall, dark mayor. He looks down at me hesitantly, wondering if I'll judge him for the story he's about to tell but seemingly decides on telling me anyway.

"By now I assume you're familiar with the history of Martha Brant?" He confirms.

"Lived in Havenwood in the 1690s, was accused of witchcraft during the witch trials, died. Now she's some sort of urban legend around town, Elsie's terrified of her." I recite, searching the ceiling to jog my memory. Finn grins pridefully at me, seemingly proud that I picked up on the history of Havenwood so quickly.

"Well done," he compliments before continuing with his story. "Before we knew for certain what had become of Martha's remains, Milo and I had several hunches. All of which never panned out. Accused witches weren't allowed to be buried on church grounds and often found themselves buried in unmarked graves. Making it extremely difficult to locate her body.

"A few months ago we decided to check a random location on a whim, below a very old oak tree that dated back to Martha's time. The two of us set out and began digging, and thirty minutes later, our shovels hit something wooden." Finn's blue orbs are locked on mine, pulling me deeper into the story with each word. I take note of him being an inept storyteller, his eyes and eyebrows moving concisely with his words.

"We had gotten as far as we could with our shovels, so we bent down and dusted the dirt from the wood, and just as we had suspected, it was an unmarked coffin. We took only a second to share a look of excitement before we got to work hauling the box to the surface." Finn gives me one more deciding look before hitting the climax of his story.

"We were quick to crack the lid open but as soon as fresh air touched the inside of that coffin the wind began to pick up around us and swirl like we were trapped inside a cyclone, just the two of us. I swear the temperature dropped ten degrees like that," he snaps his long fingers. I jump at the sound, completely entangled in his story.

"Worst of all came this awful, unnatural banshee shriek. The sound felt like ice in our blood. It was horrible. Then, it all stopped at once and everything returned to normal as if it never happened. The wind slowed, the screaming ceased and it wasn't freezing anymore. Neither Milo nor I can explain what happened; if you ask him about it, he likely won't talk about it; his scientific mind has a hard time processing this kind of thing."

I blink at him in skeptical disbelief. Finn had yet to give me any reason not to believe him, and he looks unsettled as he recounts the event to me. However, his story is so far-fetched that my logical side has a hard time giving in.

Finn breaks the silence, chuckling despite himself when he sees my saucered eyes.

"I promise you, I'm telling the truth," his smile is alluring, mirth evident in his icy eyes. His amusement calms once again as he tacks on. "Kids would claim to hear Martha wailing as she wandered the streets late at night. Most of us assumed it was just some story our parents told us to make us go to bed on time or be home before dark. But since that day, almost everyone in town has heard her cries."

I open my mouth to speak, unsure of what exactly will come out but am abruptly cut off by a loud, haunting feminine lament echoing throughout the house. Finn and I meet each other's surprised gaze, fear paralyzing me in place.

"Are all your windows shut?" He demands, jumping into action mode almost immediately. A brief look of terror flashes across his face as I force my head to shake itself. I raise an unsteady hand, pointing upstairs.

"The bedroom," I inform him in a whisper. *Jesus fucking Christ,* had talking about the witch's ghost summoned her here?!

Finn shoots me a wavering look of false confidence before breaking himself free from the safety of his blanket. He stands to his full height, taking in an unsteady breath before heading for the stairs.

"Wait!" I interject before I have a chance to change my mind. "I'm coming with you." Finn doesn't protest my company but issues a protective, "stay behind me."

I nod and we ascend the staircase together.

As we take the steps one by one my knees almost clatter together comically and I fully regret asking to exchange ghost stories, *who even does that?* I'm too terrified even to attempt to comprehend how Finn intends to defend us against the ghost of a witch who has been dead for 300+ years. Finn is a tall man standing at about six foot and seems well built under his nice clothes but even I know he's probably pissing himself right now. What is brawn against the supernatural?

We reach the second-floor landing, my darkened bedroom now directly in front of us. We enter the room cautiously, with Finn still in the lead. I slip my hand into his for moral support, the electricity buzzing between our palms keeping us somewhat grounded through our fear.

The room is coated in darkness, save for the thin strips of moonlight shining in through my open window, making it nearly impossible to determine what is right in front of our faces. I had opened the window after my shower in an attempt to let some of the steam out and had forgotten to shut it, something I was deeply regretting now. My eyes are glued to the window as I anticipate another spine-tingling howl to be carried in through it.

I watch through the dimness as Finn reaches his free hand towards the nearest wall, rubbing over the smooth surface in search of the light switch. As soon as he locates it and I hear the click of the switch shifting into the on position, another piercing screech erupts. As the overhead light illuminates the room, a shrieking black mass charges us, nearly smacking us in the face.

"Fucking Christ!" Finn exclaims as he raises an arm defensively, shielding his head. I instinctively begin to duck as well, but once the light exposes the creature, all the fear dissipates from my body, quickly being replaced with annoyance.

"Olive!" I reprimand, straightening my posture. Finn slowly lowers his raised arm, taking in the situation and watching the little bat flutter around the ceiling, squawking in her displeasure at the light. He looks at me with a raised brow; under his gaze, I realize just how crazy I must look at this moment. We both take note of his arm wrapped protectively around my middle. At what point had he let go of my hand and wrapped it around me instead? Most likely when Olive had launched her blitzkrieg and sent the two of us into flight or fight, either way, I'm glad for it.

"Often keep rodents in your bedroom?" Finn jests as he clears his throat, walking over to the window and locking it shut.

"Normally, I make them take me on a few dates first," I joke back, watching his back muscles as he closes my bedroom window. I watch those same muscles tense as he comprehends my joke, is the mayor upset at the thought of me letting other men in my bedroom? If he had been, he'd fixed his face by the time he turned around, and there's no hint of any evident disdain.

"I guess I'm an exception," he offers a shy smile. I open my mouth to tell him *yes, you're so much different than any man I've met. You're sweet and compassionate and not a selfish prick. You're perfect.* But it doesn't come out; there's still that part of me holding back, waiting for him to give me a sign of reciprocated feelings.

"She normally lives in my attic," I change the subject, awkwardly fidgeting with my sleeve. I flick my eyes to Olive, who is nestled into the corner of my room, glaring at Finn for turning the light on.

I pause to contemplate that sentence as realization hits me over the head like a log. I knit my brows together and retreat a few steps into the hallway. Sure enough, the door to the attic is open, barely cracked enough for Olive to squeeze through but still ajar. The sight sends a shiver down my spine. That door was closed when I came upstairs earlier for our blankets and Olive sure didn't open it herself.

I decide not to mention it to Finn. I'm not sure exactly why, but I keep it to myself, not wanting any more weird distractions for the night.

Finn helps me wrangle Olive back into her domain, and I ensure the door latches shut before retreating downstairs to collect our blankets. Both of us are ready to end the night and forget about our tense, *almost* paranormal encounter.

Now came the most nerve-racking part of the night, sharing one bed.

13

All Good Sides

Finn

After the bat scare, Courtney and I mutually agreed that it was time to end the night. After retrieving our blankets from downstairs, I found Courtney had retreated to her en suite to begin her skincare routine.

I lean against the door frame, just out of sight, and watch her reflection pat her bare face dry before she begins to massage retinal into her beautiful sun-kissed skin. It seems like a tantalizing, multi-step process, and yet, there is such beauty in watching her do something so mundane. It's like watching a doe graze in a meadow; there's nothing particularly exciting happening, but being so close to such a beautiful and skittish creature is exhilarating enough.

I'm falling for Courtney much harder and faster than I had previously imagined even to be possible; I've never felt this hopelessly lost for any woman before. It feels like the more I try to suppress my feelings, the deeper I'm sucked into them, like fighting quicksand. The more I try to remind myself of the reasons why I can't keep Courtney, the less and less memorable those reasons become. I silently step away from the door with a head full of regret and take a seat on the edge of her mattress that is lying unceremoniously on the floor. I close my eyes, envisioning a life where I end each day watching Courtney complete her captivating regimen and pull her into bed with me right after, the two of us drifting off to sleep together with my arms wrapped around her. A life that I know is out of reach.

How different things could have been between us if I were an honest man, if I didn't have the fate of an entire town riding on my shoulders, and if lying to Courtney wasn't the damn key to solving it all. But it doesn't hurt to pretend I'm worthy of Courtney for a little while longer. Does it? I'll find a way to tell her the truth somehow when the time is right. She deserves that and so much more yet I'm too selfish to do it now, just as she's starting to warm up to me and her hard facade is beginning to lower, it's too soon.

Since the moment I met Courtney at Mystic Brew, she's been my first thought in the morning and my last thought before sleep overtakes me each night. The fruity scent of her hair, the galvanic feel of her skin on mine, the way she would fit perfectly in my arms. It all feels as if I've already known her forever, and the magnetic pull between us only reinforces the ridiculous notion that it was love at first sight with her.

"Bathroom's all yours if you need it," Courtney emerges from the en suite wearing fuzzy pink pajama pants and a thin tank top that clings to her perky breasts. My throat dries as my gaze peruses her gorgeous figure, getting stuck on the two pebbled peaks below her shirt. I snap my eyes back to hers as quickly as I can but it's too late, the subtle blush on her tan cheeks tells me she caught me staring.

"I know it's a big leap from going to dinner together to sharing a bed. If you're uncomfortable, and I mean *at all*, I have no issue leaving." I offer her a final excuse to kick me out, searching her face for even the smallest sign of hesitation. Courtney is offering me a place to stay out of the kindness of her heart and to allow myself to sleep beside her; feeling the way I do feels like taking advantage of that kindness. She shakes her head fervently, sending her caramel tresses sweeping her shoulders.

"I'm not uncomfortable, Finn," She dismisses my offer, her doe-like eyes searching the room for something. "I'll sleep below the covers, and you sleep on top. It won't be weird. It's like a sleepover. Here." She reassures me as her sight lands on a thick blanket resting atop a suitcase in the corner of the room.

"Use this one; it's my favorite." Courtney struggles to fit the entirety of the heavy brown blanket in her arms as she carries it to me, dropping it in my lap. She pauses momentarily, regarding the spot where she had just dumped the blanket. I freeze as she does. Admittedly, a little blood had rushed south upon seeing her in her pajamas, leaving me silently praying she hadn't noticed the bulging below my zipper.

"You're wearing jeans."

"Yes.." I respond, unsure of the meaning behind her words, hoping that her seemingly out-of-place statement has nothing to do with me sailing at half mast.

"I'll find you something more comfortable." She blinks a few times before toddling off to another suitcase tucked inside her closet. I let out a small sigh of relief, conscious of how narrowly I avoided an awkward conversation.

"I don't think we're the same size," She jokes as she digs

111

through her luggage, examining each pair of bottoms as she goes.

I watch as she does, comprehension dawning on me as she carefully inspects each piece of clothing. She's distracting herself. From what, I'm not exactly sure, but the way she takes her time with each article of clothing tells me she's trying to keep her thoughts preoccupied.

I tilt my head in contemplation as she casts the suitcase aside, starting to ruffle through another. She refuses to let her eyes stray, keeping them glued on the task before her. I crease my brow as I study her. *Is my presence what she needs distraction from?* The idea causes a warmth to radiate from within me and a festering heat begins to settle low in my stomach. One that I quickly attempt to dowse.

I hold the blanket tighter against myself as I feel my cock begin to lengthen; I can't allow myself to get excited when I know I'm supposed to be platonically sleeping beside her in mere moments. But if there are signs that she reciprocates my feelings, I can't help but be enthralled.

Courtney hesitantly dips her hand into her luggage, pulling out a pair of light gray sweatpants that look to be made of cashmere or some other similarly expensive fabric. She turns them over in her small hands, a glint of unreadable emotion dancing across her eyes before she passes them to me.

"These might fit," she offers, trying to keep her tone light despite the tightness in her throat.

I silently take them from her, holding them out in front of me as I inspect them, my jaw clenching as I do. These are men's pants, it's clear from their size and cut and the thought of Courtney having another man's pants sends a small stream of unwarranted jealousy trickling into my system. I don't let

Courtney see my discontent, however. What right do I have to her?

I hold the sweatpants up in front of her and squint one eye, comparing the size of the pants to her small frame, playfully letting her know that I know they don't belong to her.

"You sure their owner won't mind me borrowing them?" I pry slightly, keeping my tone casual and light. I have no right to her but I *do* have morbid curiosity and maybe some masochistic tendencies.

"I'm sure." She answers shortly as she turns her back to me, giving me privacy to change into the pants. I rise to my feet and unzip my jeans, allowing them to fall to the ground beside the unframed mattress. I step out of them and pull the cushy cashmere sweats up to replace them, looking quite ridiculous in my button-up shirt and sweatpants. Courtney turns once she's sure I'm decent and pauses at the sight of the pants.

"They look good on you." Is all she offers before crawling onto her side of the bed. "Will you hit the light?"

"Of course." I flick the light switch off, immersing the room in shadow. I tenderly find my place on the bed beside her, making sure not to brush my skin against hers as I pull the brown blanket over my long torso.

In the faint light provided by the moon, I can discern Courtney's beautiful face. She looks deep in thought as she stares up at the ceiling. *Is she thinking about the original owner of these sweatpants?* Jealousy rushes in once again at the thought. I prop myself up on an elbow and turn in Courtney's direction.

"Tell me about Mr. Sweatpants," the words leave my mouth before I have the chance to vet them. This is way overstepping and I know it. This isn't a topic I would normally broach but I have to know. Some weird part of me feels like I'm competing with this mystery man, and knowing more about him will decipher my chances.

Courtney's bark brown eyes find mine in the darkness. Even in the faint moonlight, I can tell her expression is one of surprise. If she doesn't want to answer, I'll understand, but a little piece of me will never be satisfied if I don't ask.

Instead of telling me to mind my own damn business, like I thought she might have, Courtney takes in a contemplative breath.

"We were seeing each other for a while. A long while."

Envy trickles into my chest cavity as she confirms what I had already assumed. Courtney had dated a sweatpants guy and, from her sad tone, it seemed he had hurt her. We sit in brief silence as she decides how much of the story she wants to tell me. I allow her all the time she needs.

"I only saw the parts of him that I wanted to and because of that, I overlooked the bad parts. Eventually, he forced me to see who he really was and it was almost entirely bad. Scratch that, it was entirely bad—manipulative parts, image-obsessed parts."

Hearing the hurt in Courtney's voice has the same effect on me as if someone were to pinch off the blood supply to my aorta. Pain cramps in my chest, and at the moment, I'm overrun with the desire to pull Courtney into my chest and comfort her any way I know how. Simultaneously, I feel my jealousy melt into guilt for forcing her to relive and explain a traumatic part of her love life, and even more guilt mounts as I consider her words. *Manipulative*, that's exactly what I am. If Courtney knew the truth about me, would she believe that I'm made of entirely bad parts, too? I know I am; I must be if I'm willing to manipulate her to get something I need.

"I'll never let a guy deceive me like that ever again. Next time I let myself fall for a man, it'll be for a man with all good sides." Her eyes are on me once again but this time they feel like they're burning holes into me. The guilt causes my stomach to flip in a truly unpleasant manner. If she looks too hard will she be able to see I'm not that guy? Will she be able to see that I *want* to be?

"You said the next time you let yourself fall," I repeat.

"Mhm," she nods her head, a yawn falling from her full lips. I hold my breath as I ask my next question.

"Does that mean you're not falling right now?"

Her lips part in hesitation and her eyes widen slightly but she gives no answer, shocked into silence. I bite the inside of my cheek until I taste iron, my heart hitching on its beat.

"Goodnight, mayor." Is all she offers before rolling over, absconding my view of her face.

"Goodnight," I say quietly, spending the remainder of the night reflecting on the massive hole I've dug myself into. Courtney had been burned by the men of her past, which explained her original cold demeanor towards me and her drive to keep me away.

I don't want to hurt her like they had but I already have, whether she knows it or not. I've befriended her with ulterior motives and though everything since then has been genuine, she'll never be able to see that once she knows the truth and I can't fault her for it. From the moment I sent her that first email I soiled my chance to be a man that is good enough for Courtney Berrycloth.

Yet, for some reason, knowing all that isn't enough to stop me from trying to be.

14

Sugar and Spice

Courtney

The mayor had left as soon as the rain let up, around 5 a.m., citing the excuse that he had important mayoral duties he needed to tend to early this morning. I didn't believe that for a second and, admittedly, missed him when he was gone, but I knew it was ultimately for the best. I had had my experiment, I'd spent time alone with him, and I learned that the more time I spent with Mayor Finn Abernathy, the harder it was to keep my feelings for him at bay. Every part of me ached for him when I was in his presence; I wanted to curl up in his lap like a house cat and listen to his every thought. At this point, I was borderlining on obsessed.

Last night, he had asked me if I was falling for someone right now. Admittedly, it had caught me off guard. The question, and the mayor himself, confused the hell out of me. Why would he ask me that if not for the fact that he liked me, too?

I had consistently tried to swallow my attraction to Finn as well as deny the possibility that Finn was attracted to me because I was scared to be vulnerable again. Carter had hurt me deeply but it wasn't fair to make Finn live in that asshole's shadow. Finn deserved a chance to prove himself and I grappled with whether or not I was ready to give him that chance. I had laid wide awake for hours contemplating whether or not I should've even told Finn about Carter - Mr. Sweatpants, as he knew him. I worried that he would now see me as a bitter ex-girlfriend, incapable of discerning any other man from Carter and his shortcomings but I could. Couldn't I?

What I had told Finn about only letting myself fall for a man with all good sides is true. What he didn't know, however, was that I was describing him. The more I got to know the reserved mayor, the deeper I found myself infatuated with him. But my time spent in Havenwood hadn't only strengthened my feelings for its mayor but for the humble town itself.

The thought of Havenwood's qualms and hardships had weighed heavy on me since learning of them and I wanted to use my skills to help the dying town any way I could. The bookshop is a good start, but there has to be more I can do. The perfect idea hit me that morning on my jog - I'll use my skills as a writer to write a guidebook to Havenwood! That way, when I get back to LA, I can use the book to promote Havenwood as a niche, rustic New England town. The perfect place for a fall retreat for Californians who barely know what the changing of seasons means aside from a 5-degree change of temperature.

As I'm preparing to round the redbrick corner of one of the downtown buildings, a familiar voice causes me to freeze just before my turn. I pause and remove the one headphone I'm wearing to better hear from my hidden position.

"You cannot rent to her!" Starr's irritatingly smooth voice

is raised in annoyance as she engages in a heated discussion. I flatten my back against the building, not wanting to be caught eavesdropping.

"I'm sorry, dear. She's a nice girl and I've given her my word, our lease starts in a couple o' days." Another familiar voice. This one is rickety, kind, and much less angry than Starr's. I recognize it from our phone call as belonging to Landlord Gable.

"Gable, she's an outsider. She doesn't care about Havenwood! I'd give it one week until she's back in Cali. Enjoying avocado toast, traffic, and spin class."

"As long as she pays her rent on time, I don't give two hoots. G'day, Starr."

I hear the shuffle of footsteps and the sound of a cane clacking heading in the opposite direction, paired with Starr's growl of indignation. I take it as a sign that the conversation is over and that things did not go as Starr had hoped.

Feeling overly confident and delighted by the musician's inability to get rid of me, I pick up my knees once again, resume my jogging pace, and round the corner. Sure enough, Starr is standing in the middle of the sidewalk, her arms crossed against her chest, fuming like she'd never heard the word "no" before.

"Oh, hey, Sun, right?" I feign being out of breath as I casually greet the irritated singer, tossing her the same disrespect she afforded me last night. Starr doesn't acknowledge my intentional mistake; instead, she takes a quick, threatening step toward me. As we go toe to toe, I can clearly see the white-hot ire burning behind Starr's juniper green eyes.

"You're going to stay away from Finn," she hisses. Who does she think she is to tell me what I'm going to do? Finn is a grown-ass man. He can decide who he wants and doesn't want. Clearly, Starr can't handle the fact that he doesn't want her. I try to restrain myself, but anger clouds my better judgment, and I don't hold back.

"Oh really? Y'know where he was last night?" I challenge, tipping my head as if posing an innocent question. "Because I do."

Starr's dark red lips part, venom ready to spew from them when a thought seems to lodge itself somewhere in her malicious brain. Just as quickly as she was in my face, she's now taking a step back.

"You're going to regret getting in my way, Hollywood." Her calm, collected tone sends a warning chill up my spine.

Starr shoulder checks me as she makes her exit past me, the click of her boots echoing off the pavement as she goes. Just before she's out of earshot, I swear I hear a giggle come from her, the sound sending a nasty feeling straight to my gut. I shouldn't have flaunted the fact that Finn stayed over at my place last night. It isn't only my business to be sharing, but something told me that Starr won't be passing that information around, not wanting the public to know her attempts to regain the mayor's favor were faltering.

A sensation of unease continues to linger in the back of my mind as I resume my jog, B-lining for Elsie's coffee shop.

* * *

I slow my pace to a walk as I approach the dated glass front door of the Mystic Brew, holding it open for the older gentleman who is exiting. His aged, weathered hands are full, holding a comically large mug in one and a newspaper in the

119

other. "Thank you kindly. Say, you must be Courtney?" The old man's face lights up with recognition as he slowly shuffles through the open door. His voice and slight Boston accent strike a chord of familiarity once again.

"Hi, Mr. Gable, yes I am. It's great to meet you in person." He shifts his mug into the crook of his elbow, extending his now free hand to greet me with an unsteady handshake.

"I was just stoppin' by for some fuel," he nods to the empty mug, "I like to bring me own mug. The ones here are barely big enough to qualify as a sample for an old sailor like me." Gable grumbles, giving me a glimpse into the particularity of the old man's personality. "I'm glad I caught you, girl. I have your key to the rental."

He reaches into his pocket and retrieves a small silver key that he pushes into my outstretched palm. He gives my hand an encouraging squeeze after depositing the key, the small gesture solidified my liking for Landlord Gable.

"Thank you, Mr. Gable." I beam down at the small piece of metal, my cheeks protesting the stretch caused by my smile, already mentally selecting a color palette for my new bookstore.

"I'm headin' out fishin' this morning or else I'd stop by the space personally to bring you the contract. However, Mayor Abernathy was kind enough to offer to do that errand for me, so he'll be by sometime this afternoon." I feel my face heat at the mention of Finn, even so casually as Landlord Gable had said it. "Mayor Abernathy offered?" I clarify, my fingers nervously finding their way into my brown tresses.

After the mayor's early exit this morning, my imagination had begun to run wild with assumptions, but if Finn had offered to do a chore that would intentionally put himself in my path, then maybe he hadn't ran away from me after all?

"Yup, good man he is. Always willin' to help us old geezers out. Have a good day, girl." Gable bids me goodbye, continuing his shuffle back towards the residential portion of town. I watch him for a moment until I'm confident he can manage the short walk himself and then duck into the empty coffee house. Before my eyes can even fully acclimate to the dimness of the shop, I hear Elsie's teasing voice.

"How was dinner with the mayor who's *not* into you?" A smirk is plastered on her freckled face as she towel dries a mug. I bridle my laughter, keeping my face unreadable until I cross the short distance to the counter. But once I'm close enough to feel the heat of her smug gaze, I crack, the two of us erupting into a fit of girlish giggles.

"How could you possibly know about that?" I question, attempting to bay the blush that has crept onto my cheeks.

"The entire town knows about that! Danielle is a certified yapper, ya know." She rolls her small eyes as she mentions the hostess but quickly returns her laser-pointed focus to me. Her stare demands answers or blood or maybe both.

"Okay! Okay!" I laugh, doing my best not to make assumptions about what exactly the hostess had to say about me. I prop my elbows up on the counter, resting my chin in my hands.

"So maybe he *is* into me? Last night, he asked me if I was falling for anyone, and it felt like he wanted me to say yes. I don't know, Els. Everything is really confusing right now." Elsie's eyes widen at my confession but I decide not to tell her about Finn sleeping over, at least not yet. Despite Elsie being my closest friend in Havenwood, it feels too personal to talk about.

"How about your feelings for him? Are those confusing too?" She pries as she begins to make me a chai latte.

Are my feelings for Finn Abernathy complicated? No, not really. I like Finn; I like how special he makes me feel, I like the way he's kind to everyone and dedicated to his position as mayor. I like the way his warm body felt beside mine last night, and I really like to imagine what he looks like naked. All that I understand, *that* is straightforward. What is complicated is whether or not I'm ready to open myself up again to a new relationship and a new person. Although I hate to admit it, I'm still hurting from Carter and don't know if I'm ready to trust someone new, to give all of me to someone again and Finn deserves all of someone.

"How have things been here?" I change the subject as the barista sets my latte in front of me. She smirks softly, acknowledging my conversation pivot but complying anyway, leaning against the counter.

"Nothing new, besides that Micah's been in here several times the last few days trying to convince me to give up your number." She raises an eyebrow at me as she crosses her arms across her dainty chest. "Are you going to leave any men in Havenwood for the rest of us?"

"To be fair, I get the impression Micah would fuck anything with a pulse," I reply. She bobs her head in agreeance, ginger tresses bouncing around her shoulders. "I got the key to the bookshop." I offer her an excited grin. I had filled Elsie in on my plans to open a bookshop last week as we passed the rental space on one of our walks.

"Courtney! That's so exciting!" Elsie squeals, clapping her espresso-stained hands together in excitement. "Let me know if you need any help getting it into tip-top shape."

122

"Thanks, Els." I look down at my phone and note the time. "I should probably go, Finn is supposed to be dropping the rental agreement off for landlord Gable at the shop sometime soon."

"Ooooh, have fun." Elsie teases before dancing back to the dish sink, shooting me an encouraging wink. I shake my head at her disapprovingly but feel my cheeks involuntarily heat at her implication. A big part of me would love to "have fun" with Mayor Abernathy but that will have to wait until I can figure my shit out.

I give her a farewell salute and push my way out of the coffee shop door and back onto the empty sidewalk. I glance up to observe the sky, now murky and gray compared to its previously blue and sunny disposition. The threat of another rainfall has the town park devoid of seniors, amplifying Havenwood's ghost town appearance.

I make the short walk to my new storefront, inserting the key. A wave of excitement rolls over me as the lock clicks open. I allow the door to swing open inwardly, revealing the old-fashioned beauty of the shop's interior.

The shop is in better condition than I could have hoped for. Its layout is rectangular with the door and bay window placed on one of its longer, street-facing ends. An upholstered chair had been left behind and occupied one of the dusty corners. The chair and a beautiful golden floral chandelier are the only indications the space had been previously occupied. I envision what the place will look like once transformed to fit my own design: tall white bookshelves lining the long back wall, a reading nook nestled alongside the large window, and a register counter tucked into one of the end corners.

In my zealousness, I barely hear the soft knock at the door.

15

Everything Nice

Courtney

"What do you think?" Finn's tall frame fills the doorway. One of his large hands is tucked into his pocket, the other holding a small stack of documents. His pensive eyes study the gold crown molding that lines the ceiling then trickle down to me. A current runs up my spine in response.

"It's perfect," I answer honestly, not bothering with a formal greeting. I turn my attention towards him, my hand coming up to rub my arm in a comforting motion.

"You left early this morning."

"I apologize," his voice is professional as if bridling his true emotions. "Being mayor means working at odd hours, unfortunately." I nod, casting my disappointed gaze down to his shoes.

Finn takes a few steps further into the shop, closing the door behind him. My eyes snap back up to his as I clock the movement. Shutting the door is a perfectly normal thing to do, especially with bad weather brewing, but the act makes the space feel much smaller and much more intimate, pushing a shot of adrenaline straight into my nervous system.

"You amaze me, Courtney Berrycloth." He admires, his tone low and almost ominous as he sets the small stack of papers down on the ledge of the bay window. I feel my heart flutter at the sultry words of praise and a low heat begins to boil in my stomach.

"Why's that?" I keep my voice casual, ignoring the moisture between my thighs. He continues his slow creep toward me, a hunter stalking his prey.

Finn rubs his chin through his beard as his glacial eyes bounce from me to other points of the room; as if looking at me for too long makes him lose a focus he's desperate to hold onto.

"You found an old, beat-up flower shop in a dying town and saw its potential." He's standing right in front of me now, I can feel his warmth bleeding through the space between us. The scent of his cedar wood cologne is so rich and delicious, mixed with his deep voice, he becomes entirely intoxicating. There's no way I'm getting turned on by a hot mayor praising me over my appreciation for his town. Except, there *is* a way and the puddle in my panties is proof.

"I wonder if you could do the same for a person."

"I-," I attempt a sentence. *What exactly was I going to say? What does he mean? I'm not sure.* I feel my eyelids flutter as I inhale a deep whiff of his delicious musk.

Finn makes the first move. His large hand reaches out and cups my cheek softly but firmly, I nestle into it before he slowly trails his long fingers down my neck. A wave of static rushes over me and I shutter at just how good his touch feels, his palm comes to rest flatly on my chest above my breasts. Now he can definitely feel how hard my heart is beating against its cage, threatening to break free. There's no hiding the way he makes me feel.

We lock eyes as he leans in, lowering from his height and connecting his lips with the goose-bumped skin of my neck. I let out a small moan and tip my head back, exposing more of my flesh for him to kiss. Every ounce of me is struggling against myself, I should stop him, I'm not emotionally ready for this but physically..

He hooks a finger into the waistband of my leggings and all rational thoughts go up in flames. I wrap my arms around his neck and he moves quickly, instantly reduced from respectful public official to carnal need.

Scooping me up by my ass, he deposits me into the abandoned chair, I settle into the old piece of furniture with a plop, and Finn's hands are once again around my leggings, tugging them down. I watch as he peels them down my legs, leaving me in my lacy navy thong, his smoldering eyes look much hungrier than before as he keeps eye contact with me. I risk a look away from him and glance straight ahead, out the bay window directly in front of us. If someone were to walk past, they would get an eyeful of what the mayor and I were doing.

"F-Finn," I warn in a stutter as he places a kiss on my bare thigh. He looks up at me through his dark eyelashes and traces my line of sight, noting my concern.

"Don't worry. No one will be walking around with the weather like this." As if to back up his point, thunder cracks loudly outside the shop. I bite my lip, contemplating only momentarily before giving him a consensual nod to continue.

He spares no time, gripping either side of my thong and ripping it apart down its seam. The sound of shredding fabric engulfs the silence that follows the next clap of thunder and I stare wide-eyed down at him. Before me, is not the well-mannered mayor that the townspeople knew; he's the rugged, primeval God I had fantasized about. Finn takes in my shocked expression before tossing the two sheer pieces of fabric to either side and gripping my knees in his large hands, pushing them apart savagely so that I'm on full display to him. Only now do his eyes dare to stray from mine, dipping low to see the wetness of my core.

"Mmm, Courtney." He praises just above a whisper, his voice deep and gruff, almost a growl. His words cause another stream of wetness to flow from me. "You're already wet, baby. Do you want me as badly as I want you?"

That is all I needed: a few words of confirmation, and suddenly, I don't care about being the best person possible. I don't care that I have my own emotional unavailability and issues to work through before I can fully commit to him. I don't care about anything aside from fucking Mayor Finn Abernathy.

"I want you," I admit to him and myself, running my hand down my own thigh and over his hand that still rests firmly on my knee. The veins on the back of his hands bulge from how tightly he's gripping me, his knuckles turning ghostly white after my confession.

"That's all I needed to hear." Without warning, Finn slides his hands up my thighs and dips his head in a swift motion, his tongue darting out and coming into perfect contact with my clit.

I gasp as he gently circles the swollen numb like a shark locked in a feeding frenzy, encircling its prey. My core tenses with anticipation and desire as he works me slowly, teasingly.

I peer down my stomach at him, watching him taste me conservatively. Small whimpers fall from my parted lips, begging him to stop the teasing and devour me whole. Without needing words, he translates what I'm asking of him, beginning to lap at me more fervently. His rougher and more calculated licks force me to hook my fingers below the seat, desperate to find something to ground me. Through my pleasure, I keep a hesitant eye on the window, still anxious that someone will walk by and get a full view of the mayor's face buried between my thighs. Finn lashes his tongue quickly over my clit, causing me to cry out and return my attention to the beautiful blue-eyed deity in front of me.

I shove my fingers into his raven hair.

"You're taking it well so far, baby. Can you handle more?" His icy pools are focused on my face but his mouth remains on my entrance, his lips brushing my folds as he speaks. My brain is so muddled with emotion I can hardly conjure a single thought or word, so a few syllables will have to do."Mm-hm," I'm practically begging him to give me more through the desperation in my voice.

A pleased smirk creeps onto his face; it's so sinfully hot that I'm convinced I could come just by looking at him. He reaches forward, sliding his middle and ring finger between my lower lips, dragging them up and down until they're sopping in my excitement. I watch in anticipation as my tongue juts out to wet my bottom lip. I can only imagine what wild, sex-crazed animal I look like in this moment but, whatever I look like, Finn can't seem to get enough of it. His gaze has been locked on mine the entire time, relishing the way I'm falling apart at his touch.

He slowly begins to massage my entrance open, teasing me

with only the tips of his long fingers and then pulling them back out again, gauging my reaction as he does. I whimper out a complaint of annoyance. I'd spent the entire duration of my stay in Havenwood fantasizing about his fingers being inside me and now, on the precipice of going full feral, he dares to only taunt me with them.

Just as I'm about to complain again, he shoves his fingers unforgivingly deep inside me. His eyes darken with lust as I gasp at the unexpected, yet welcomed, trespass.

I straighten my back with a pleasure-filled cry, my jaw dropping entirely as the pain of being stretched and the ecstasy of being penetrated mingle, I shutter as I attempt to regain my bearings. Before that can happen, Finn is retreating his fingers and plunging them back inside me with merciless force. My grip on the rim of the chair tightens as he uses his thumb to apply pressure to my clit, his fingers continually slamming into me and curling ever so perfectly to hit that spot inside of me. An inexorable pressure is mounting inside me much sooner than expected.

"This morning," Finn bends at the waist and trails soft kisses along my stomach. He knows I'm close and he's keeping perfect tempo, a feat most men can't seem to accomplish, pumping his fingers in and out of me at a consistent rhythm that has me teetering on the edge.

"I left because I couldn't bear to be so close to you and not touch you. I had to go home and fuck my hand and pretend it was you." He dips his head low once again and replaces his thumb with his tongue, his long fingers continuing to work me.

"F-Finn," his lascivious words doom me, and with a few more gyrations of his tongue, I'm melting, pushed over the edge into euphoria. My orgasm hits me like a fucking tidal wave and I find my hazy vision locked onto the icy blues in front of me as my voice breaks on a silent scream.

"Good girl, come for me." He encourages as I ride his fingers, prolonging the already unceasing waves of my orgasm, more breathy praise falling from his lips.

As I collapse into the chair, my chest heaving to regain my breath, Finn steadily removes his fingers, as if savoring the feeling before he can't any longer. For a beat, we sit in stunned silence. Me, unraveled in the chair and him, sitting on his knees between my legs.

Without so much as a word, he raises his drenched fingers to his mouth and drags them down his tongue, allowing my liquid to pool into the curve of his tongue. I watch, mesmerized, as he rises to his feet and stands over me. With his mouth still slightly ajar, he laces his fingers into my brown hair and yanks at its roots, forcing my head to tip back. Using his free hand, he squeezes my cheeks, coaxing my mouth open. I do what he wants with little push back, curious to see where the mayor is taking this.

Once my mouth is open expectantly, he extends his tongue, my liquid that had previously pooled inside his mouth now dripping from the tip and into my mouth. The first strands of glistening liquid hit my tongue and I'm met with the piquant, delicate taste of my own orgasm. Before I can process what the actual fuck just happened - and how hot it was - Finn is back in front of me, gingerly pulling my leggings back over my expended legs.

"I thought you should taste how delicious you are." Is the only explanation he offers me in his husky voice. His glorious eyes look me over once more before he excuses himself, exiting the shop into the rain. I open my mouth to protest but he's gone before the words even form.

I stare at the chipped pastel paint of the shop's front door long after Finn has departed. I'm disheveled, exhausted, and desperate for more of him. My thoughts refuse to silence themselves as I gnaw relentlessly on my innocent inner cheek. Why did I allow that to happen? There will be absolutely no hiding from my feelings for Finn now, now that I'd let him touch me and prove every dirty fantasy I had about his sexual abilities was correct.

I rise from the chair onto flimsy legs, unaware of exactly where I'm going but knowing I need expert advice- and maybe a wheelchair.

16

Pumpkin Cookies

Courtney

I inhale a deep breath as I enter the bakery, the warmth and sweet smell of the shop greeting me affectionately. The tinkling bell above my head draws Agnes' attention to my arrival, her old chocolate-brown eyes taking me in. I squirm under her gaze; despite the benevolence of her stare, I wish she would look away, afraid if she looks at me too long, she might somehow find out what just happened between me and her adopted son.

"Hello, sugar," Agnes beams. She pops her tray of pumpkin cookies into the oven, their earthy autumn smell wafting towards me as she approaches. She wraps me in a tender hug, not seeming to mind the layer of dried sweat on my skin. Her smile is still bright as she releases me.

"Hey, Agnes. I came for advice, I guess?" I say as I take a seat on one of the counter stools. The baker stifles a knowing look as she returns behind the counter, beginning to prepare her ingredients for another bake.

"You guess?" She echoes, raising an eyebrow that tells me I'll have to be more forward if I want her help. I'm grateful that she keeps her gaze on the condensed milk she's measuring out as I formulate what I'm going to say next. How do I tell her that her son just finger fucked my soul out of me and that I don't want to lose him but I haven't healed from my last breakup.. in a roundabout way? I scratch the back of my head below my ponytail, debating on my delivery.

"It's, um, boy stuff." Is the only way I can even think to begin to broach the delicate conversation. Agnes eyes me, taking in my obvious distress before putting down her supplies and pulling up a stool on the opposite side of the counter to face me.

"Having two boys, I never had a child to have these *boy* talks with, so forgive me if my elocution is a bit rusty." Agnes ticks her tongue, dipping her head to one side before correcting herself. "Well, Milo likes men but he never comes to me for this sort of thing."

A small smile splits across the tense surface of my face. I feel the fear and anxiety evaporate as Agnes quickly reminds me why I chose to come to her for advice. Agnes is a strong force, she reminds me of the local oak trees that refuse to bend or sway to anyone or anything. Yet she manages to stay comprised of a maternal and gracious presence just below her protective bark. She's the kind of woman I assume all women want to become one day.

"Okay, well, here it is, buckle in. I got burned in California by this guy I'd been with for a while, and I thought I had sworn off men. They're manipulative, they hurt you, they lie. But then I met *someone*," I wince. "Who is the complete opposite of that. He's amazing and dedicated, with a heart of pure gold. He's the kind of guy you can only dream up in a fairy tale."

133

The words fall out before I can even process them.

"But?" She encourages me as I pause.

"But I don't think I'm ready for a relationship again. I'm still so afraid to get hurt and I don't think I can open up the way he deserves. I don't want to lead him on or ask him to wait for me to heal, but I want him so badly, and he deserves everything. And... and... what if I just can't *be* everything right now?"

Agnes offers me a thoughtful look. Her expression briefly resembles one of pity as she rolls her lips together, she folds her hands between us before she speaks again.

"My late husband passed six years ago, God rest his soul. We met when we were thirteen and got married the instant it was legal. Some people would say we weren't ready." Her knowing gaze falls from the ceiling and lands on me. My stomach tightens in remorse at the mention of Agnes' deceased husband, the knowledge only adding to the strong image I had of her. "If I could have started our love and our life together even five minutes sooner, I would in a heartbeat because moments, opportunities, people, they're gone before we know it." I see her waterline fill before she blinks away the forming tears.

"I'm so sorry for your loss, Agnes." I reach out across the counter and squeeze her hands. The baker responds by patting mine to assure me she's okay, but she doesn't speak.

"I understand what you're saying, I really do. *Seize the moment because it's ever-changing.* I'm just afraid to be hurt again, or worse, I'm afraid to hurt him."

"You will," she says as if it were a matter of fact. My expression twists into one of confusion as I stare at her from below my creased brow. I thought this was supposed to be a

134

pep talk?!

"Love is painful, child. Everyone has these bad or deceptive sides you're afraid of but they're not something to hate or fear, they're something to grow from. Sometimes you can help your partner grow through them; other times you just have to call them out on that bullshit, and they need to do the same for you." I audibly cackle over hearing Agnes swear for the first time. As we had sat by my fireplace last night, Finn told me stories about how, as a boy, Agnes would make him and Milo hold bars of soap in their mouth if she heard them cursing. Something told me that she'd probably inflict the same punishment today.

"By the way," I watch the baker rise slowly from her seat, weighed down by her age only physically as her brown eyes gleam with a mother's knowing. "I hope this little boy you're torn up over is my son or else Finn is going to be very disappointed."

My jaw almost smacks itself on the counter with how fast it drops. Agnes is an intelligent woman, of course, she isn't blind to spark the between Finn and I. And clearly, she has some insider knowledge.

"You'll catch flies," Agnes circles her grinning mouth with her finger, prompting me to snap my mouth shut.

"That reminds me," After the shock runs its course and allows me to regain control of my motor functions I pull out my phone from my sports bra, opening it to my notes app. "I'm starting a little project, can you tell me about Havenwood's folklore? Including all the bedtime stories and all the witchy woo-woo stuff you can." I pose my thumbs over the small, glowing letters on my phone's keyboard, ready to pad away any stories the old baker has to share.

"Where to even begin."

* * *

After an hour or so of listening to Agnes' tales, full of mythical forest creatures and pestilent house elves that plague Havenwood homes, I say my goodbyes and thank Agnes wholeheartedly for her stories and advice. I make my way back to 2213 Queens Avenue, grateful that the sky has begun to clear and allow small streams of sunlight through the moody clouds.

My notes app is contently filled to the brim with helpful half-truthed histories and fables. Most of Agnes' stories correlated with a period in Havenwood's past that could help explain where these urban legends originated but I'd have to cross-check all of my info with Milo before concreting it into my guidebook.

"Hey, cutie!" The chipper voice drags me from my thoughts and I turn to face the source. Micah stands a few feet away from me, an unfairly attractive smile on his chiseled face. Suspenders hang on his bare shoulders because, despite the unpredictable weather, he isn't wearing a shirt.

"Hey, Micah. Are you going for a sexy Johnny Appleseed vibe?" I question playfully. He chuckles and jogs to catch up to where I'm standing.

"One of our turkeys got loose," he informs me. "I was taking a nap when mom woke me up to go chase it down, didn't have enough time to grab a shirt but you called me sexy, so I think it was a win in the end." Being this close to Micah allows me to take note of his pointy canines as he grins down at me;

honestly, I'm trying to look anywhere but at his tanned chest that is on full display.

"It's really cool that your family raises turkeys," I say, smirking at Micah's disappointment at the change of topic, knowing he'd prefer to continue talking about how sexy he is.

"They sell well around Thanksgiving. Helps us make some extra cash in a dying town." He shrugs his muscled shoulders, his traps looking extra beefy weighed down by the straps of his suspenders. I try to ignore his comment about Havenwood dying, not wanting to think of this place fizzling out of existence. Not right now.

"Do you save one for yourselves for Thanksgiving dinner?" I ask, glancing up into his hazel eyes. He shakes his head, sunlight shimmering off his black hair.

"Not quite; we're Indigenous, so Thanksgiving isn't something we celebrate."

"Oh, that's cool. I'm sorry, I didn't know." I feel the heat rise to my cheeks, a bit embarrassed and hoping I didn't offend him. Micah elbows me playfully, his handsome smile never leaving his face. "But yeah, we do save one or two for ourselves." I beam back at him as we hit a crossroads.

"I'll catch you later, beautiful. Holler for me if you find my turkey?"

"Promise." I give him a wink before we split paths. Micah follows the gravelly road back toward the apothecary shop and I take the more paved one leading to Havenwood's one suburb.

My run-in with Micah was a nice distraction, but now that I'm once again alone with my thoughts, I'm fighting to ignore the nauseating feeling of guilt that accompanies my memories of today. If Agnes is right, and relationships are a matter of growing together, why do I have these feelings of self-condemnation for giving into my desire for Finn? I have so many questions and no answers, I'm pulled in so many directions and have no resolution. I'm driving myself mad trying to balance what I want and what I think is right by him.

As I let out an exhale of confused frustration, the wind whips in tandem with my breath, swiping my hair across my face and blinding me momentarily. The eerie feeling of being watched settles deep in my bones and I swear I can almost hear the sound of breathing coming from behind me. I desperately swat my hair from my face, feeling suffocated in the darkness of it, half expecting to see a face pressed to my own once my vision is cleared. But as I whirl around, my gaze darting around the empty street, I don't see a single person watching me or any cause for the feeling, which is gone just as fast as it arrived.

My heart is still pounding as the uneasiness dissipates, leaving a strange feeling of clarity in its wake. The message is crystal clear and coming from within my own head: *Everything will be okay.* It feels as though it isn't my own consciousness speaking the words, but nonetheless, they bring me comfort and a strange feeling of peace.

I rush the rest of the way home, my conscience feeling lighter but the rest of me feeling majorly weirded out by that experience. As I step onto Queens Avenue a wrinkly face glowers at me from three feet off the ground, the displeased scowl distracting me from what had just happened.

"Someone is looking for you," I remark as I walk past the rusty brown-colored turkey. The animal garbles out a gobble at me as I near it, ruffling its plumage and fanning out its white-tipped tail feathers in an attempt to intimidate me. I chuckle at the ridiculous display as I hop the few steps up onto my porch and let myself into the rental.

I kick my shoes off in the entryway and retrieve my cell from its spot my bra, intending to call the apothecary shop and let Micah know I found his rogue turkey, but a text notification on my lock screen detours me.

It's from Kashvi. I tap my passcode in and read her message.

Kashvi: No. Effing. Way.

I click the link attached to her message, prompting a YouTube video to load on my small screen. The title of the video informs me that it's the official movie trailer for this year's best-selling fantasy book. For a brief second, I question why Kashvi is so concerned about the book receiving a movie adaptation until unnecessarily dramatic music overtakes my phone's speakers, and a familiar face appears on my screen.

There, in all his chiseled, blond glory, is Carter reciting some sappy sonnet in pointy prosthetic ears. He had done it; Carter had finally convinced his uncle to give him a leading role, and he was acting his little black heart out.

"No effing way.." I echo Kashvi's sentiment as I watch Carter kiss and caress the face of his rising B-list actress co-star. The sight causes a pinprick of anger to jab into my side as I realize that I am watching Carter act for the first time. He's playing pretend, yet the way he's delivering his lines feels so familiar because he was *acting* the entire time he was with me. He had pretended he cared about me to get me to be his damn booty call, and somehow, it had worked for so long.

I feel ire now as I watch him perform because I fully understand that that's what our relationship was: performative. I want to slap myself even harder now that I can clearly see Carter isn't even a *good* actor, I was simply too naive and trusting. I was a means to an end for him; I was an easy fuck who looked good on paper, I helped elevate his social rank in the L.A. scene, and once I was no longer useful to him, I was tossed out.

I'm fuming by the time the short trailer ends on a melodramatic beat. The credits roll after announcing the film's release date and my eyes snag on Carter's uncle's name as it flies by, confirming what I already know.

"Son of a bitch," I scoff as the puzzle pieces magnetize to one another inside my head. It's all making sense now. Carter had dumped me knowing he was going to land this main role and he couldn't have any of the focus landing on his striking screenwriter situationship. That would highlight the fact that he's crossing picket lines and is a scab. *What a strategic, manipulative motherfucker.*

I'd done a great job ignoring Carter and the pain he'd caused me, thanks in part to a certain mayor, but I can't keep the emotions at bay at this moment. A growl of anger rumbles in my chest as I clench my fists, my acrylics digging into my palms. I'm angry that Carter never truly cared for me, I'm angry that he landed this role that he doesn't deserve, I'm angry that I still have such an adverse reaction to him and I'm angry that I didn't see through him from the beginning.

I storm into my bathroom, cranking the faucet and splashing the cold water onto my face. The refreshing sensation allowed me to calm down enough to regard my reflection in the mirror. I see my messy, windswept caramel hair and angry chocolate eyes, the clenched muscles of my jaw. But more importantly, what I don't see is *myself.* I'm not this angry, hurt person Carter has made me. I don't want to be, not anymore.

My thoughts flick to Finn, I don't ask or wield them to

but he appears anyway. Finn doesn't invoke anger or pain, he makes me happy, he genuinely listens, and he gives me flowers for crying out loud! I've been shutting him out and punishing myself in the process for Carter's mistakes. I decide that that ends here and now. I close my eyes, inhaling a deep breath and banishing the angry woman in the mirror.

On the exhale, I tell myself, *I'm expelling every feeling I've ever had for Carter. The good, the bad, the painful, it's all getting out of me. From here on out, Carter is evicted, and I'm making room for Finn.*

I let my breath out in a slow stream, opening my eyes to examine myself once again in the mirror. Just like a maple tree, which has shed her angry, red leaves and is left with bare branches, ready to begin new growth, I see a familiar yet changed woman in the reflection. Looking back at me is messy caramel hair, calm chocolate eyes, and a hopeful grin. Now that I've officially expunged the disease that is my ex, I want to see Finn again. I want to tell him about my idea for a guidebook, I want to tell him to stop running away, and I want to tell him that I want him.

My gaze tracks back to the messy mop of hair on top of my head and I decide a shower is definitely necessary before going anywhere. I let the shower warm up as I undress, the steam fogging the glass of the mirror and filling the small room. Once the temperature is right, I lather up quickly, rushing in an attempt to minimize the time before I see Finn again.

I bend down to clean my legs and flinch as my calf muscle tenses, a side effect of being a runner. Many of my muscles are tight or achy from my morning jogs around Havenwood, and thanks to my extracurricular activity this morning I'm extra tight. I consider Googling a nearby massage parlor once

141

I'm done bathing but a more enticing thought overtakes me. What would it be like to get a massage from Finn? How long could I possibly last with those long fingers kneading into my skin before I become overwrought with horniness and fuck him on the massage table? Were his other appendages as lengthy as his sexy fingers?

During my intermission my hand had somehow found itself between my thighs, playfully swiping my enlarged clit. The little strokes of pleasure fueled my desire to see Finn's face.. and hands, once again. I pull away from myself and lodge my fingers into my shampooed hair, locking them in my tresses before my shower gets steamier.

17

Tangled Webs

Finn

I ruffle through the stack of papers before me, calculating the numbers over and over and over again as if that will magically prompt them to change. The city budget has dropped 10% since last quarter, and Havenwood is mere margins away from going under financially.

I cast my fatigued gaze past the budget and to my desk before me, where my calendar stares back. Another stark reminder that I'm running out of time, only 30 days until Halloween. I only have 30 days to find a solution, 30 days to save my home and all the amazing people in it. 30 days and I let Havenwood, and my parents, down. Admittedly, my encounter with Courtney in the bookshop earlier today helped to relieve some of the stress that had built up within me. But finally confirming her feelings for me is only a topical solution to a much deeper issue. If I lose Havenwood then I'll have ruined my chances with Courtney for nothing, I can't lose them both.

An incessant buzzing in my pocket clears the fog of somber

thoughts long enough for me to retrieve my cell phone from my jacket pocket. I answer the call without bothering to check the caller ID.

"Hello." I bark with more grit in my voice than expected. I've never been good at hiding my emotions but they become nearly impossible to disguise under strenuous circumstances.

"Hello, sunshine." Milo chirps. He's in one of his overly bright moods, the kind where he can convince you that the world is made up of rainbows and cotton candy. The kind of mood that I most certainly am *not* in.

"Yes, Milo?" I love my brother but I don't have time for his cheery disposition when I can actively feel the weight of Havenwood crushing my vertebrae.

"Lighten up, would you? I have good news." I readjust in my chair, the promise of good news perking up my ears. "I explained our situation to the state this morning and they said that Martha's remains are practically ours, so long as we can get a determinate DNA match between her and Courtney by the due date."

My hand flies to my goatee, my fingers anxiously rubbing at the dark hair on my chin. Milo doesn't verbalize what comes next but he doesn't have to, I know I will have to be the one to convince Courtney to take this DNA test. The security and stability of Havenwood is dangling right in front of me, packaged within a tanned brunette goddess who wears adorable fuzzy pajamas.

"This is the part where you celebrate." Milo reminds me, some of his initial excitement having already dwindled at my reaction or lack thereof.

"Great news. Thanks, Milo." I keep my voice flat, hoping my brother won't pick up on my grim nature.

"Finn," Milo's voice softens on the other end of the line, proving my acting skills need major improvements. "This is a huge step; if we can get solid proof that she's an ancestor and has the right to sign those remains over to us, Salem won't be able to do a damn thing about it. We're going to save Havenwood." His words compel my eyes to flick back to the severely lacking budget.

The plan we had hatched months ago was genius, foolproof even. A plan that had begun to crack the instant a vibrant, beautiful Los Angelean woman with a passion for writing and a pussy that tasted like fine wine arrived in Havenwood and carved herself out a space in my heart.

I'm running out of time, I have to make decisions. Either I tell Courtney the entire truth (including the fact that I may have loosened the pipe under her kitchen sink before she moved in as a ploy to get into her house) and pray that she might forgive me for lying to her, hope that she'd be willing to continue our relationship and beg her to sign over the remains. Or I chicken out, convince her to sign the papers, and continue to let our relationship grow from a bed of deception, all the while hoping that none of my lies come to light.

I know which option is certainly easier. If I tell Courtney the truth not only do I risk her not signing the papers and ending Havenwood, I risk losing her. I can't bear the thought of Courtney hating me, not after I'd fallen so deeply for her. But I also can't fathom the thought of lying to her anymore.

"You really are falling for her," Milo translates my silence as an answer. "Look, man, she'll still like you after you confess. But only AFTER we get DNA confirmation and she signs those documents. If Salem gets their grubby, tourist-hogging hands on those remains, Havenwood is good as dead." I sigh.

145

As I release the breath I'm holding, hot tears pricking at my eyes.

"You don't need to remind me of that, Milo. I'm not the perfect mayor but for the first time in my life it's difficult to put Havenwood's needs before my own."

"I know you'll do what's right," Milo reassures me before we end our call.

I sit in silence for a beat after we've said our goodbye, every emotion under the sun stewing in my chest. Anger, guilt, frustration, sadness, pain. They all come to a crescendo as my trembling hands reach out and snatch the budget off my desk, taking the calendar with it as I chuck the stack across the room. A formidable growl rips from my throat as I assault the stationary. I watch the papers seesaw in the air before landing delicately on the floor in front of my desk, mocking me with their unbothered slow descent as my chest heaves in annoyance. My little temper tantrum did little in the way of relieving any of my trepidation.

I plant my palms on my desk in an attempt to mitigate the shaking that refuses to cease. My thoughts fly by my brain at 60 miles a minute, searching for a way, any way to fix what I've broken. Instead, each passing thought hurls a colorful insult at me, insulting my honor for lying, reminding me that I've let my parents down, questioning why I thought I'd be good enough to be mayor, questioning why I thought I'd be good enough for Courtney. *It's all your fault.*

Just when they've become excruciatingly loud, a soft knock sounds at my office door, silencing them in an instant like magic.

Courtney

For the second time since moving to Havenwood, I'm nervous to pick out my outfit. Both times I found myself very concerned with what the mayor would think of my clothes, whether or not he would like them. I have a strange suspicion that he really liked my pajamas but that doesn't narrow down much unless fuzzy pink pants are his thing.

I hastily decide on a blue sweater dress that shows a flirtatious amount of cleavage. The dress is similar in color to the thong Finn had tarnished and I'm hoping something about this color is good luck for me.

Now that I've decided I'm ready for a relationship with Finn, it's time to start playing the game. The game that men and women have played for centuries, a game of courting and a game of desire. My competitive nature will be an asset and with Finn as my prize, nothing can stop me. Not Carter, not Starr, not even myself.

Finn had mentioned in passing that the mayoral office is located in the town square and I know I'd seen the aging building weeks ago when I'd arrived in Havenwood but I'm not sure of the route there. Regardless I walk at a brisk, determined pace, making sure to take the time to appreciate the smell of wet pavement from this morning's drizzle.

My eyes track the vibrant orange and yellow leaves sticking to the contrasting dark road as I go. Those are the little things I had started to love about Havenwood. It feels like every time the sun rose and set over me, I became more and more enamored by the charming town and its little treasures. I know I'd never be able to pass a colonial-style house again and not think of my historic rental or appreciate the oranges of a sunset and not relate them to autumn in New England. I'd never again be able to enjoy a Southern California pool party without comparing the cool water's color to a certain mayor's eyes. But I don't want to think about going back, not now.

City hall comes into view in all its derelict glory; the directory sign out front informs me that Havenwood's fire department, police department, and mayor's office are all located inside the large building. I tug open the stubborn, rickety front doors and am immediately greeted by the main hallway. A small, wooden desk sits directly in front of the doors with a familiar woman attending it. I recognize her face as one I've seen once or twice before, at the coffee shop and on the street as I ran my morning jog. The receptionist perks up upon noticing me, straightening her posture.

"Hi there, Courtney." She raises her eyebrows in surprise, exposing her bright blue eye shadow that had previously been concealed by her folded eyelids.

"Hey, Cathleen? Right?" I pull deep from within my memory to remember the woman's name. I'd heard Elsie greet her at the coffee house and I'm almost confident I remembered it correctly. Her bashful head tilt confirms my suspicion.

"Where you headed, sweet pea?" Cathleen asks, tucking a few papers into a maroon envelope before crossing her hands over the scratched-up desktop, giving me her undivided attention.

"I was hoping you could direct me to the mayor's office?" I regret asking as soon as the words leave my mouth. Cathleen is barely able to control her facial expressions as her jaw smacks her desk. She quickly picks it up but doesn't bother reigning in any of her other expressions.

"Take that staircase up; his office is the entire second floor. " She points behind her with her neon pink nails. "Have fun!"

Cathleen's sing-song words cause a small blush to creep onto my cheeks and extend to the tips of my ears. I force myself to swallow my embarrassment, reminding myself that I should only be embarrassed if I don't want people to know how I feel about Finn. Now that I'm sure about how I feel, everyone should know, right?

I offer the receptionist a quick "thank you" and ascend the stairs, desperate to escape the now awkward environment. Each step I take up the carpeted stairs amplifies the sound of my heart beating in my ears. *Why am I so nervous?* I had accepted my feelings for Finn but admitting those feelings to him, playing the game, that's a whole new ballpark. Now I'm entering an arena of possibilities and danger, I can't control this part of the process, I can't control how Finn will react. Most of all, I'm anxious because I feel like *me* again. I am not guarding or putting up a hard front anymore; I'm allowing myself to be Courtney in all her hopeless romantic glory. And I know it will hurt ten times more to be rejected as myself.

I reach the second story landing before I feel ready. I take a steadying breath, reading the shiny gold plaque on the door that officially reads, **Mayor Finn Abernathy**. I drag my fingers over the inscribed letters, something about seeing his name written so formally makes me want to laugh, nothing about the charming, affable man is as formal as his nameplate suggests. That thought sends a calming wave over my nervous system; I'm not confessing my deep, dark feelings to Mayor Abernathy; I'm just going to talk to Finn. That's all.

With a confident preceding knock, I turn the handle to his officer door, pushing it inwards as I enter the space.

I'm greeted by papers littering the floor and a desk calendar lying haphazardly. I look up from the mess to the desk across the sea of papers. There stands Finn. His raven black hair looks slightly tussled, and his cell phone clutched in his long fingers—the same ones that I definitely wasn't fantasizing about earlier. He lifts his gaze from the mess on the ground, his icy eyes widening upon seeing me, sending a fleury of butterflies ripping through my stomach.

"Courtney." Finn runs his free hand through his dark strands, attempting to domesticate them. I smile at him timidly, tucking a caramel strand behind my ear.

"H-hi," he stutters out his greeting, looking me over with indecision evident on his handsome face. Finn has never seen me as bashful as I am in this moment, not even when his face was buried deep in my thighs and I assume this is the reason for his strange reaction. During my time in Havenwood, I refused to let myself be anything but strong and stoic for my own protection, but now, seeing this softer side of me for the first time, it's evident he is determining how to react.

"Hi," I greet back softly, filling in the comfortable silence. I'm admittedly confused about the mess of papers before us but more than anything I'm just happy to see Finn. Despite seeing him less than six hours ago, I feel like I'm now seeing him through a new lens. Although we'd greeted each other half a dozen times before this time it felt like the start of something new.

Or perhaps the start of the end.

18

Wicked

Finn

I attempt to dry my sweating palms against my slacks discreetly, not wanting my surprise guest to see how nervous her presence is making me. Normally I would be overjoyed to see Courtney - especially after our rendezvous earlier - but her showing up immediately after ending my phone call with Milo feels like an omen. And not a good one.

I'd also be the first to admit that Courtney's timid disposition has me feeling muddled. Don't get me wrong, I rather liked knowing this more intimate and vulnerable side to her, but I'm stuck trying to figure out what had changed for her to act this way around me. The obvious answer is that any woman feels exposed around a man who had put his face between her thighs less than four hours ago but that just doesn't seem like Courtney. I don't pin her as a woman who would allow sex to crumble a shield she was so adamant to hide behind. There must have been some other change I'm not privy to.

"I'm surprised to see you here," I admit, pocketing my flip

phone. "A good kind of surprised, um." That is also the truth. I loved seeing her even though she was the root of my moral turmoil. *Get out of your head*, I instruct myself. Closing my eyes, I give my head a slight shake, my attempt at dislodging my guilty thoughts. "How can I help?"

Courtney studies my expression for a prolonged moment, making me squirm in my own culpability. After a beat, she's seemingly found whatever answer she was searching for and extends her firm leg, taking a step over my tossed paperwork and advancing a step closer to me. Her chocolate eyes are set on mine and they look.. hungry.

Just like they had moments before I made her climax.

I attempt to keep my resolve as I recall the memory but I can't stop my gaze from wandering down to her full hips that sway ever so sassily as she approaches and *God damn. How does she fill that dress so fucking well?* I mentally scold myself for the objectification and cursing, in that order but how can I do any differently when Courtney Berrycloth is looking at me like *that*? If she is hungry, I'll merrily volunteer to be breakfast, lunch, and dinner.

"Did I interrupt something?" She answers my question with one of her own, her voice sounding more like a low purr. With her this close to me, I can smell her fruity scent, the sweet aroma beckoning me closer. When was the last time I jacked off? I will need to add that into my schedule ASAP.

"No," I say, adding another lie to my long list. I clear my throat, watching her every move like a hawk. "I was just wrapping up some..." My eyes drift to the town's budget littered about the carpet. I chew on my bottom lip, searching for my next words. "Mayoral stuff."

Courtney offers me one of her signature full-lipped smiles

before she's suddenly reminded of something. Her eyes lower to my chest as she wets her lips. Her voice teetering from that of a sultry dominatrix to a more timid variety, reminding me of the pitch a school girl's voice takes when she's confessing to her crush. Then she says the very last thing I expected her to.

"I wanted to apologize if talking about Mr. Sweatpants made you uncomfortable last night; it just felt good to rant. I came to Havenwood dejected and wounded from that relationship. I tried to shut myself out from romance entirely, but in doing so, I shut out parts of myself—parts that I actually really like. I also shut out people who I really like."

She releases the last sentence slowly as her eyes find mine once again, a glimmer of vulnerability behind them. I can tell she is attempting to be open with me and explain her hot and cold behavior toward me, though she's the last person who owes me an explanation or apology.

"Spending this time with you has made me realize that there are still good men out there without secret agendas." She laughs softly, tucking another soft strand of brown behind her ear. The bile in my stomach is set ablaze by her misplaced trust in me but she continues before I can stop her. "I was hoping you'd give us a chance. If I haven't scared you off entirely *but* our encounter this morning tells me I might still have a shot." She giggles flirtatiously, the sound so beautifully alluring.

"Courtney, I.." My eyes dart around her face, looking for some easy way to tell her that I'm the opposite of what she's looking for. I am the antithesis of a good guy who deserves her affection or a chance to be her man. I am literally the relationship Trojan horse in a button-up shirt!

153

Her face drops, most likely interpreting my silence as denial. I take a deep breath, choosing once again to be selfish and pretend I'm not the worst man on this planet.

"Of course. I would love nothing more than a chance with you," her bright smile creeps back onto her face, sending my heart fluttering at the sight. "I promised to make a trip to the community gardens around noon tomorrow. I know dirt doesn't make for a great second date but the gourds this year are supposed to be-."

"I'm there." She cuts off my painful rambling with a kiss on my cheek. The feeling of her warm lips pressed on my cheek, freezing me in my place.

"Could you stop by my place after you're done with mayoral stuff? I have something I want to run down you- BY you! I have something I want to run BY you!" A light blush flushes her cheeks, making me chuckle. I slide my hands into my front pockets and lean against the edge of my desk, admiring the gorgeous woman before me. I need to tell her the truth but I also need to save Havenwood, both those things can't be accomplished all while still being her dream guy. But that's a problem for a different day today I'm the man Courtney wants and that's enough for me.

"I'm there."

Courtney

I lift the lid off my crock pot, steam immediately assaulting my face before it dissipates into the air around me, causing me to swat at it ridiculously. I've never been a great cook but putting meat and veggies in a crock pot is one of my more well-rehearsed dinners so I feel confident serving it to Finn.

I poke at a piece of roast with my fork to test if it's ready, sure enough, the meat practically falls apart at the prodding, signaling a well-done pot roast. I use a ladle to scoop some of the gravy and pour it over the meat and carrots, allowing its flavor to soak into the dish.

As I cover the pot once again, anxiety and anticipation dig their nasty claws into me. I'm excited to see Finn, but now, with my cards out on the table, I'm also extremely nervous. Our interaction earlier seemed off for a reason I can't quite put my finger on but he had agreed to a formal date. So nothing can be *that* wrong, can it?

I switch the pot from SIMMER MODE to OFF and walk over to my newly purchased dining room table, one of my many new goodies. On the tabletop sat my notebook that I had spent the afternoon filling with Agnes' local legends. Tomorrow, after visiting the community garden with Finn, I intend to bring the notebook to Milo to see if he can add a factual perspective to the stories written inside. It's not that I don't believe the factual and fantastical can't exist simultaneously, I know they can. The witch trials that had run rampant through these parts are a great example of the two coexisting. The logical side will tell you innocent women were murdered and the more supernatural folks will claim those women practiced witchcraft. I believe both things to be true in unison, but it's always interesting to see the overlap.

Almost as if summoned from my thoughts a haunting wail sounds from the impending darkness outside my open kitchen window, yanking me back to the current moment. I reach over quickly and slam the window closed with a shiver. I say a silent prayer for Finn to hurry up and get here as I pull my cardigan tighter around myself.

* * *

I just finish setting the table when my doorbell rings, alerting me to what I believe to be Finn's arrival. I can't fight the smile that battles its way onto my lips as I anticipate seeing him again. Our relationship had changed drastically over the span of one day from awkward acquaintances to hook-up buddies to giving our relationship an actual chance. Despite the inconsistencies in our relationship dynamic I'm really excited to see what this leg of our journey has to offer us, with a relationship like Finn and I's I assume it'll never be a clear-cut path but I'm eager to see where things go.

I run my hands down the front of my dress, smoothing out the defiant wrinkles that have formed. I had noticed the mayor watching my hips earlier today in his office, so I specifically changed into this dress due to its unbeatable ability to make my waist look snatched and my hips look curvy. I check myself over once more in the entryway mirror before I reach for the door handle, swinging the thick wooden door open eagerly. My enthusiasm quickly escapes me when I realize it's not Finn at my door. It's fucking Elvira.

Starr stares back at me with her arms folded across her chest, her wicked green eyes searing a hole into my own sockets. Needless to say, I am less than pleased to see Starr's monochromatic ass on my doorstep.

"Sorry, the auditions for the new Tim Burton movie are that way." I point in a random direction.

She scoffs, shifting her weight to one hip as she peruses my outfit. A look of disgust solidifies her opinion of it. "You're meddling, Courtney and you need to leave Havenwood before

156

you get yourself hurt."

"Is that a threat?" I practically laugh in her face. Starr has about an inch on me but I'm more toned and not afraid to go for the hair.

"Not in the way you think." There she goes again, saying ominous shit that she doesn't bother to explain.

"I don't have time for riddles. Get off my porch, Morticia." Part of me wonders why she's here or what she means by *"there's a lot I don't know,"* but I'm not going to jump through hoops to figure it out. Especially not when I have a super hot dinner guest due to drop in any minute. Starr being here when he arrives is the last thing I need. She raises a thin black eyebrow that is unnecessarily pointy on both ends.

"I know you can't be that dense. Finn and I have a history, a very long, very deep history." She smirks as if remembering good times that I don't want to picture. The thought of Finn touching her makes me feel nauseous and even jealous but I'd rather get hit by the metro than let Starr see that.

"History is in the past for a reason, babe. People learn from their mistakes." I offer her a look of faux sympathy. I didn't pride myself on starting cat fights but I *do* pride myself on finishing them.

"A mistake is something that happens by accident. People try not to repeat *mistakes*. If I'm a mistake, then I'm a mistake Finn Abernathy has been making since junior year."

I can feel my cheeks redden in anger as I consider the fact that she has been Finn's booty call since high school, a fact I could've gone an eternity without knowing. Obviously, there was something he liked about her if he had continued to hook up with her for so long but I can't pinpoint what it could be. Who's to say it was even just hooking up, what if he actually had feelings for Starr? What if he *still* has feelings for her?

Insecure thoughts flash across my mind in less than a second but it's already too late, I know Starr saw the way her comment had chipped away at my tough outer facade.

"You're getting in the middle of something you don't even know the half of. Finn and I are meant to be together and your big-city girl routine is not going to get in the way of that. There is so much you don't know about and when you find out you're going to wish you had listened to me and not messed with things that don't belong to you."

I narrow my eyes at her as she lowers her voice to a condescending tone, that sickening smirk only spreading on her annoying mouth as she speaks. I want to slap it off her smug face but decide neither the jail time nor the amount of white foundation on my hand after the fact would be worth it.

I decide I'm done being belittled and more than done with this conversation.

"Good night, Beatlejuice." I attempt to slam the door shut in her face, reminding myself not to say her name three times in a row but Starr slams a hand against the door. I stare at her in surprise, my brows shrouding over my eyes at her audacity.

"Last chance, Hollywood." She hisses through clenched teeth. I huff out a laugh in her face, taking a step into her.

"Get your fucking hand off my door," I say darkly. A haunting wail echoes through the neighborhood as if to emphasize my point, causing Starr to look over her shoulder. When she turns back to me, a strand of her black hair is strewn across her face, adding to her look of disdain.

"You've been warned." She looks me up and down before turning and making her exit down the sidewalk, the fading sound of her chained boots clanking in the distance. I'm never one for getting high, aside from doing so to help write scripts for kid's shows, but some California weed would seriously help in this moment. I consider calling Micah but he might take a late-night phone call the wrong way and that isn't a situation I want to explain to anyone.

What had Starr meant by *there is so much you don't know about*? Like any old town, I'm sure Havenwood has its gossip and skeletons in its closet, but what could be so bad that it would scare me away from Finn, and why did Starr know about it? I attempt to compartmentalize my anxiety, wanting to enjoy the rest of my night without Starr's mind games getting to me.

Not even ten minutes later, the doorbell rings once again, and this time it is Finn.

"Hey," he greets calmly. I mentally pat myself on the back when I see Finn's eyes trace down to my hips and back up to my face. I knew they looked amazing in this dress, and that is one thing Starr can't take away from me!

"Hey," I respond, attempting to mimic his cool and calm demeanor even though I'm screaming inside.

I notice the bouquet of peonies in his hand as I invite him inside and a grateful smile settles deep on my lips. A single thought solidifies in my mind as I stare up into the mayor's inviting blue eyes: nothing Starr can do or say will turn me away from this man.

19

Cedar Wood

Courtney

Our greeting is slightly tense as we fumble over whether or not to hug, this new gray area of "giving our relationship a chance" having us both flustered and unsure. We finally settle on hugging and I'm a bit too enthused when his arms loop around me, submerging me in his woodsy scent. I revel in the warmth of his body before he pulls back, offering me the bouquet of peonies with his charming, lopsided smile. Any insecurities that linger over my conversation with Starr melt away, at least temporarily.

"You look amazing," Finn compliments me as we move our conversation into the kitchen. "Thanks." I peek back at him with a smile and find he's once again watching my hips sway as we walk. I smirk to myself as I turn my attention to my new dining table, I make a grand gesture towards it with a prideful, *"ta-da!"*

"Look a you!" Finn exclaims with a chuckle upon seeing the new table, running a large hand over the smooth top of it. "Finally putting down some roots, you're practically a local now." His genuine laugh makes my heart skip a beat as his baritone rings in my ears. My excitement falls off of a cliff and dies when I remember that I'm not a local and, when the writing strike ends, I'll have to return to my fast-paced life in LA. Thousands of miles away from Finn.

I push the thought to a far corner of my mind. I just want to spend tonight enjoying the company of a particularly sexy mayor. I'll go back to Los Angeles eventually. I have to. Right?

"This is what I wanted to tell you about," I say, picking up the notebook of local legends off the table and handing it to him. He gives me a quizzical grin before flipping the cover open and reading a few lines.

"These are stories about Havenwood."

"Yes, I plan to use them to write a guidebook. I'm going to include the town's history, the highlights, the ghost stories. So that when I go back to LA, I can tell everyone-." I stop myself from going any further. Hesitantly I look up at Finn only to find him already looking down at me, his handsome face is dowsed in a somber expression and I don't have to ask why. The thought of me going back home to California is plaguing him just as much as it is plaguing me.

"I made us dinner," I inform him, turning away quickly. I serve him a plate from the crock pot to distract myself from the topic.

"It smells amazing, thank you but you didn't need to do that." He responds politely as I hand him his plate. Finn and I don't currently have a label for whatever we are, but it would be difficult to continue with whatever it is from opposite coasts.

"That's what makes me so awesome," I tease as I motion for him to have a seat at the table. I serve myself, despite Finn's protests, and we dive into conversation like two lifelong friends picking up where we had just left off. We mull over the details of my guidebook as well as my renovation plans for the bookshop and it feels *normal*. Like we could do this every night for the rest of my life, almost like we're *meant* to. Things are so easy with Finn; he fits seamlessly into every aspect of my life, showing me the stark contrast between him and Carter (who made it very clear that fitting me into his busy schedule was a chore).

After our meal, I clear our plates, laughing over some dorky joke Finn had made as I place them in the sink. I return to my seat beside him and for the first time tonight, we find ourselves with nothing to discuss. We only sit in silence, trying desperately to interpret one another's body language, attempting to translate each movement. Both of us desperately curious whether or not we both want the same thing in this moment.

I observe Finn's full lips, internally debating with myself on whether they are an apricot pink color or more of a misty rose and whether or not the tip of his dick matches that delicious color. I notice my eyes have inadvertently dropped to his zipper and I try quickly to focus them elsewhere. *Did he see that? Shit.*

In my haste to redirect my stare, I unintentionally land on his eyes and our gaze locks. His arctic blues now emoting a completely different feeling than before. Something had settled in them, something raw, something demanding. The warmth and welcoming are long gone, replaced with a presence threatening to devour me whole.

He's a predator and I'm the prey, unable to do anything besides simply waiting for him to strike.

His velvety voice snaps the tension between us. "There's

no storm tonight, Courtney." I can't help but repress a small moan as he coos my name in his deep voice, still unable to look away from him. "If you want me to stay, you'll have to ask. Nicely."

Just like in the apple orchard, the mayor is commanding me to ask him nicely, setting the feminist in me ablaze, all while pleasing the parts of me that long to be dominated. I barely give any notice to the fact that I had begun to caress myself below the table but it isn't a surprise considering I'm soaking my panties from the sound of his voice alone. I can't control myself any longer.

"Please."

No sooner have the word left my mouth before Finn yanks me from my chair and into his lap. I drop my legs on either side of his thick thighs, straddling him as our lips crash together in a hot mess of need. I greedily drink in his lips and mouth as his tongue darts out, swiping across my lower lip to request entrance. I comply, parting my lips and allowing him in as one of his large hands tangles itself into the hair at the base of my skull. A moan escapes from me as he tightens his grip on my strands, the pinpricks of pain at my roots elevating my arousal.

"You sound so hot, baby," Finn's voice drips with appetite as he whispers against my parted lips. He positions his spare hand respectfully on my lower back and I can feel his rock-hard cock through the thickness of his slacks. I can't stop myself from grinding against it, *disrespectfully*.

"Finn, please.." I whine as my hips glide up and down the length of his erection. Knowing that I'm the cause of his arousal adds to my own tenfold. In my frenzied state, all I know is that I want him. I want to claim him. I want to mark him so deeply and fully that he won't be able to remember Starr's name in the morning. Now is not the time to be thinking about Finn's ex-girlfriend but the jealous side of me can't help it. Something else to address in therapy.

"I love how you sound when you beg for me, baby. Tell me what you want." He instructs slowly as he catches my earlobe between his teeth, nipping at it softly.

If any other man wanted me to beg for him, I would tell him to go to hell, but if Finn Abernathy wants to hear me beg, then I'll get on my hands and knees and fucking grovel.

"Please, Finn. Fuck me." I manage between jagged breaths and sloppy kisses as my chest heaves with titillation. That should feel demeaning but instead, I feel the liquid heat boil low in my stomach at the sound of my own impure pleading.

"Fuck, Courtney." He hums from low in his throat. His zipper poking me is the only proof necessary that he truly does like my pleas.

He stands, taking me with him as he does, forcing me to wrap my legs around his sturdy core for support. He holds me up by my ass as he heads for the living room but we both synchronously have the same realization, *no couch.* He's already pivoting, heading for the stairs and my bedroom. "Wait," I instruct before he can reach the first step.

Finn halts immediately in his tracks, searching my face for any sign that I'd changed my mind. I certainly had not, I'd simply had a better idea. "I know you're headed for my bed but there's a perfectly usable table right there."

He pauses for a beat before his lips curl into a smirk of comprehension. "You're right, naughty girl." He chuckles as he readjusts my weight into one of his arms, holding me as if I'm as light as a toddler on his hip. He uses his now free arm to slide his forearm across the table, unceremoniously yet effectively clearing the tablecloth and decorative candles I'd put out. The objects barely hit the floor before my ass is propped on the wood tabletop, Finn's cool blue eyes admiring me as if I'm a work of fine art. I can't stand it any longer, I need the gap closed between us, no distance or irritating clothes in our way.

I free my arms from the thin straps of my dress and begin to pull at my undershirt when Finn's large hands grip my own, freezing them mid-move. Now it's my turn to be confused.

I look to him for an explanation, the blazing lust in his eyes telling me all I need to know. I remove my grip from my shirt and he takes over, beginning to undress me himself. He doesn't strip me immediately, however; instead, once my shirt is off and my dress is pulled down to my stomach, he trails one of his long fingers from the side of my face down my neck. His soft, taunting movements causing goosebumps to break out over my skin and my nipples to harden into pebbles. I groan as his finger trickles down further, over the curve of my breast and down my exposed stomach, his proximity to my pussy causing the muscles to pulse with need.

With my chest exposed to him, I watch as Finn takes in the pink peaks of my nipples, his tongue swiping his bottom lip. At this moment, he no longer resembles a reserved, respectable mayor but instead a man, half-starved and salivating. My nipples tighten painfully under his stare, begging for his attention. His gaze remains transfixed on my breasts as he reaches behind his neck, tugging on the back of his shirt and unceremoniously tossing it to the floor once it's over his head. With Finn now shirtless and on display before me, it's my turn to stare.

I examine his torso, loving the way the overhead kitchen light casts dramatic shadows across the grooves of his strong body. Even with the flattering lighting, I can see that his biceps are sizable bumps on his arms, strong enough to easily toss me around like a rag doll—a trick I might ask him to demonstrate later.

I rake my eyes across his powerful shoulders down to his well-defined chest, which sports a light dusting of dark chest hair that deliciously contrasts his pale skin. I allow my gaze to dip further to his core, my excitement burning hotter as I force myself to savor each part of him instead of attempting to greedily drink him up like I want to. Despite how solidly built Finn is, I'm relieved to see no trace of a six-pack on his middle. The softness evident in his lower stomach turns me on in a way I haven't felt before. By my third SoCal hookup, I'd lost interest in abs entirely since Los Angeleno men tended to make them their entire personalities. I'm happy knowing there's more to Finn than his muscles (although they are fantastic as well).

My eyes pour down him in seconds despite my best efforts to luxuriate in his beauty. With a mere step, Finn closes the distance between us just as I finish my objectifying examination of him. With him so close to me, I reach out, unable to stop myself from touching the God in front of me and allow my finger to delicately trace the dark hair of his happy trail into his slacks that hang carefree on his hips, knowing just how mad it will drive the man inside the mayor. His lips brush my own as we share a fleeting moment of tenderness before crashing together once again in an insatiable frenzy. Finn runs a hand deep into my hair, his fingers curling around the strands as the other fills with one of my breasts. I feel the softness of his palm tightening around my sensitive flesh as he gives my breast a rough squeeze; I cry out an unchained, pleasureful yelp, his uneven breathing exposing just how much he's enjoying touching me.

"You have beautiful fucking tits, baby," Finn growls against my kiss-swollen lips. That's something I already know, but hearing it from Finn is a whole different level of validation that I didn't know I needed.

His lips move from my own to my throat, planting kisses along the side of it as his warm breaths spill down my neck. I can only manage to respond in approving purrs, hooking my arm around his shoulders to draw him in closer to me. The warmth of his chest against my own ignites the desperation inside of me. I need him inside me. Now.

I react on impulse, snaking my hand down in between us and unbuckling his belt with ease. The metallic clink of the prong and bar separating sounding like victorious music to my ears, one step closer to my prize. Finn examines my work with a naughty grin of approval.

"That's impressive." He chuckles softly, genuine surprise underlining his flirtatious tone. He lowers his hands to meet my own, unbuttoning and unzipping his slacks. His erection is now only shielded by the thin fabric of his boxers. I grab his hands before he can make any more moves to undress himself, shrugging casually.

"I know how to take what I want." I use the arm that's wrapped around him to pull him into another kiss, catching him off guard. He stumbles into me perfectly, his hard cock pressing into my stomach. I like Finn's praise but I love to surprise him with my control and sexual prowess even more.

I can tell Finn is trying to take his time with me and start slow, like a true gentleman. I'm not trying to rush us either, but after coveting this man so desperately for weeks and only getting a brief taste of him this morning, the anticipation feels like torture.

I guess I'll have to show him how much of a lady I am *not*.

I hook the heel of my boot into the front pocket of his pants and skillfully extend my leg straight down, effectively peeling his pants down his legs. Finn breaks away from our kiss, once again admiring my creative ability to undress him.

"Where have you been all my life?" He laughs and runs a hand through his raven hair, showing off his perfect smile. *Trapped beneath lying blond men*, I respond in vain in my head. Tormenting myself once again for allowing someone to treat me so badly when I could've been here, getting my guts rearranged by a hot small-town mayor on my kitchen table.

My eyes must have momentarily gone distant because Finn rests a curled finger under my chin, lifting it so our eyes align. There's no need to punish myself right now when I definitely shouldn't be thinking about my past or Starr or anything else besides Finn fucking Abernathy. Finn's blue eyes search my own, silently checking in on me before we advance any further. That's something else I love about him, several times now he's put my comfort above his lust. Something I didn't know the modern man was capable of.

I conjure up my flirty smile once again, beating down the self-deprecation. "We're just getting started, Mr. Mayor."

A devilish laugh escapes him. The timber of the noise mixed with the way his core tightens as he laughs causes me to face the music for the first time. Finn has barely touched me, *hell*, we're both only naked from the waist up but I'm the most turned on I've ever been in my life. I wouldn't even be shocked if he told me there was a puddle forming below me on the table right now and it's because I genuinely like him. *A lot.* Maybe too much.

I won't say I'm falling in love with Finn Abernathy because it's way too soon, but as I look up into those icy blue eyes filled with lust and adoration, I know I can't hide from the truth much longer.

I am falling in love with him.

20

Black Lace

Finn

Courtney's lust-filled eyes lure me in once again and I lean down to connect my lips to hers. They're soft and plush and slightly parted, inviting my tongue inside.

Courtney is beautiful, intelligent, and talented, all of which encourage me to take my time with her. *Be slow. Be kind. Be a gentleman.* But Courtney is also red hot with sinfully full curves and gorgeous tits that make my cock ache. All of which encourages me to pound myself into her until she's blind from pleasure and screaming my name as she rides through the waves of her third or fourth orgasm.

I push on her small shoulders a bit harsher than intended, coaxing her to lie flat on her back. She does so complaisantly, looking up at me with those doe-like brown eyes that have haunted my dreams since the moment she set foot in my town. She's awaiting instruction but I know there's only a 50% chance she'll follow them even if I were to give them. Courtney's bratty disobedience is something I love about her.

She's a mountain you can't bend or move against her will; she has to want it for herself, and the fact that she's here with me now means she wants it. She wants *me* and that turns me on more than I care to admit.

I grab at either side of her dress, which is now clustered around her center, keeping my eyes on hers as I pull the material down. She raises those glorious hips to help me slide the fabric off of her, and once she's free of it, I toss the dress to the floor alongside my shirt. Leaving her only in black lace panties that are far too easy to see through. Did she wear those specifically for me? Or does Courtney Berrycloth live her day-to-day life in frilly, sexy panties? Either way, both possibilities make me impossibly harder to the point where my balls are screaming at me for release.

I drop to my knees to level my head with the table and her lace-clad opening. "I'm ready for my dessert."

My words are the only warning I afford her before I tear her panties in half. They rip away without resistance, just as they had last time, causing Courtney to gasp in shock as I discard the torn lace over my shoulder. I can practically see Courtney's words die on her tongue as her jaw hangs open in stunned silence, her mouth drying out as I watch its moisture travel to her lower region. Without allowing her a moment of reprieve, I dip my head and lick her sweet cunt from its tight entrance to her swollen clit. My tongue fluctuates from flat to a point as I ascend her pussy. I'd gotten a taste of her sweet honey this morning and it had ignited a hunger in me that nothing will ever satisfy aside from her.

"Oh fuck," she heaves as her core tightens, her body curling in an attempt to watch as my mouth works her.

"Your cunt is so sweet," I speak freely, feeling comfortable enough to tell her all my impure thoughts that she deserves to hear. I've been described as rather reserved and quiet and, under most circumstances, I don't like to use foul language. As a titled member of society I'm almost forbidden to but here, in this kitchen with Courtney, I'm just a man with a million dirty thoughts on his mind.

I tear myself from her pussy before I risk devouring her entirely. I gently touch my fingers to my beard which has been doused in her liquid heat. I pull my hand back, admiring the glistening creamy liquid now transferred onto my fingers.

"I-," Courtney attempts to speak, maybe even apologize, for soaking my face but I cut her off before she can do something so unnecessary.

"Looks like you're as excited for me as I am for you." My voice is much lower and more sultry than I remember it being but the look on Courtney's face tells me that that's okay with her. "Show me how excited you are," she demands breathlessly. My ears perk as if finally hearing the magic words.

"Gladly." The word sounds like a threat and I suppose it is.

I dip my head once again and begin to enthusiastically lap at her pussy, worshiping her gorgeous body with each feverish pass of my tongue. I watch as the harsh pleasure pulses through Courtney's frame, forcing her back to arch against the hardwood of the tabletop. Whimpering cries break from her mouth like little encores demanding I continue. I latch my hands to either side of her hips, holding her pelvis still enough for me to hit all those necessary spots.

Her right leg begins to quiver as she rolls herself against my tongue, aiding me in setting the perfect tempo to accompany her crescendo. She kicks her feet up onto my shoulders; the heels of her thigh-high boots dig into my trap muscles, but I hardly notice.

I dig my fingers unkindly into her flesh and bury my face deeper between her legs, attempting to drown myself in her honey and make her cum all at once. As I attack her clit more greedily, her leg begins to shake more violently, a primeval, feminine sound ripping from her.

"Oh, Finn, just like that. Don't stop!" *I didn't plan on it, baby.* I don't move a goddamn centimeter or change my rhythm in the slightest, instead, I follow her exact instructions and within seconds I feel her pussy begin to pulsate below my tongue.

"Finn! Finn! Finn!"

She cries my name as her heels dig painfully into my muscles. I glance up at her face, watching as waves and tsunamis of ecstasy roll over her contracted body. I don't dare stop until her muscles have relaxed and I'm sure she has finished for the first time but certainly not the last. She lies stagnate on the tabletop for only a beat of recuperation before she crunches into a seated position, staring at me in bewilderment. I only allow myself a second of pride before lowering my face once more so that I am again engulfed in her feminine scent. "Ready to come again?" My eyes dare her response, already in my readying stance.

"Not yet," she lowers her heels from their position on my shoulders, prompting me to stand up straight. I rise to my full height without question, what Courtney wants Courtney gets. We both know her second orgasm will come, if not now, then later, and I don't mind prolonging our time together one bit.

Her eyes trace the outline of my hard cock still trapped inside my underwear, sending a jolt of excitement to my enlarged member. Her gaze stays there, entranced, as she scoots to the very edge of the table and begins to peel my boxers down my thighs slowly. As she lowers the hem, my cock springs free from its taut confinement, mere inches away from Courtney's face. Her eyes drink up the sight in a way that makes me want to propose here and now, the look of disbelief in her expression fueling my need to be inside her this very instant.

"God damn," she mutters to herself, running her delicate fingers up and down my length, sending a shiver racking through my entire body. I let out a faint hiss caused by the pleasure that erupts from the trails left by her fingers.

Setting her awe aside, she motions to the table behind her. "Lay down," she commands. I obey my little tyrant and lay back, my naked skin against the cold wood. I inchworm as gracefully as I can until my body is in the center of the table. Courtney wastes no time crawling on top of me, her arms pinned to either side of my head as she stares down at me contemplatively.

"Can you swim?"

"When required." It seems like an odd question to pose right now but I answer truthfully.

"It's required." She states before pivoting on her knees and turning herself around so that her legs replace where her arms just were, spread wide on either side of my head. Her syrupy little cunt levitating inches above my face, the honeyed smell of her arousal flooding my senses. I feel the warmth of her plump lips wrap around the head of my cock, circling her tongue around my tip. I moan, now understanding exactly what is happening, and oh my God, am I ready for it. Courtney spreads her knees further apart, lowering her core closer to me, allowing my tongue to dive back into her as her mouth works me from the other end of the table. Now I understood the swimming question because damn, is she wet, soaked in fact; as soon as my tongue had found her swollen clit, candied liquid leaked down my chin. I feast on her once again, losing track of what is her arousal and my own drool as I do, pleased to have the flavor of her back on my tongue.

Although I can't see her head bobbing, I can feel her mouth sliding up and down my cock, massaging it into euphoria as she uses her tongue to flick over the thick veins that rope around my shaft and the sensitive part below my tip. She knows exactly what she's doing and the idea of her being well-versed in male pleasure admittedly makes me irrationally jealous. I have no claim to Courtney Berrycloth and I attempt to remind myself of that while my face is acting as her throne but that doesn't mean I don't *want* to stake my claim.

As I lap ferociously at her rosy bud, fighting for my resolve, I feel her leg begin to twitch once again beside my head. She's close, and thank God because if we continue any longer, I might come directly into her pretty mouth. And that's not where I want to leave my seed tonight.

Within seconds her lips are tightening around my base as she hums out moans as best she can with her mouth stuffed with my dick. I wrap my arms around her center and hold her still so that my mouth can fuck her until the very last second of her orgasm. I can almost swear I hear her moaning my name as she unravels on top of me.

Her seizing calms, and once I know she's finished for a second time, I relinquish my hold on her middle and allow her to crawl off of me. Courtney rotates so that she is straddling me once again, this time with her entrance hovering above my well-coated cock.

"I loved you coming on my face, baby," I tell her as I position my hands firmly on either of her full, sassy hips. "But I'm going to love you coming on my cock even more." I use my grip to slam her down, effectively impaling her with my cock.

Her mouth falls into an O as she cries out in shocked pleasure. I admire the way Courtney looks in this moment, disheveled and raw, probably not dissimilar to myself. The two of us, just man and woman, reduced to our basic forms in this moment as I thrust up into her. The pleasure pulsing through me from one stroke of her precious pussy is unlike any glory I've ever experienced before. Maybe I'm biased but I just know that Courtney Berrycloth will be the best fuck of my life.

Her hands reach out for my chest, her long fingernails dragging down my front as she rides me, gyrating circles on my hips. Her cries and whimpers only intensify as she bounces on me, her tight walls squeezing me as she does. I can't help but moan back in harmony as she works me deeper inside of her, using gravity to aid her. My cock fills her so perfectly, my tip stimulating her cervix as she seats herself completely flat on me.

She does her best to hide her exhaustion but I can see her muscles begin to grow weak. After multiple orgasms and the effort she's exerting now, I can only imagine how tired she is. Now it's my turn to put in the work.

"Allow me," I offer. She hops off of me with a kiss and I push her forward sternly, coaxing her into the position I desire, on her hands and knees. Her beautiful ass and defined slopes of her muscular back are on full display to me now, as well as her entrance. I pause for a beat to take in the beauty of her glistening opening, her dark rose-colored lips, and her slightly more pink inner folds. It's better than anything my mind could make up on its own - despite the multiple porn videos I had watched and jerked off to in order to get Courtney out of my system. My searches had read *"tanned Cali brunette"* and *"fit brown-eyed girl,"* but none of them were worth anything compared to Courtney.

I lean over her back, allowing my cock to slide past her soaked rose-petal-soft lips and brush her clit. My lips graze against the shell of her ear as I tease her.

"Please.." She begs in her soft voice, barely above a pant. Her arms are shaking with anticipation and fatigue as she waits patiently to be properly fucked.

"I'll give it to you, beautiful. You'll never have to work for your own orgasms again." Another harsh exhale of approval from her. "I will always be the one to give them to you, I promise you that, Courtney." I vow before I plunge myself deep inside of her. Courtney and I release unison hisses of pleasure as I roll my hips into her, ramming my length inside her, not allowing her time to acclimate to the pressure I'm causing inside of her.

"Fuck, Finn," Courtney coos as her front half dips lower, her perfect tits smashing against the tabletop.

I reach around her waist and dip my fingers into her groin; I locate her clit and begin to massage it, earning me an approving cry. I coordinate my thrusts with the way I touch her, syncing my motions into a perfect melody of sensuality. Courtney's shallow breaths and cries of eroticism alert me that she's on the precipice of her next orgasm and honestly, so am I. I can feel the pressure building in my chest and my balls beginning to constrict. I'm not typically one for coming quickly but between the way I had been fantasizing about this moment for weeks and the way that Courtney's pussy feels like heaven, I'm not surprised. Hell, I'm not even ashamed, I can't imagine any man being able to last longer than an hour with Courtney. But then again, I can't imagine any man with Courtney besides me.

I pump into her more aggressively, using this time to commit the tan lines of her muscular back and ass to memory, forcing myself to sear the image into my brain in case I never have the opportunity to see them again. As much as I don't want to admit it, or think of it, right now especially, Courtney disappearing from my life is a real possibility. Either she'd be called back to the writing rooms of Los Angeles or she'd flee from me of her own accord, unprompted by anything other than my deception.

The mounting release in my lower stomach and the pulsing of Courtney's inner walls bring me back to the moment as she screams my name once again but I barely hear her. Specks of darkness threaten the edges of my vision as I feel myself pouring into her, all my senses dulling except for one. My moans of pleasure mix with hers as my release overrides any resolve I have left in me. I fuck her disgustingly rough until the last drop of seed is milked from me and I've emptied into her entirely.

As I fall back from heaven and back to my drained body, I register Courtney's flushed face looking back at me over her shoulder. Her caramel hair is a mess, and her mocha eyes are filled with an emotion that I haven't seen in them before.

"You are going to ruin me."

21

T.P.

Courtney

Finn's warm body beside mine kept me asleep until nearly 10 a.m.. After a night like ours, sleep was desperately needed for recuperation. When deep, dreamless sleep had finally released me, I was unsurprised to find that I was sore in most places. Now would be a great time to get that massage I had fantasized about.

I stretch my arm across the bed, feeling for the naughty mayor who had occupied the space last night, but he's gone.

I peek open a heavy eyelid and sure enough, where Finn had once laid is now just empty mattress. I sit up and rub the sleep from my eyes, scanning the room. He isn't here. A scathing ball of anxiety begins to claw its way from my stomach up into my throat as worst-case scenarios infiltrate my thoughts. *Did he not enjoy himself last night? Did he regret it? Did he only intend to hook up and never speak again?* Starr's ominous words come flooding back without invitation. *"There is so much you don't know about."* Does his disappearing act have something to do with her warning?

Sneaking out while I was asleep is a major dick move, but unfortunately, if that were the case, it isn't the first time it's happened. The last asshole to pull that even had the audacity to leave his business card on the pillow!

I risk a glance at the pillow beside me, just in case.

I try to remind myself that Finn isn't like the other assholes I had the misfortune of dating. If he had to leave urgently and without telling me, there was a reason.

A distant sizzling sound catches my attention. *Shit! Had I forgotten to turn my crockpot off last night and caused a fire?* I quickly spring from my bed, not bothering to dress before making a B-line for the kitchen. I take the steps two at a time as I internally panic, trying not to imagine what my neighbors will think about me fleeing from a burning house stark naked.

I'm bounding halfway down the stairs when a familiar whiff breaks through my mania. Bacon? I slow my pace as I step onto the cold hardwood floor and am immediately relieved to find my house perfectly *not* on fire.

"Good morn-," Finn begins to greet me, clad in yesterday's clothes and a dorky apron that reads *Life Is What You Bake it.* His greeting is interrupted as his eyes drop down to my breasts and I remember just how completely bare I am. The mayor wets his lips in an unintentionally attractive way before returning my gaze.

"Um," he stutters, blushing as he forces his attention back to the breakfast meat on the stove. "I'm sorry." He rubs the back of his neck in embarrassment, a cherry color highlighting the tips of his ears.

"No, no I'm.." I blink a few times in astonishment before crossing my arms over my exposed chest. Why are either one of us apologizing right now? I rub my arm as I realize that this is the awkward "morning after" part, or at least, in my experience, it was always awkward. But it doesn't have to be.

"I thought the house was on fire," I giggle despite myself. I watch Finn's broad shoulders relax at the sound of my laugh, had he been worried?

"Well don't relax yet, I'm no chef so a house fire is still possible." He smiles but keeps his gaze glued respectfully to the pan.

"Nice apron," I tease, nodding to the well-worn garment.

"Be nice," he shoots me a warning smirk. "It's Agnes' so I didn't get a choice in the color."

"Purple definitely suits you, I meant the cheesy pun." I'm able to breathe a sigh of relief knowing my house is not being devastated by a fire and that Finn didn't run away after our hookup. Not only had he not run away, he appears to be making us food. "Breakfast?" I question.

"Yeah I, um, ran to the grocery store down the street to grab some stuff. I thought you might be hungry." The small blush that is returning to his high cheekbones causes a bubble of adoration to burst inside of me. Had it really taken me an entire move across the country to find a man who would make me breakfast the morning after phenomenal sex? "It'll be ready in just a minute. Why don't you get dressed so I'll be able to have a single pure thought during our meal?"

"Where's the fun in that?" I joke but ultimately oblige, retracing my steps up the stairs and slipping on my pink robe before returning to the kitchen. Finn had served maple oatmeal with blueberries, toast, and ever so slightly overcooked bacon. As I sit at the table in awe, Finn sets a mug in front of me. I look up at him with a questioning expression.

"Your completely offensive oat milk chai," he clarifies,

fighting a smile before taking the seat across from me. "I might have also stopped at Mystic Brew."

"Finn, I don't know what to say." I laugh in disbelief as I look over the assortment, unable to remember the last time someone had done such a nice and sincere gesture for me. A delicate bushel of Russian sage sits in a thin vase, decorating the center of the table that Finn and I had blessed last night.

"You don't have to say anything," he places his large hand on top of mine, cautiously rubbing the top of it with his thumb as if he's unsure if the intimacy of the gesture is allowed. We had spent a good portion of last night doing the most erotic and unspeakable acts, yet somehow, we are both extremely skittish when it comes to the little things.

I lean across the table and kiss his cheek, the soft pricks of his morning stubble against my lips warming me from the inside out. It's good to know he isn't completely perfect; he still has to shave like normal people and may even suffer from morning breath. Knowing that Finn is capable of being flawed makes the idea of him being with me easier to swallow because, while I'm a confident woman, I'm finding it hard to believe I deserve a man like Finn Abernathy.

Finn raises his hand to his cheek, his fingers tracing the spot I had just kissed, a demure smile spreading on his lips. It's time to admit, I'm falling in love with this man.

* * *

We don't discuss last night's events or the status of our current relationship over breakfast. Instead, we talk about our favorite movies, Finn's being E.T. and I respect that choice since Spielberg directed it, as well as parts of our childhoods, hobbies, likes, and dislikes. All the inconsequential stuff that makes up a large part of who we are. It feels like a proper date; it feels like I'm Finn's girlfriend, and that scares me as much as it excites me.

I feel so strongly for a person who is living in what was supposed to be a temporary part of my life, but I'm not going to run from my feelings. Even if our future together seems complicated and out of reach, I promised myself that I was going to give Finn and I's relationship a chance and not lean into my self-destructive tenancies. When the time comes to go back to California, I'll figure my shit out then. For now, the only thing I want to do is accompany Finn to his plans at the Havenwood community garden, a spot I'm very curious to check out. I've never heard of a community garden and wonder how it's possible for a group of people to grow plants together. The individualism of Los Angeles culture could never.

As I dress for the day, Finn waits patiently on the edge of my bed, which no longer consists of just a mattress on the floor. It had received an upgrade, including a handmade bed frame made of wooden slats. As I had slept this morning, Finn had called in a favor from Micah, who had brought over the frame after breakfast, and the two of them set it up together. It was funny to watch them interact; it seemed like Micah was simultaneously proud yet a bit jealous of Finn for being in my bedroom. Micah made himself scarce quickly after the bed was finished, which I was grateful for. It had allowed Finn and I time for a quickie before getting ready for the day.

I dig into one of my many suitcases and fish out a pair of short denim overalls.

"Are you planning on unpacking? You have a lovely closet that's probably desperate to be used." Finn chuckles, watching me dig through dozens of garments to find a matching sock.

"But then you wouldn't be able to stare at my ass while I bend over into my suitcase." I shoot him a teasing look over my shoulder and sure enough, his icy blues are studying my backside. He looks away quickly, yet not quick enough, caught in the act. I giggle as I triumphantly find my second sock.

In truth, the thought of unpacking makes me uneasy. It feels like if I unpack then I'm making my stay in Havenwood permanent and abandoning my life and career back in California. But if I continue to live out of my suitcases, then I can stay in this fantasy limbo and pretend that my time here in Massachusetts is unending, much like the way time behaves in a dream.

I do a dramatic spin to give Finn a 360-degree view of my farmer's-daughter-inspired outfit, complete with brown leather lace-up boots. He gleams in approval, applauding as I strut down my imaginary runway.

"Beautiful as always." He compliments genuinely.

"Sorry, were you planning on wearing overalls, too? I can change," I quip, taking a seat on his knee. Finn wraps his muscular arm around my center, his soft blues looking up at me lovingly. "It's okay; you wear them better."

He squeezes me, signaling it's time for our departure. We have just enough time before we're due at the community garden to make a stop at Finn's house so that he can change his outfit. Turns out, it's bad PR for the mayor to not only be seen in yesterday's clothes but to arrive in yesterday's clothes with a woman on his arm.

Finn steps out onto my front porch first and I follow,

fiddling with the archaic lock on the front door. Just as I click the lock into place, I notice Finn's figure stiffen out of my periphery; I turn to him, noting the shocked stare melted onto his handsome face.

"What-?" I don't immediately register what he's glaring at, instead, I first notice Agnes standing out on the side walk, a matching expression on her round face. I assume Finn is simply embarrassed that his mom caught him sneaking out of a woman's house but that's not what has them upset.

I take a few steps off the front porch and turn around to face the rental house. That's when I see it. Streams of white coat every peak and corner of 2213 Queen's Avenue, where the grass was once visible is now a sea of snowy strands. Even the innocent red oak tree in the front yard was not spared. Its once vibrant sprouting leaves are now encased in layers of white. My house had been T.P.ed.

"What are we? Twelve!?" I growl in irritation, envisioning how long the cleanup process will be. Finn wraps an arm around my shoulders, his look of absolute bewilderment slowly fading as he attempts to comfort me.

"Who did this?" He questions softly as he surveys the damage.

"That's what I would like to know." Agnes looks genuinely pissed off, her normally soft eyes alight with annoyance. *"You've been warned."* The words rang in my head. I have to applaud Starr for her cleverness, covering someone's house in toilet paper is hardly enough of a crime to get the police involved but just enough of an inconvenience to ruin someone's day. That someone being *me*.

Finn studies my face as the revelation hits me. "Probably some teenagers from Salem," He turns to address Agnes, reassuringly wrapping his free arm around her shoulders as well. "I'll get this cleaned up ASAP, neither of you worry." Finn squeezes Agnes' and I's shoulder in tandem.

"Funny," Agnes raises a graying eyebrow to Finn, her expression knowing as it always is. "I wonder why teenagers from Salem are upset about you staying the night at Courtney's house."

I sink my teeth into my bottom lip, holding back a snort as the color drains from Finn's caught face. He stumbles over his next few words before Agnes raises a hand, silencing him. "Clean it up, mayor!" She calls as she walks back to her house, decidedly washing her hands of the situation.

Once she's inside, Finn turns to me, his questioning eyes meeting mine. I sigh, knowing I'll have to fess up to him about Starr and I's unpleasant encounter last night.

"Starr paid me a little visit last night before you got here," I relent. His raven eyebrows knit together, concern draping across his features.

"What did she say to you?" His tone is protective as he searches my face for answers.

"Nothing important, stupid shit to try to make me insecure and drive a wedge between us." My eyes drift to the strands of toilet paper swaying in the gentle breeze. "Although she did warn me she would exact her revenge. I just didn't know it would be in the fashion of a prepubescent boy."

"T.P.ing is a Havenwood tradition," Finn shakes his head at the immature custom. "You piss someone off, your house gets T.P.ed. You join a sports team, your house gets T.P.ed. It's your birthday, T.P.. It's a hazing sort of thing; just ignore it. In fact, ignore *her*." Admittedly, my chest warms at the annoyance present on his face when he tells me to ignore

Starr, any remaining jealousy draining from me entirely.

"Maybe I should take it as a compliment then? My official baptism as a Havenwoodian." A smile pulls at Finn's lips as he presses them to my forehead, the action speaking for itself.

"I'll make sure this gets cleaned up before the next rain, c'mon, we'll have to hurry to make it to the gardens by noon." He takes my hand in his and we set off at a brisk pace, the dangling pieces of toilet paper waving us goodbye.

22

Warm and Fuzzies

Courtney

Finn lives in an unembellished two-story house in the middle of his street. It's exactly the kind of place I would expect a nonmaterialistic man like Finn to live. Nothing too flashy, but the house still boasts ample space and a cozy vibe. His front lawn is maintained and green, although patchy in some spots, most likely from forgetting to water it after a long day of work, but overall, it's respectable for being owned by a bachelor.

"How am I scoring so far?" Finn's eyes remain trained straight ahead as we approach his place, the curl at the corner of his lips exposing his attempt to hide a knowing smile. It's like he can read my thoughts and tell that I'm taking notes on his property.

"So far, so good," I answer honestly, a cocky air to my voice. I lift my chin to glance up at him. "The inside is the real test."

Finn unlocks the front door with an intricate key that would look more natural in the 19th century. The key rejects today's standards of sleek, modern minimalism, as much of

Havenwood itself does. "Be gentle on me," he winks, that irresistible half-smile returning as he holds the door open for me.

I cast him a cheeky smirk as I step past him, wasting no time in inspecting the living room, shamelessly allowing my critical gaze to cascade over the space.

The layout of the first floor is uncomplicated, with a thin staircase directly in front of the entryway, a living room to the right, and a decent-sized kitchen tucked in the corner of the house. I take a few steps into Finn's living room; the space is furnished with a wall-mounted TV and a sectional couch that looks well-loved but clean, with a beautiful painting of a forest hanging above it. The wall furthest from the front door sports a bookshelf filled with genres ranging from political science to fantasy to popular SciFi titles. The space is simple but effortlessly posh.

I'd heard that there is a lot to learn about a man based on the way he keeps his place and, based on the fact that there isn't a single hard sock or sports team-themed couch in sight, I would say Finn had superseded my expectations.

Finn watches me observantly as I finish my inspection, no doubt fighting the urge to make me vocalize my approval of his furnishing abilities. "I'm going to go upstairs and change, I promise to give you the grand tour later." He says, taking my hand in his own and kissing the back of it. I bite my lip as I watch him trot up the stairs. I have half a mind to follow him, but I know that will lead to things we don't have time for at the moment.

I try in vain to distract myself by continuing my snooping but the lingering idea of following Finn upstairs and watching him undress is debilitating. My brain won't allow me to focus on anything other than the mental image of the delicious mayor shedding his clothes in the room right above my head. *Screw it*, I decide, making my way up the staircase.

I try to remain silent as I climb to the second-floor landing. Once there, I'm faced with three identical doors. I start with the one to my left and find it to be an empty guest bedroom, the door in front of me is the upstairs bathroom, which leaves the door to my right. I slowly twist the knob and push the door inward. This is the room I was looking for.

Finn stands with his toned back facing me, his shirt already on the floor, giving me an excellent view of his bare muscles. I'd been so quiet in my ascent that he hadn't even noticed me watching him. I stare in silence as he pulls off his belt, the leather snaking around his hips before being dropped at his feet. As he reaches for his pants, a longing noise escapes from me, the sound drenched in horniness - and unfortunately - loud enough to reveal my voyeuristic position. Finn casts his gaze at me over his pale shoulder, surprise evident on his handsome face.

"Couldn't wait for the tour, hm?" He chortles, turning to face me properly. His pants are unbuttoned and unzipped, hanging open and revealing boxers that manage to hug his bulge disgusting well. I try to respond but the words evade me. I wet my lips, my eyes glued to the magic that I know is hidden below his briefs. Finn notices my distracted nature, honing in on what exactly has my attention. He smirks pridefully, taking a step closer to me. "Tell me what you want, baby."

"I want your cock to fill me up," I answer honestly, my voice breathless as I drink in the sight of him. Even after the multiple rounds we had gone last night and our quickie this morning, I still did not have enough of Finn fucking

Abernathy.

"As you wish," he coos, deceivingly soft. He trails a gentle touch from my cheek into my hair as I stare up into his icy blue pools. I'm completely lost in their depths and the sweetness of his breath when a disorienting pain at the base of my skull brings me to my knees. I yelp as my hands fly to the source of the ache, only to find Finn's fist buried in my tresses. I stare up at him wide-eyed, aggrievement strewn across my features. He had yanked me to my knees by my hair. "What the f-," his grip tightens on my strands, ending my exclamation in another sharp cry. "You said you wanted my cock to fill you," his thumb digs into his waistband, lowering the hem of his boxers and allowing his erection to spring free. "You didn't specify *where* to fill you."

I glance anxiously between Finn's eyes and his hardened length. The initial shock had passed and, instead of being pissed off that he had practically thrown me to the floor, I'm wildly turned on. I love that he is mild-mannered, compassionate, and executive, but in the bedroom, he's dominating and rough, all while meeting and surpassing my needs. And I love that even more. It feels like I get to see this secret, unhinged side to him that no one else does. This is our own little fantasy where he doesn't have to be a mayor with the weight of his town on his shoulders and I don't have to be the transplant torn between the safety and distance of her home and the man she's falling in love with.

I lean forward and lick his tip, sending a shutter racking through his toned body.

"Such a good girl," he praises before thrusting harshly into my mouth.

* * *

Half an hour and two orgasms later, we emerge from his bedroom, both of us in desperate need of a hair brush. Finn holds back a laugh as he attempts to soothe my wild brown flyaways, his eyes full of admiration.

"I'll be right back." He kisses my forehead before heading into the bathroom. I smile lazily in his direction as he disappears behind the restroom door, endorphins and other post-climax hormones giving me those warm and fuzzy feelings.

Seeing as we're now running significantly late I decide to make my way down the stairs. I let my footsteps fall heavy as I descend, my body tired from our activities and in need of a nap. The promise of seeing the Havenwood garden is the only thing preventing me from turning around, going right back up the stairs, and sleeping the day away in Finn's bed. As I wait at the base of the stairs, a golden shine catches my attention.

In the small space between the front door and the stairs rested a small wrought iron table adorned with gold picture frames, the light shining in from the windows causing a reflection to bounce off the frames. I smile to myself, knowing a sentimental man like Finn would have kept photos of his friends and family somewhere in his house. I drag myself over and peruse the photos, noticing a few familiar faces. Agnes, with fewer gray hairs, hugging a young Finn and Milo, who are sporting more acne and even braces! I knew Milo couldn't have been born with such perfect teeth, it simply wouldn't have been fair. I glance to the next frame and stumble upon a pair of faces I don't recognize.

A man and a woman with a toddler version of Finn, the trio smiling wide for the picture, their coordinating shirt colors telling me it must have been a planned family photo. I observe the beautiful features of the woman, who I assume to be Finn's mother, with her raven hair, glorious green eyes, and high cheekbones. She could have easily been a model with her stunning features and attractive dimples, her elven features reminding me of one of the characters from Lord Of The Rings. Finn's father was a handsome man, despite rocking a less-than-desirable hairline, with a strong nose and jawline and icy blue eyes he had passed down to his son.

Finn makes his way down the stairs with a brush in hand, interrupting my snooping as he does. His pace slows as he takes notice of which picture I am admiring.

"You look so much like your mother," I offer, unsure of how Finn will react to discussing his late parents. His lips twist into a reminiscent smile as he approaches the small collection of pictures, stepping behind me and wrapping his arms around my waist.

"She would have loved you," He says softly. No, *sadly*. I reach behind me to place a comforting hand on his cheek.

"They were the best parents a kid could ask for - save for Agnes and Phil, of course." He lets a small exhale of air out through his nose.

"If you don't mind me asking, how did they pass?" I question delicately, not trying to pry any further than necessary or rake Finn across painful memories.

"Fire," he responds shortly. "It took them, our house, almost everything we had. I only have this picture because it was our Christmas card one year, and luckily, Agnes saved it."

The idea of young Finn being orphaned without any home

or belongings to speak of pulls the corners of my mouth down into an empathetic frown. *Thank God for Agnes and her husband,* I think silently to myself. Not only had they welcomed their son's orphaned friend with open arms, but they had done so without hesitation despite Finn not having a single thing to his name. Who's to say what would have happened to him if they hadn't stepped up? My perception of Agnes is already a great one but this moves her up to saintly status in my eyes.

"I'm so sorry, Finn."

He kisses the crown of my head and gives my core a reassuring squeeze.

"Let's get your hair brushed out before we go or else we'll really be the talk of Havenwood."

23

Harvest

Courtney

We enter the community gardens through a grand granite archway detailed with beautiful stone flowers carved into its facade, only the deep visible cracks revealing the arch's true age. As I step past the stone curvature, I'm shocked to see how bountiful and lush the garden is despite the harsh New England weather. Each planter box I pass is effervescent with gourds, determined fall flowers, corn, potatoes, and other produce. Almost every other plantar has someone tending to it, with the crowd ranging from late thirty-something-year-olds with their toddlers to folks in their eighties, working as diligently as their bones will allow. The best part is the small pasture just past the planters that consists exclusively of endless rows and rows of pumpkins sprouting from the rich brown earth.

They range from white and round to orange and lumpy and every variation in between, no one is tending to them, however. Finn later explained that the pumpkins were ripening for Halloween and that at the end of the month, the local children would come and select their pumpkins for carving. Yet another adorable Havenwood tradition that had stood for generations.

"This is beautiful," I remark, mostly to myself, referring not only to the gardens itself but the sense of community that clearly stemmed from it. I watch in awe as planter box neighbors share seeding techniques while less busy community members entertain and hold children for busy gardening parents and older kids freely roam the rows of blooming pumpkins, calling dibs on their favorites. From this view, it's easy to see Havenwood as the tight-knit community it is and heartbreaking to know it's all on the verge of extinction.

I already knew I had fallen in love with the town of Havenwood, but somewhere down the line, I'd fallen even harder for its mayor. A familiar rock weighs in my stomach as I remember that, eventually, I'll have to snap the roots that Havenwood and Finn have grown into me and return to California.

I pull my gaze from the gardens and risk a glance up at Finn. Luckily, he's too preoccupied surveying his fellow Havenwoodians to notice my stare, pride and somberness warring on his conflicted face. I love this man and there is no use in denying it. I had spent the last two months rebuking my feelings for him, trying to protect myself from the vulnerability that relationships bring but there's no hiding from the way I feel for Finn Abernathy.

Do I really *have* to move back to California? On multiple occasions, I had been given the opportunity by my managers to write and work from home but I had always opted to come into the office for the social aspect and connection building.

Seeing Kashvi's beaming face each day at 7 a.m. and being caught up on the work gossip of the week was the highlight of my mornings but I've started to feel a shift in my priorities, a shift in what makes me happiest. As I stand staring down the barrel of Cupid's gun, I feel ready to let go of the fear of the unknown. I'm ready to trust Finn and ready to trust myself.

"Finn, I lo-."

"Some of our friends are here, let's say hello." Finn laces his fingers into mine, unintentionally halting my confession. I bite my lip as he directs us towards a patch of potatoes. In hindsight, this isn't the best place to profess my love and Finn's intervention, though accidental, is a blessing in disguise. The right time will come and it probably won't be in a public setting such as this.

I smile with recognition as we approach rippling bronze back muscles plowing a hoe through loose dirt, several female onlookers gawking at Micah's physique as he works.

"Hey, kid," Finn greets pleasantly as we approach.

I keep my eyes firmly planted on Micah's as he twists to face us, wiping sweat from his forehead with the back of his hand. "Oh, hey you two," he acknowledges us with a wave, eyeing my outfit. "Look at you, cowgirl."

"Yee-haw," I throw an imaginary lasso around Micah; playing along, he hobbles towards me as if ensnared in my pretend rope. Before he can come much closer Finn holds out an arm, aligning his spread fingers with our imaginary rope, and clamps down, cutting our imaginary lasso.

"Snip." He gives Micah a sarcastic look, warning him to proceed with caution. The apothecarian throws his hands up defensively, a playful smirk on his lips. Elsie's welcomed presence disrupts the testosterone flying around in the air.

"Hey all," her cinnamon strands bounce beside her shoulders with each approaching step, I release Finn's hand to greet her with a hug.

"No Milo today?" Micah asks Finn, leaning his body weight against the planted hoe. I note the subtle look of discomfort on Finn's face before he responds.

"No, he has… historian stuff he's working on today. Besides, he's already heard everything I have to say during the town hall."

"Town hall?" I raise an eyebrow at the towering mayor beside me, squinting as the sun assaults my eyes.

"We have one every couple of weeks," Elsie explains with a shrug. "It's a way for the mayor," she nods at Finn, "to get out any necessary information, kind of like a newsletter. Why can't we just have a newsletter again, Finn?" Elsie asks in annoyance, tipping her head to one side in faux exhaustion. Finn offers her a grin in response, crossing his arms over his chest.

"If I sent out a newsletter, you would never leave the coffee house, Elsie Murphy." He teases playfully, pointing an accusatory finger. She rolls her eyes, huffing out a small complaint under her breath.

"Town hall meetings are also a great way to hear what concerns the community has and for me to ease as many of those concerns as I can." He continues, addressing me in a tone far less sassy than the one he gave Elsie.

"Why have a town hall?" I ponder out loud as Micah prods at the ground with his tool. "I just mean that you see these people every single day. Why don't they voice their concerns to you then?"

"It's somewhat of an unspoken rule that when people see

me on the streets I'm just *Finn*. In return for that kindness and casualty, I host one of these town halls every six weeks so that they can formally address any qualms with *Mayor Abernathy*."

I nod, acknowledging that that logic seems to check out.

"I heard landlord Gable gave you the key to your new shop, Courtney?" Micah changes the topic, clearly bored of the last one.

"Oh yeah!" Elsie's eyebrows shoot up in excitement. "How was the place? Is it still in decent condition?"

I almost choke on my spit. Neither Elsie nor Micah had made any mention or reference to what had gone down between Finn and I in my new book shop but the memory alone causes me to blush. "Um, it's in great condition."

"Ooookay?" Elsie scrunches her brows at me, picking up on my awkward energy. "So, have you thought of any names for the shop?"

"I have, actually; I'm going to call it Courtney's Cover to Cover." I declare confidently, talking with my hands to add pizzazz to my shop name. Micah's amber eyes flick immediately to Finn as if attempting to telepathically convince the mayor to persuade me to pick a more palatable name. Finn takes no notice, his prideful blue pools glued to my face.

"That's a perfect name," Finn seconds my idea, lacing an arm around my waist and pulling me close to him, earning us a few prolonged stares. I know the smile on his face is attributed at least in part to knowing my bookshop is another commitment to keep me in Havenwood but what he doesn't know is I would stay with or without the shop. I'm staying for him.

An artificial redhead parts the crowd of gardeners, her head on a swivel until she spots us.

"Hi, Cathleen." I smile as I recognize the receptionist.

"Hi, kids," she greets, giving us all a rushed nod. "Mayor, it's time for the town hall."

* * *

I look around at the small sea of faces gathering towards the center of the garden, many of which I see on a daily basis and all eager to hear what Mayor Abernathy has to say.

"Are you nervous?" I ask as I look up at Finn, who's subtly gnawing on his bottom lip. I mentally smack my wrist for the dirty thoughts that fester at the sight.

Finn nods, cuffing his sleeves around his elbows and exposing his forearms.

"Is it that obvious?" He jokes. Even in stressful moments such as this, I appreciate his ability to try to keep things light. That quality is probably one of the things that makes him such a great mayor.

"Not at all," I tease, grabbing his hand that had begun to rub anxiously at his chin and holding it in my own.

"Public speaking has never been one of my strong suits, but unfortunately, it comes with the territory. I'll meet you right here after I'm done." He kisses the back of my hand before leaving me to take his place in front of the group. I nestle in amongst the locals, curious as to what needs to be addressed today.

"Hi folks, thank you all for being here today. Without further ado, let's get into it." Finn's greeting is short and to the point but he makes intentional eye contact with as many people as he can.

"As always, I want to remain completely transparent and honest with you all, despite the upsetting nature of what I have to address today. The town budget is looking very tight for this quarter."

The group immediately begins to mummer and whisper amongst themselves and I see a few people shaking their heads. I know Finn sees it too based on the upset look that he swallows down quickly.

"There is some silver lining, however. Tourist season is fast approaching so let's be ready for that and be on our A games. We also have a few upcoming events to look forward to that I am confident will drive some folks and revenue into Havenwood. Starr and Soul will be holding their concert in the park on Halloween night and Ms. Courtney Berrycloth has taken over the old floral shop to open her new book store, Courtney's Cover To Cover."

My cheeks light up red as Finn mentions my name and I try not to acknowledge the faces that turn to look at me. Finn plasters a hopeful smile on his face as he opens the floor up to questions. One hesitant hand raises, belonging to an older gentleman close to his seventies.

"How long've we got, Finn?" The old man asks in earnest, his face concerned and sad but extremely tired. Finn examines his shoes before looking back into the faces of the crowd, furrowing his brow he says, "A year. At most."

His answer hushes an already silent crowd but a buzz of uneasy energy can be felt as dozens of citizens begin to face the reality of Havenwood's situation. Even the children, too young to comprehend the severity of Finn's words, stay silent, sensing the tender ambiance. I swear I even see a woman shed a tear but I don't fault her, this is my first time hearing this news as well and I'm not composing myself much better than she is.

The reality is crashing down on me that I might not have the choice to call Havenwood home at all if Havenwood is no more than abandoned buildings and littered streets, all of its residents displaced into nearby towns and cities. Finn has been doing all he can to save the town from financial ruin and it still isn't enough. I always intended to find my own way to help Havenwood but it seems I'm running on borrowed time and that guidebook isn't writing itself.

"Excuse me," I repeat multiple as I make my way out of the back end of the crowd, my feet moving without my command. It's time to do my part and I know where I need to start.

24

Accused

Courtney

Before my knuckles can even connect with the front door of the historic center Milo has it swung open, the swift movement startling me.

"Hello Courtney, what are you doing here? Where's Finn?" He peeks his head out of the doorway, scanning for his adoptive brother. The historian seems more high-strung than normal; even his signature gold glasses hang haphazardly off his round nose.

"Finn's still at the town meeting," I answer distractedly, taking in his slightly disheveled appearance. I've never seen Milo anything less than stylish and on point; something has to be amiss, but whatever is agitating him will have to wait since saving Havenwood is my first priority at the moment.

"I want to use my skills to help Havenwood, so I figure I'll write something. A guidebook, specifically. I got your mom's account of all of the local folklore and I need you-."

"You're writing a guidebook? To Havenwood?" Milo raises a sculpted dark brow dismissively. A few noticeable unplucked strays further reinforce my suspicion that something is off with him. I cross my arms over my chest defensively.

"Well, when you say it like *that*.." I huff, knowing I should be used to Milo's sass by now, even though I definitely am *not*.

Amused by my reaction, a wide smile breaks across his face as he opens his mouth to speak again but quickly snaps it shut. The words die on his tongue and the humored smile drops from his lips as a serious thought seems to cross his mind. Milo scratches at the small tuft of dark hair adorning his chin, peering at me thoughtfully behind his lenses.

I sigh, rolling my eyes in surrender, assuming he's thought of a new way to insult my idea. "Look, it's not that bad of a-."

"What if I told you that you *could* save Havenwood single-handedly? *Instantly*."

I crease my brow, feeling the furthest thing from wanting to play games right now. How can a transplant like me save the town from financial ruin not only by myself but also instantly?

"Milo, I'm really not in the mood to be fucked with. You know the severity of the town's situation and I'm trying to help the only way I know how." He ignores my remark, continuing his tirade of riddles.

"Do you remember when you first came to this center and I told you Salem's historical guild was on our asses about wanting something from us?"

I nod with a sigh, knowing there will be no shortcut to getting answers out of him.

Milo's eyes search behind me before his long arm darts out, grabbing my bicep and pulling me towards the building. "Let's talk inside." I stumble into the old church, dragged by my arm until Milo lets go and shuts the door behind him. "Ouch," I remind him that I do, in fact, have pain receptors, but he pays my complaint no mind.

"Finn and I searched tirelessly for years to find the remains of the accused witch Martha Brant. Four months before you moved here, we found her." Milo's voice is serious, missing his normal whimsical tone. I remember the ghost story Finn had shared the first night he had stayed over, he had told about them finding Martha's remains.

"*She* is what Salem wants so desperately. The Massachusetts State Historical Conservancy Foundation is of the mindset that Salem has better facilities and equipment to preserve her remains." He crosses his arms and rolls his eyes, muttering an insult to the state of Massachusetts under his breath. "But they agree that under ideal circumstances, Martha's bones should remain in Havenwood, where she was born and died."

This conversation is hitting weirder and weirder curves and I'm suffering from whiplash attempting to follow Milo's train of thought. I try to conjure up all the knowledge I have about Martha to understand why exactly he's bringing her up here and now but I can't find a connection between the accused witch and me saving Havenwood.

"Well, it's great that the state's historical foundation knows she belongs here; that will help draw in tourists," I offer, raising my eyebrows in the hopes that that was the answer he was searching for.

"It would be great *if* the state's historical foundation hadn't tacked on a little clause." Milo dots the air with his finger to emphasize his words.

"We have to find a descendant of Martha A. B. Brant and get that descendant to sign the remains over to Havenwood by Halloween in order for us to keep her here. If we don't get that signature by then, Martha's remains legally belong to

205

Salem."

"So we find a descendant and explain to them the issue and what's at stake." I reason, excitement bubbling in me at the prospect of finding this mysterious Brant heir. Forget my guidebook; if we find this heir, that would be our golden ticket to securing Havenwood's future.

"Exactly!" Milo claps once, showing his normal colors for the first time this evening. "I've been doing some research." He gives me his back, thumbing through old leather-bound books on a bookshelf. Carefully selecting a particularly dusty one, he places it on the table between us, particles of dust drifting away as he swipes quickly through the pages. He hands me the book, its pages splayed open to one in particular that seems to be some sort of old roster. I give him a displeased look before relenting and examining the page more closely. Getting a better view of the yellowing page I can now interpret it as a list of names, attendees for a Havenwood town hall meeting dated in September of 1689. One attendee's name, in particular, is highlighted. My eyes freeze on the name as Milo reads it out loud.

"Martha Abigail Berrycloth Brant."

"Woah," I breathe, physically recoiling from the page as if the coincidence might reach out and slap me in the face.

"Getting the picture?" Milo twirls his finger in the air in a sassy motion.

I scrunch my brows, searching for a different answer because the one in front of me isn't computing.

"I'm a descendant of Martha Brant?"

"She was a Brant by marriage but a Berrycloth by blood. So, potentially, yes. We'd need a DNA test to be sure."

"I-I'm not sure about this, Milo," I warn as my stomach

begins a contortionist act, slapping nausea across my face. Something about this situation feels far from organic and more like a booby trap. I try to remind myself that Milo is Finn's brother and has been a good friend to me; he has no reason to lie to me. I fight to swallow the feelings of deceit that continue to claw their way up my throat in the form of acid reflux.

"Okay," He closes the book with one hand. "I just thought you wanted to save Havenwood. What questions do you need answered for your little guidebook?" He lazily leans over the table, resting his bored face in his palm as he looks up at me through his dark lashes. He's attempting to gaslight me right now, I can recognize the manipulative tactic but in all honesty, it's working.

If I truly am a descendant of Martha and I don't even agree to get my DNA tested, I'd personally be signing Havenwood's death warrant.

"That's not fair, Milo. This is a lot on me all at once," I advocate for myself as best as I can. I scrutinize his features, trying to sort out the myriad of emotions I feel colliding inside me. This feels wrong. I know there is some puzzle piece that is being intentionally hidden from me. I can feel it.

Finding out that I could be the key to saving Havenwood couldn't have been this simple or have worked out this perfectly in just the nick of time, this had to have been a premeditated plot. I take a steadying breath, trying to clear the fear that I might be the victim of some scheme Milo had thought up and focus on the things I do know for certain. I know I'm in love with Finn, I know I love Havenwood and I know I might have the only opportunity to rescue it. The rest I will have to figure out later and I *will* figure it out.

"What kind of DNA test?"

Finn

The town hall went as well as one could expect when telling residents that the town they know and love is going broke and is essentially counting down to extinction. It was depressing, to say the least. Actually admitting out loud how dire our circumstances had become felt like acid on my tongue, I had fought desperately to save my home and I had failed. It seems as if Havenwood's fate is sealed.

I had hoped to be with Courtney immediately after delivering the blow, to get lost in her sweet perfume and forget everything for just a few seconds but once the crowd had dispersed she was nowhere to be found. I had searched the gardens for any hint of caramel hair or warm brown eyes, and in their absence, I felt the dark, empty feeling of loneliness pooling in my chest. The nasty feeling made itself home there as I reminded myself that this was a grim glimpse into my future. This is what each day will feel like when Courtney inevitably returns to California.

Her absence will leave a stark crater in my heart and I know I won't be able to fill it with anything, not duties nor hobbies nor alcohol. No other woman will be able to mend the Courtney-sized gap left in my chest and no one will ever be able to measure up to her in any capacity. I'm in love with Courtney Berrycloth. I knew it from the moment I met her in the coffee house but I had been too much of a coward to admit it until right now and now that I had, I want to tell her.

But first, I have to find her.

I keep my expression neutral while still in view of the townspeople but survey the remaining group of gardeners until I find the flash of auburn I'm looking for.

"Hey, Elsie," I call out to her retreating figure as she strolls towards the stone archway. The barista glances at me over her shoulder before coming to a gradual stop. She doesn't appear concerned by my announcement but rather something else, some other unplaceable emotion.

"Are you okay? Given the news?" I decide to check on her before berating her with questions about Courtney's whereabouts. She shrugs, her red hair scrunching as her shoulders rise.

"I've dealt with worse, I always find my way. Coffee is my passion and although Havenwood is my home, every city needs caffeine." I laugh at her statement, acknowledging the truth in her words. "Besides, dad and grandmother won't ever leave so maybe this is my out, ya know, my chance to get away from them and start my own coffee house someplace else. Maybe I could follow Courtney back to California." She doesn't mean to but her words slice me like thousands of little paper cuts, causing me to wince in pain. I clear my throat, physically feeling my expression harden.

"Have you seen Courtney? I'm not sure where she went."

"I remember her saying she needed to see Milo to help her with her guidebook. Maybe she's there?"

I nod, remembering Courtney telling me the same thing yesterday when we had discussed our plans for today but I hadn't expected her to be there *right now.* Why had she left so suddenly? I decide not to dwell any longer in my own dark thoughts and to ask Courtney for myself.

I give a gloomy goodbye to Elsie and thank her for the information before heading in the direction of the historic society. I spend the entire walk contemplating how I'm going to tell Courtney I'm in love with her. *Should I just come out and say it? Should I lead into it with some smooth pickup line?* I had never told a woman that I loved her before and I'm petrified that I'll mess it up.

How had Mr. Sweatpants told her? However he had done it I certainly want to top it. My thoughts keep me preoccupied for the duration of the walk. I approach the building and don't bother to knock, instead opting to swing open the heavy door of the old church and let myself in. My eyes widen as I observe the scene before me.

"Milo.. What are you doing with my girlfriend's mouth?"

Courtney turns her attention from Milo, who is holding some sort of swab that he'd been using to scrape the inside of her cheek, to glance at me. Her warm eyes round as I refer to her as my girlfriend. *Nice move, Finn; what kind of weirdo publicly calls a woman his girlfriend without having a prior conversation about said relationship status?* I feel the tip of my ears redden.

"Milo discovered something kind of... Crazy, hard to believe, actually." Courtney stares Milo down with an untrusting leer. I suck in a sharp breath, my heart picking up pace as I anticipate my response. What exactly had my asshole of a brother told her?

"What's that?" I ask cautiously.

Now it's my turn to stare Milo down, knowing the answer has something to do with Courtney and her relation to Martha Brant. Something I'm not ready to address. I silently question him on how much he's told her about our plan, wondering how much blame he absorbed to keep me innocent, how many more lies he told her to protect my name. Or worse, wondering just how much of the truth he told her.

I cross the room and wrap a protective arm around Courtney's waist, relief washing over me when she doesn't pull away.

Milo's hazel eyes flick to mine, the emotion behind them is a combination of apologetic and stoic as he bottles the swab that he just took from Courtney's mouth. He had made a decision he knew I wouldn't approve of but one that we both know needed to be made. He pulled the trigger when I wasn't willing to and, in doing so, effectively killed any chance Courtney and I had.

"I might be related to the accused witch, Martha Brant." She says with a smile that doesn't reach her eyes. "If my DNA is a partial match to the remains you and Milo found, then I can sign to keep her here in Havenwood. Tourists would almost have to stop here in order to get the full history of the witch trials, Martha is an important part of that story. This could potentially save Havenwood." Her tone is optimistic as she explains to me a plan I'm already very familiar with. But there is an aura of hesitation as she recites it, twisting my stomach into an even tighter knot.

"I wouldn't ask you to do that," I reassure her, peeling my eyes from my brother to look down at her. Her own gaze trained on her hands.

"I know, and luckily, you don't have to. I want to."

I'm not sure what to say or do. I came here to tell Courtney that I love her but instead, I walked into a mess that I had created, one I tried to avoid for as long as I could. Courtney turns to face me and her eyes meet mine. I give her a look to tell her I'm not sold on this situation.

"Havenwood is important to you but it's also important to me." She raises a dainty hand to my cheek, her thumb mindlessly passing over my stubble as her warm eyes gaze up at me. They're looking for something, searching for an answer to a question she isn't asking.

God damn it, I did not want things to go down like this! I lament inside my own head. I wanted to lay everything out in the open, tell Courtney the truth about how I lured her here with those emails, and be completely honest with her when the time was right, way before even considering asking her to sign over those remains. But now I'm out of time and it's clear that Courtney is suspicious.

How can I possibly hope for her forgiveness now?

25

Skeletons in the Closet

Courtney

"Now we're waiting for the results to come back. As long as my DNA matches Martha's to a certain percentage, I have the legal right to choose for her remains to be kept here in Havenwood." I finish the story to an intently listening Elsie, her bright brown eyes widening and narrowing appropriately during my recounting of events. For the last twenty minutes, she's been hanging off every word that leaves my mouth, yet now, as I end my story, she sits there silently. Her freckled face warped into an expression I can't read.

"What?" I laugh dryly, nursing the now lukewarm oat milk mocha in front of me.

"I don't know, nothing." She shakes a thought from her head before anxiously looping a finger through her cinnamon hair. I sigh; my patience for avoidance and half-truths feels very short these days.

"C'mon, Els." I encourage, curious as to what cat is holding the barista's tongue for the first time ever. I watch her rake her bottom row of teeth down her thin top lip, contemplating an unpleasant thought.

"It all just seems too... convenient, I guess. Thought out? Planned? Intentional?" My stomach tightens as Elsie voices the very same concern that has been plaguing me since allowing Milo to swab my mouth three days ago. I had barely left my bookshop since then, choosing to avoid the harsh truths staring me in the face and instead bury myself in renovations, hence why Elsie is just now hearing this all for the first time. I had avoided her too, knowing she'd be able to sniff out the bullshit quicker than anyone.

"What do you mean?" I ask, attempting to keep my voice even despite my blood's rising cortisol levels.

"Think about it. A few months before you move here Milo and the mayor find the witch's body." I have half a mind to correct her and tell her that Martha *wasn't* a witch but I remind myself that my correction would do little to help my ancestor's image. *Ugh, look at me, getting defensive over a potential relative I never even knew.*

"And once you're here and head over heels for Finn, Milo *randomly* discovers Martha's maiden name was Berrycloth and that you're the magical key to saving the town?"

"Honestly, when you say it like that, it makes it almost impossible to deny that this *wasn't* a trap," I bury my face in my hands, a stressed growl escaping from me as I rub my eyes. Suddenly, I find myself wishing that there was a shot of whiskey in my coffee. Or two. Or three.

Elsie places a comforting hand on my shoulder, her expression telling me she has no idea how to comfort me.

"But Milo couldn't have orchestrated my breakup with Carter; he did that all himself and that's what prompted me to move here. Well, it was the *main* reason." I remind her.

"True," she agrees thoughtfully. "Why did you pick Haven-wood out of all places anyway?"

I think back to those random emails and my stomach drops to a new low I didn't even know existed as I consider the fact that they might not have been so random after all.

"I had gotten several emails about Agnes' rental house and the crazy low rent, all from different spam email addresses. I kept blocking them but every time I did a new one would pop up." Elsie's ears prick up as I explain, clearly coming to the same hypothesis as me.

"What if they sent you those emails to lure you here?"

"They?" I crease my brow, looking Elsie over skeptically. I understood that we were accusing Milo of scheming but who else did Elsie suspect to be in on this plan? A soft kiss on the crown of my head abruptly ends our conversation. I jump slightly out of shock and turn around to see a soft face and a pair of icy eyes staring back at me.

"Sorry," Finn apologizes sweetly, resting a protective hand on my lower back. "I didn't mean to startle you." His voice is calm but something about his demeanor is off, just as it has been the last few days. He's nervous, antsy even. He reminds me of a jack-in-the-box, one twist of the knob away from springing.

"Speak of the devil," Elsie mutters just above a whisper before shielding her face with her coffee cup. She reemerges from behind the white ceramic mug, wearing a tight-lipped smile that is miles away from genuine. She and Finn exchange greetings. Elsie's brown orbs knowingly flick to mine and the world slows as I finally catch on to her meaning. She thinks Finn is in on this plan.

Is Finn capable of lying and deceiving me to save his precious town? My own answer nauseated me.

After an awkward and strained conversation with Elsie, Finn and I leave the coffee house and head toward my bookstore. I had managed to use bookshop renovations to distract myself from the weird tension between Finn and I over the last couple of days. But it still feels like he's walking on eggshells around me and now I finally understand why. There really are no coincidences in this world or perfect men.

I look around my quaint store as we enter, admiring our handiwork. My new bookshelves are due to arrive tomorrow, a prospect that had once excited me; now, my brain is heavy with a million other things to even care about stupid bookshelves. I stare blankly out the bay window at the breezy late October day, questioning whether or not it had really been less than a week ago that Finn and I had conducted less than holy activities in this very spot. That interaction had been my first sign of confirmation that my feelings for Finn were reciprocated but now I'm unsure how genuine those feelings are.

"Courtney?"

"Hm?" I hum back distractedly. *Shit*, had Finn been talking to me? I'd been too caught up in my own thoughts to hear him. *What had he said? Whatever it was, it was probably a lie..* I know it isn't fair to label Finn as guilty without giving him the chance to defend himself but the evidence had already begun to pile against him and I can't deny the obvious truth much longer.

Finn takes a concerned step toward me, his delicious scent of spice and cedar wood dancing on the air around us, effectively intoxicating me. I close my eyes and allow myself an inhale of his sweet, tempting aroma. He might be a liar but he's a damn sexy one and I can't blame my body for the way it reacts to him.

"What's wrong, baby?" His deep voice is laced with genuine concern, confusing both my brain and my hormones. I force myself to look up at him through my lashes, my bottom lip popping out in a subconscious pout.

"Hold me," I instruct, giving into the side of me that needs comfort and, despite being skeptical of him, knows Finn is the only one who can properly provide it. He doesn't ask questions; instead, he reacts instinctively, wrapping his arms around me and pulling me close. I press my ear against his firm chest, using the soft beat of his heart to help clear my head and soothe my thoughts. I might be doubting him and he might be the reason for my distress but he is still the only person who can bring me any semblance of solace. I feel the tears prick at my eyes as I mentally rehash Elsie and I's conversation, unsuccessfully trying to find any holes in her theory.

"Talk to me," Finn runs his large hand into the hair at the nape of my neck, gently circling his fingers along my roots in a soothing motion. I don't even know where to start. I lift my head off his chest and look up at him through watery vision, a look of worry overtaking his handsome face as he spots my tears. "Courtney-?"

Before I can begin any sort of interrogation, Finn's cell phone chimes loudly from within his pocket.

"Answer it," I instruct with a nod. He shakes his head, attempting to speak again but I don't afford him the opportunity. "Answer it."

Finn's eyes search mine for a beat before he resigns to

retrieve the device, flipping it open and pressing it to his ear without bothering to check the caller I.D..

"Hello?" A beat passes as he listens to the person on the other end of the line speak, a look of hesitation crosses his face. "Okay." He responds shortly and snaps the phone closed. My breath hitches as his expression hardens from concern to solemness, his icy orbs tracing over my face.

"That was Milo. He says we need to get down to the historic center."

My stomach triple somersaults as I read between the lines. It's time to figure out whether or not I am related to the town witch.

* * *

The tension in the room is thick enough to cut with a knife.

I sit at Milo's desk above the main floor of the historic center, pleading with my internal organs to quit doing the jig they'd been doing since Finn got the call. Finn stands behind me, leaning against the wall stoically with his arms crossed in front of his chest. I can feel his eyes bouncing nervously between Milo and myself but that's the only indication of his emotions that he's allowed to break through his collected surface.

Milo stands facing both of us, repeatedly smacking a manila envelope against his palm, carefully eyeing us. It's easy to see he is nervous as well. Not only does his home hang in the balance, but so does his career. I imagine it would be quite embarrassing for an anthropologist to make an amazing historical discovery such as finding long-lost remains just to have that discovery snatched from you by a more qualified and funded establishment.

"Results are in," Milo announces theatrically.

Finn scoffs and crosses the floor, snatching the envelope from his brother.

"You've been watching too much Drag Race again."

"I resent that." Milo's hazel eyes narrow as he crosses his arms, feigning a wounded ego. Finn slides a finger under the lip of the envelope, breaking the seal. He hesitates as his eyes flick to mine, a look of sorrow mixed with anxiety perforating his perfect blues. He looks at me as if he knows, regardless of whatever answer is in that envelope, that our relationship will change drastically after the results are read.

He studies my face like he's attempting to commit it to memory, his unyielding attention causing me to catch my bottom lip between my chattering teeth. I watch his Adam's apple bob as he takes a harsh swallow, opening the envelope and retrieving the white page from within. My heart feels like it might explode from how hard it's beating against my ribs as he silently reads the results, like a caged animal desperate for its freedom.

It's now, in this moment, that I know I have to decide what I'm going to do upon hearing the results. If it comes back positive for a match, it will confirm that I was being used from the start, that Finn had prioritized his town over me, and that I truly had no idea how much of our relationship was real and how much of it was an act to get me to comply. Regardless, I would still sign the papers. I would do it out of respect for Havenwood and out of my love for Finn as one last gift to him. Then I would go back to California out of respect for myself. I couldn't stay here and pretend all is well after my trust had been so viscerally violated and I'd been lied to by a man I love and trusted.

I hold my breath and try one last time, in vain, to convince myself that this is all an impossible coincidence.

Finn's lips move rapidly, silently mouthing the words as his eyes scan down the page. He finishes reading and his gaze turns to me, a blank, unreadable expression masking his emotions. I feel the oxygen suck itself from my lungs.

"Well?"

"It's a match."

Milo lets out a whoop of excitement, throwing his arms around me in celebration. He squeezes me suffocatingly tight as he repeats, "Oh my god! Oh my god!"

Despite the oblivious celebrating happening beside us, Finn and I do not share the same triumphant attitude. Our eyes are locked, just as they have been since he read the verdict. The look on Finn's guilt-stricken face tells me everything I need to know.

He used me.

I could barely hear anything happening around me. It feels as if a grenade has detonated right beside me, stealing my hearing and drowning out all sounds with a high-frequency hum. I'm having a hard time comprehending my surroundings as everything now has a hazy glow to it - or is it just that my eyeballs are vibrating from pure emotion? I vaguely hear Milo call my name off in the distance.

"Huh?" I force my eyeballs to stabilize enough so that I can see his face and read his lips. He's holding a long-necked green bottle in one hand and a glass flute in the other.

"I asked if you wanted champagne. To celebrate?" His words come into focus after a prolonged silence on my end.

"Oh. No." I shake my head, wrapping my arms around my middle for comfort, subconsciously attempting to self-soothe away all the harsh realities falling upon me. *Finn lied. He doesn't love me. I was used. Again.*

"I think I should get Courtney home." Finn's words are soft but his tone is anything but. He sounds angry, most likely with himself or even Milo. He rises from the seat he had taken to steady himself and holds the office door open for me. I say nothing as I walk through the door and down the spiral stairs, my movements feeling robotic, like I'm on autopilot as opposed to commanding the movements myself.

* * *

We walk in tangible silence, the sun barely peeking over the horizon to light our way back to 2213 Queens Avenue, a place that I will be saying goodbye to very soon. The cold October breeze pinches at my ears as I feel my heart shattering in my chest, completely unable to look anywhere but down at my feet.

As we round the corner onto my street, I sneak a peek up at Finn. His eyes are also fixed on the pavement just ahead of his shoes and not daring to stray. I watch as he nervously rubs at his goatee, looking as if he's searching to find any sort of justification for his actions, decidedly unable to find one and smartly choosing to remain silent.

He stops uncharacteristically on the front step of my porch as we approach Agnes' rental. We had practically been living here together since the town hall meeting so his sudden discomfort spoke volumes.

"Um," I watch as the mayor shoves his hands into his front pockets, his expression pained. "We'll have to head to Boston as soon as possible. Me, Milo, and you. You'll have to sign the consent papers in front of the state notary there-"

"You sure know a lot about this process, especially with this all being so random." My tone is sassy with a hint of accusation but I don't care right now. I've come to my boiling point, my hurt quickly dissolving into anger and I deserve to know the truth. I look up at him. Finn's gaze is hanging low, not daring to look at me. His face is twisted into a flat expression but I can see the pain right below the surface. Whether he regrets his decisions or not, the bridge is crossed and he knows he's about to watch it burn.

"Is there something you need to tell me, Finn?" I ask pointedly.

He matches my gaze and for a moment, we just stare at one another in silence, confirming a sentiment I already knew deep down. He opens his mouth to speak, that hidden pain now clearly visible on his face as the words seemingly die on his tongue. My phone chimes loudly from my purse, the noise signaling the end of Finn's one and only opportunity to explain.

"Goodnight, Finn." I will my voice not to crack as I push into the house.

"Courtney!" Finn pleads desperately as I slam the door behind me. As soon as the door is shut, I collapse against it, sliding down the unforgiving wood just as hot tears begin to cascade down my cheeks.

Today had given me all the confirmation I needed to know that Finn was part of the plot to lure me to Havenwood. He hadn't pursued a relationship with me because he was genuinely attracted to me or liked my personality, he did so as a strategic move to get close to me so that I would sign those damn papers. Less than two hours ago, I had plans on moving my life across the country and uprooting my entire career to be with Finn, and now I felt like an idiot. A broken idiot.

Regardless of whether Finn had developed real organic feelings for me during our time spent together or not, it didn't matter. We could never have a relationship built on a foundation of lies.

I sit like this, with my thighs tucked into my chest and my forehead pressed into my knees, for what feels like hours. Tears are repetitively falling and drying in a vicious cycle when another chime from my phone pulls my attention. I wipe the wetness from my face with my sleeve as I dig in my pocket, retrieving my cell. I have two unread text messages from Elsie.

Elsie: 911
Elsie: I'll be @ your house in 20

26

Trunk of Secrets

Courtney

I hadn't been able to gather the emotional strength to move from my position against the door when a quick rapping against it rattled my brain, forcing me to stand and answer it. I reluctantly open the door to wide-eyed Elsie, her head turning side to side on a swivel as she waits to be let inside.

"Are you okay?" I question in a meek voice that has gone hoarse from crying. Between Elsie's frantic behavior and her cryptic texts, you would think someone had put a hit out on her or something.

"I'm fine. I just don't normally walk anywhere after dark because, you know, the witch. Sorry! I know she might be your relative but she still freaks me the heck out."

My relation to Martha Brant is the last thing I want to hear about right now. A small part of me blames her for this fucked up situation I've found my way into but deep down, I know I just want to blame anyone but myself. I roll my eyes at her superstitious nature but step to the side, allowing her inside the house. She wastes no time getting through the doorway and lets out a quiet sigh of relief when I close and deadbolt the door behind her.

"So what's the 911?" I try to act casual as I pass the spot on the floor where I had spent the last half of an hour falling to pieces. I super glued myself back together in Elsie's presence to try to hide the agony but I'm still so fragile, that a mild gust of wind would send my shattered pieces right back to the floor.

"So at work tonight- Oh my God, are you okay?!" I had done a decent job of disguising my emotions but my puffy eyes and a traitorously pink nose gave me away. My act wouldn't have lasted long anyway, Elsie had become too close of a friend not to be able to see the signs of my distress. I had never felt this level of betrayal in my life, not even when Carter had broken up with me, I can only imagine how much of a wreck I look based only on how I'm feeling internally.

Elsie's thin arms wrap around me in a tight, sisterly embrace. To my surprise, I accept the comfort almost immediately, hugging her back tightly. I'm not really the type to accept comfort or physical touch, but it's clear I need some support right now. The ugly tears are now back with a vengeance causing me to crack apart once again, revealing my distraught and wounded center. I don't want to cry on Elsie, she has her own struggles and I don't want to be an added burden on her. But right now, it feels like my whole world is burning from the inside out.

"It's okay, you're okay." Elsie coos softly as she holds me tenderly against her bony frame. She doesn't bother asking what I'm upset about, allowing me to tell her in my own time, which I am hugely grateful for. We stand together as she strokes my hair and I silently sob into her shoulder. I manage to regain my composure enough to stifle the waterfall of tears.

"I'm sorry to cry on you, Els." I sniffle as I pull away from her, swiping at the salty tears.

"Don't be," she offers me a pitiful smile before her small eyes drop to my shoulder.

"It just makes what I'm about to tell you even harder."

I give her a look that screams, *"Kill me now."*

Elsie and I sit on the new couch I purchased two days ago when my life in Havenwood was feeling a lot more permanent. After our hug, the barista had scurried off to the kitchen and concocted two chai lattes, which I'm more thankful for than I care to admit.

"Alright, you've procrastinated as long as you can. Tell me what's going on," I urge as Elsie sinks into the cushion beside me, her gaze still hesitant to meet mine. She takes a deep breath, searching for the proper words; seemingly having found them, she turns her entire body towards me. She searches for bravery in her latte before letting out her breath.

"Soul and Starr were at Mystic Brew today," She starts slowly, her knuckles turning white around her mug. *Great*, I groan internally. Starr is at the top of my list of people I do *not* want to hear or think about today.

"I overheard the two of them talking. I could only hear parts of the conversation over the coffee grinder but based on what we talked about, about the mayor luring you here and the discovered remains and the custody battle over them?" She reminds me as if I could've forgotten. I just nod, not wanting to take my sour mood out on her. "It just all makes sense now!"

"What makes sense, Els? What did you hear?" I ask, putting her back on track. She twists her cinnamon ponytail around her fingers anxiously before speaking in rapid-fire; as if ripping off a painful but necessary bandage.

"Starr said that sooner or later you would realize the mayor was just using you and that you'll be crying your way back to Hollywood before November 1st."

I press my lips into a firm line to prevent them from quivering. Starr knew that Finn was using me and that's the final confirmation needed that Finn is a willing participant in this scheme. That is the last nail in the coffin of Finn and I's relationship and I'm livid that Starr fucking Iglesias is the one to hammer it in.

"Even Starr knew about his plot and I was completely blind to it. I'm such a fucking idiot," I huff out a hoarse breath, dipping my head into my hands and once again letting the traitorous tears fall. Elsie rubs my back as she racks her brain for the proper comforting words.

"No, you're not. There's no way you could have known. Starr and Finn have a past together; I'm sure that's how she found out. There's no way you could've known." She repeats, rubbing circles into my upper back. For being so young, Elsie is great at bringing solace. It makes me wonder what her life at home looks like with her dad and grandma. Is anyone ever there to comfort Elsie when she needs it?

A loud squeak from upstairs sends the barista back into fight-or-flight mode as she clutches a couch pillow to her chest, her brown eyes darting wildly around the room. Her insane reaction to Olive's squeak almost pulls a laugh out of me despite my misery.

"Relax," I sigh, tucking a caramel strand behind my ear and

heading to the kitchen. "That's just Olive; she wants her strawberries."

* * *

I crawl up the stairs with Elsie clung to my back, still terrified that the noise she heard wasn't a bat but instead, a 300-year-old witch coming to eat her. She had requested a flashlight, citing that witches were afraid of light. I happily provided her with one, demanding that she stop being such a pussy in exchange. She did not like that much.

I open the slim door leading to the attic and proceed up the narrow stairs, not paying attention to or caring if Elsie is brave enough to follow. Admittedly, caring for another living thing is a great distraction from everything else imploding around me, even if that living thing is a prima donna bat squatting in my attic.

I remove the previous bowl of bananas I had brought to Olive yesterday and replace it with an offering of strawberries. I had done this multiple times since moving to Havenwood, it had become part of my routine but just like everything else in my life, this too, feels different. It feels numbered because I know that I'll be leaving soon.

The little whiner must have been hungry because she glides down from her position in the rafters to ravage the newly placed fruit bowl almost immediately. Elsie squeals as Olive sails past her face, flailing her arms dramatically as if she'd seen a bee.

"Ew, ew, ew!" she chants as her arms swing wildly around her head, causing her to drop the flashlight she'd been holding. The flashlight lands a few feet away from us, its beam highlighting the disregarded trunk in the corner. Given everything that had occurred over the last few weeks, I'd completely forgotten about the trunk and its mystery contents.

I walk past the barista and towards the old box, my curiosity once again peaked by it. Elsie steadies herself and, upon seeing Olive eating out of the strawberry bowl contently, finally chills out. I squat down to examine the trunk's lock as Elsie diverts her attention to me.

"Woah," she gawks, taking up residence beside me, "that looks mega old."

I reach out and give the top a firm shake.

"Locked," I snip, still riding the unpleasant emotional waves of the day. As I demonstrate the box's impenetrability, my fingers brush against something I hadn't noticed the last time I examined the trunk.

"Elsie," I call to her, not removing my fingers from the raised ridges of the trunk. "Can you bring that flashlight over here?"

She pops up from her squat and retrieves the light, bringing it over and shining it directly where my fingers were lingering. I remove them and Elsie and I share a look of shocked disbelief. The raised markings I felt on the trunk are initials marking the box **M. A. B.**

"Oof," Elsie shutters, grimacing at the initials. "I told you the witch had something to do with this."

I sit back on my heels, studying the three raised letters in disbelief. Elsie's head is once again on a swivel, scouring for any signs of paranormal activity.

"I believe in cosmic energy, the butterfly effect, and even zodiac bullshit as much as the next California girl," I say, shaking my head skeptically. "But there's no way that I learn that I'm a descendant of Martha Brant and discover her initials in my attic on the same day by coincidence."

Elsie studies me hesitantly, knowing me well enough by now to know where this is going.

"You don't have the key to the trunk, do you?"

"Nope," I pop the P, a nefarious smile mounting on my face.

"But we're going to go find it?"

"Yep!" For the first time today, I feel my spirit lighten a bit with a sense of adventure.

"Where is it?" She winces, already knowing the answer and not liking it.

"I don't know for certain but I have a really good guess."

27

Witch's Ghost

Courtney

Elsie and I bundle in jackets, preparing to brave the cold, dark October night and whatever else we might encounter on our mission.

"For the record, I think this is a really STUPID idea," Elsie complains loudly, voicing her displeasure of our late-night adventure. I turn from her to hide my excited smile as I zip up my outer jacket.

"Come on, Els. Where's your sense of adventure?" I try to encourage.

"Dead. Like we're going to be if the witch catches us snooping around her house in the middle of the night."

"Adventure aside, if we can get into that trunk and find something of Martha's, it'll be a huge slap in the face to Milo. Who would probably kill to be the first person to get his hands on whatever is inside." I wring my hands together in an anxious motion as I continue. "As terrible as it is, a part of me wants to do it to spite him. I want revenge for his part in the plan to lure me here and for betraying the friendship I thought we had."

Elsie studies me for a moment before zipping up her own darkly colored jacket in solidarity. "Fine. Only because I'm an avid supporter of revenge. Let's go." I offer her a look of pleasant surprise as she marches straight out my front door, expecting me to follow.

The pair of us set out on foot for the decrepit two-story house on the edge of Havenwood's tree line. The very same tree line that that nasty little crow had scared me away from weeks ago, we're headed for the Witch's House. That's the last place Martha called home before she was murdered, so it only makes sense that the key that unlocked her trunk would be there somewhere.

Antsy groans vibrating from Elsie's throat act as the sound-track to our mission as we cross town in the dark, not wanting to risk drawing attention to ourselves with flashlights. Every noise we make feels amplified; even the sound of our breathing seems to reverberate off the brick buildings and echo far beyond us.

"The witch's house is considered a historic building or something so it's been persevered, almost no one has been allowed in there since her husband moved out of it," Elsie informs me in a hushed voice.

"When was that?" I question as we sneak along the side of a building.

"Like two months after she was burned at the stake. He got remarried and moved out right away, he left all of her stuff in there."

"How do you know all this?" I whisper back to the barista. She shrugs, checking over her shoulder for the fifth time.

"We learn all this stuff in school. In fifth grade, we even

went on a field trip to the house."

"With it being untouched all these years I bet the key is still in there somewhere. But I'm guessing there will be some sort of security measures in place?"

Elsie nods, a strand of cinnamon falling from her dark beanie. "There's alarms and stuff, but there's no security guard or anything. A lot of the local kids go up there to smoke or drink."

"There's two of us so we can search double as fast, that gives us a better chance of finding the key before anyone arrives to check the alarms." I devise as the surrounding houses begin to thin and give way to the more rural edge of Havenwood.

My phone buzzes for the millionth time today, the shock from the vibration causing me to almost pee myself. I hastily fish it from my back pocket and go to turn it off, the most recent message on my screen causing me to pause.

Finn: Courtney, please answer my calls. I wasn't honest when I should have been but I'm ready to be honest now. Please give me a chance.

I power my phone off. *I did give you a chance*, I respond in my head, *and you lied.* I slide my phone back into my pocket.

"How much further, Els?" I call quietly to her; in the darkness, I can hardly even tell where we are. The barista says nothing but holds up a slightly shaking hand, pointing reluctantly just ahead of us. Thanks to a lack of electricity, the historic house is pitch black and very difficult to see against its forested background, but as my eyes adjust to the darkness, I'm able to make out its familiar outline. A small rectangular-looking two-story building with a wooden door stares back

233

at me. The same foreboding feeling overtakes me, just as it had the last time I'd gotten this close to the witch's house.

I take the lead, stealthily crossing the open field that separates the house from the neighborhood, cautiously treading through the wild grass with Elsie following closely behind. As we approach, the sounds emanating from the forest become louder and louder. The humming of bugs and the distant cry of some nocturnal animal sets a freaky Blair Witch vibe.

We scout the outside of the petite house, looking for an entry point but find that all the windows are tightly sealed and the door has a cartoonishly large lock.

"We could try to pick the lock?" Elsie suggests in a whisper. The nearest occupied house is over a hundred yards away but she still keeps her voice low out of fear of something supernatural hearing her. I look down at the heavy-duty lock and then back to Elsie, my expression letting her know that isn't a viable option.

"We could.." Elsie brainstorms out loud, swaying side to side as she contemplates. We're wasting time and risking someone seeing us lingering out here. I walk over to one of the downstairs windows, sling my arm back and send my fist flying through the glass. It shatters immediately, crashing to the floor and giving us our much-needed vantage point. Elsie stares at me in pure shock before an annoyingly high-pitched alarm begins to whoop, alerting neighbors, authorities, and any lingering spirits to our presence.

"Why would you do that?!" Elsie hisses over the obnoxious siren.

"We needed a way in. Come on! We have to be quick," I beckon Elsie to follow as I slide my leg inside the broken window, followed by the rest of me. I ignore the sharp cuts on my knuckles, so long as I don't bleed all over the floor and leave evidence, the wound can be taken care of once we're safely back at Queens Avenue. Elsie hesitantly pops her thin frame through the window; even in the darkness, I can see her apprehension.

"You check this main floor, I'll go upstairs. Find that key!" I encourage, the urgency in my voice giving her no room to argue about our separation. She nods and I rush up the rickety stairs, each one creaking loudly beneath my weight. As I make it to the second-floor landing, I begin to regret my decision to split up, especially regretting leaving Elsie with the only flashlight as dark rooms stare back at me.

"Woman up.." I whisper to myself, taking in a deep inhale for added bravery. I dig into my pocket and turn my phone back on, using the flashlight application to navigate as best I can.

I breeze through into the first small bedroom, keeping conscious of the time as I move on to searching the main bedroom, the one I assume belonged to my ancestor centuries ago. I search below the dusty mattress, in the small chest at the foot of the bed, in the tiny closet—nothing. Elsie and I have been inside for at least three minutes now, and time is running out before we get caught.

I stand in the center of the room, trying desperately to think of more spots to search, when I hear a creak in the floorboard behind me. I don't dare to move a muscle or even take another breath as the air in the room turns static, the fine hairs along my arms and the back of my neck rise to attention. Suddenly I know I am no longer alone in the room and it is not Elsie behind me nor any other living person. My pupils dart to the edge of my vision but I still can't see the presence behind me.

It doesn't matter, I know who it is.

"Martha," I test my voice, unsurprised when it cracks in fear. "My name is Courtney. I found a trunk in my attic with your initials on it, I'm guessing you wanted me to find that." I hold my arms out to my sides with my palms open, a gesture meant to show that I mean no harm.

"I'm looking for the key to open that trunk. I don't have much time, I need your help."

Silence.

A beat passes and all I can hear is my heart pounding in my ears and the ragged, shallow breathing from the presence behind me. I begin to contemplate whether or not a ghost can cause physical harm when a small scraping sound interrupts my terrified thoughts. I whip around, petrified that I'm going to see a colonial ghost wielding an axe or a similarly horrific scene. Instead, I find the room empty, the night air resumes its normal temperature and the feeling of being alone settles in once again. My eyes dart around the room frantically as I force myself to remember how to breathe.

"Holy shit," I mutter under my breath, clenching my chest as I attempt to comprehend the paranormal encounter I just had. As my eyes are doing laps around the now empty room I notice a drawer that is pulled out of the tall dresser that hadn't been before. That must have been the scraping sound I heard a moment ago, the sound of the wooden drawer being pulled out on rusted wheels. I approach the small dresser drawer and peek in. I rustle through the small articles of clothing that occupy the drawer, and there it is, sitting in all its brass glory. The key.

"Thank you," I say into the open air. "We really are related, Martha. I hide stuff in my panty drawer, too." I admit with a laugh.

"Courtney!" I hear Elsie yell from the base of the stairs. "We have company!"

I quickly snatch the key and descend the antiquated stairs, I'm going so fast that I accidentally put my foot through one of the feeble steps. I yelp as I trip, but Elsie catches me before my face collides with the ground.

"Thanks," I breathe as I regain my balance and dislodge my foot from the step.

"Courtney, we need to go!" She hisses anxiously, checking over her shoulder.

"Go! Go! Go!" I urge her through the same broken window we entered through just as a cop car rounds the bend, coating the surrounding trees in flashing red and blue lights. There's no way to tell if the officer saw us but we only have one option.

"Run!" I grab Elsie's arm and we both break into a sprint, heading for the back of the residential houses closest to the woods. We both dive behind a large bush just as the patrol car parks outside Martha's house. We watch as the potbellied policeman approaches apprehensively, the beam of his flashlight slicing through the darkness.

Once we see the cop unlock the massive lock and enter the house, we take our opportunity and dart from the bush, taking the back roads to my place.

"Did you get the key?" Elsie huffs, attempting to catch her breath as we finally make it back to the safety of my porch, the space illuminated by the warm glow of the porch light. I don't respond in words. Instead, I reach into my bra and lift the brass key to our eye level.

Elsie whoops in excitement, throwing her arms around me as we both ignite into much-needed successful laughter.

28

The Letter

Finn

I sit with my elbows resting on the sticky bar. My red, stinging eyes glued to the small front screen of my flip phone, hoping, praying, begging whatever Gods are out there to see it light up with a call or text from Courtney.

I take a deep inhale as the tiny square remains black, indicating no activity, just as it has for the past several hours. No response from Courtney. She's done with me and I know it. That's why I agreed to let Milo drag me back out to the Grumpy Lobster and allowed him to supply me with round after round of beer and pump my body full of alcohol. All in the hopes of a distraction, desperate for some sort of relief from the ache in my chest and the guilt that weighed heavily on me.

I'd be lying if I said the half dozen bottles of cheap beer had helped to dull any of it. Nothing helps. Even if my head is too fuzzy to remember why I'm hurting, I can still feel the pain, and, to add insult to injury, Milo is celebrating.

"To my brother!" Milo lifts his pint of cider high above

his head, slightly slurring his words of praise. Milo is a few drinks ahead of me yet somehow less drunk. The rest of the bar follows suit, raising their drinks and awaiting a speech.

"For saving Havenwood! You are a hero, Finn. Even if you don't realize it tonight." Milo's hazel eyes stare down at me, half full of admiration, half full of pity. He knows what I lost to make our plan a reality, and even though he played a part in speeding up the process, I don't blame him. Milo's decision to act has saved Havenwood, his career, and - in all honesty - my own career. I'm the selfish one for trying to drag the process out, I tried to buy time that didn't exist in order to think of a way to justify my actions to Courtney. I tried to keep us in the blissful limbo that was truly the calm before the storm.

"TO FINN!" The bar chants in unison, downing their respective drinks. We are several towns away, no one in this bar knows me, and no one here probably even knows where Havenwood is on the map. They are all just drunk and in want of something to toast. I roll my eyes and finish off my beer, slamming the empty mug back down onto the bar. As I do, the blue square on my phone lights up. I snatch the device from its resting spot on the disgusting bar top and hastily flip it open.

A rumbling mix of a disappointed sigh and an annoyed growl escapes me when I realize the call isn't from Courtney but from Sheriff Dean Cotton. I press the phone to my ear and plug the other to drown out the increasingly loud bar. "Mayor Abernathy."

"Hey, Finn," Cotton greets, his voice old and gruff, much like himself. The hesitation in his tone, however, notifies me that something important is clearly on his mind—that and the fact that he's calling at ten o'clock at night.

239

"There's a situation at the old witch's house," he informs me before clearing his throat. "I've got it secured for now. Could you meet me here in the morning to assess the damage?"

"Sure, Dean." I drag my hand down my sweaty face, an undesired side effect from the alcohol. Milo notices my phone call and motions for me to hang up as he orders us another round of beers.

"I'll be there as early as I can," I promise, not wanting to nail down a specific time in anticipation of the hangover I'll be suffering from tomorrow. Mayoral duties don't stop, even when your heart is broken.

Courtney

Olive observes us curiously from the security of the rafters, her big brown eyes encouraging us as Elsie and I sit on the attic floor staring at the trunk, neither of us making a move.

I look over at Elsie, only to find her hesitant stare already on me. I wonder if she can tell I'm attempting to scrape together whatever courage I have left in me and use it to open this box.

After we fled Martha's house, Elsie had hypothesized close to a hundred ominous things that might occur upon opening the trunk. Amongst her most colorful ideas were curses, poisonous gas, booby traps, voodoo dolls, and the Bubonic plague. I don't believe any of those things are likely to be inside, nor probably even possible, but I intentionally did not tell Elsie about my earlier supernatural encounter back at the witch's house. I figure if Elsie hears anything confirming her belief in the paranormal, she might bust into that Scooby Doo run, where your legs move in circles, but you don't actually get anywhere and shoot off in a cloud of dust. Never to be seen again.

Despite not wanting to share my encounter, the experience had shaken me up and now left me wondering if I would be invoking some bad juju by opening the old trunk. Or *worse* juju, I should say, considering how my love life is looking at the moment.

I stare at the chest, chewing on the inside of my cheek, when a calming aura washes over me. I can tell instinctually that it isn't my own, but it is familiar. I recognize it as the same sense of calm that overcame me when I was struggling with the decision to allow myself to date Finn or not. It's so peaceful I can physically feel my shoulders relaxing and my jaw unclenching.

"*Open it.*" A calm voice reassures me from somewhere within my head. I whip my head around, looking for the owner of the voice.

"What?!" Elsie freaks, scooting away from the direction I just looked in.

"Nothing, nothing." I shake my head, attempting to keep us both calm. "I just think we should open the trunk. I don't think anything bad will happen." The voice sounded feminine, motherly, and encouraging. I know it was Martha helping me for the second time tonight. Her presence is a strong one, making her easy to recognize and for no good reason at all, I trust her. She had helped me find the key, after all.

I retrieve the rusted key from my pocket and insert it into the trunk's lock. With a steadying breath, I turn the key to the left and a distinct click tells me the locking mechanism has been disengaged. I nibble on my lower lip as I grasp either side of the trunk's lid, slowly raising it as it groans and its hinges bend to reveal its contents.

"You did it," Elsie praises. She's still sitting a cautious few

241

feet back from the trunk, probably to make her escape easier if poisonous gas had begun to escape.

"What's inside?"

I reach into the trunk and retrieve the single item that makes up its contents: a yellowed, crispy folded piece of parchment—a letter.

"That's it?" The barista raises an underwhelmed eyebrow, folding her arms at the sight of the parchment. I give her a look and unfold the delicate paper.

"This is hard to read," I remark, trying to decipher the swirly, faded handwriting. "Hand me the flashlight, Els." She does so hesitantly, not eager to let go of her protective ray of light. I shine the beam just off to the side of the letter so that the stream doesn't shine through the thin paper.

"Read it out loud," Elsie requests, scooting closer to me. "Unless it's an incantation or a spell or something. Then.. just read it in your head." I chuckle and shoot a questioning eyebrow up in her direction.

"What? You're Martha's great, great, great whatever. That probably makes you .005% witch, too. You could be casting a spell and not even know it." Elsie's stare proves that she believes what she's saying is 100 percent factual. I smile at her expense before beginning to read the letter out loud. Even Olive adjusts her position from above to hear us more closely.

"I have beene accused by mine husband, John Brant, of an offense that be anything but truth. For much time now, I have known it to be true that John beene engaging in impropriety with ye Smith's young daughter. Even on death's cold step I do not dare speak ill of my husband, yet it is of much convince to him that these accusations of witchery befall my name as he indulges in fantasies with the maiden. I am blameless. Let thyne letter expose my truths

and man's falsehood against me. Convey onto mine children mine
enduring love. Let mine truths be recounted at a more fitting hour.
Martha A. Berrycloth."

Elsie's wide eyes meet mine, her jaw resting almost entirely on the floor by the time I finish the letter.

"This is a piece of history, Elsie. This is amazing; this letter could clear Martha's name." I scoff in disbelief, rereading the words on the page for a second time. Even Olive lets out a squeak of excitement, the shrill sound causing Elsie to jump.

"You need to get this to a professional. Ooh, Milo is gonna be *PISSED!*" She comes to a full stop. Her freckled face droops with regret as soon as Milo's name leaves her mouth. Suddenly, my short-lived joy and excitement evaporate, replaced only by the reminder of Milo and Finn's deceit. The feeling of betrayal and emptiness once again smack me in the face.

"I'll drive it to the Massachusetts Historical Conservancy Foundation tomorrow; that's where I have to sign the documents to relinquish Martha's remains to Havenwood. They'll know what to do with the letter. The Historical Foundation is in Boston, so I should get some rest tonight." I look down at my overgrown acrylics, avoiding her gaze as I gently queue her into an exit. I feel bad trying to get rid of my only friend in town but I'd really rather be alone right now, I'm tired of crying in front of others. I'm tired of crying in general but it's inevitable and I'd rather do it without an audience. My excuse is true, too. I do plan on going to Boston early tomorrow morning but I don't even believe myself when it comes to getting rest.

"Thanks for breaking the law with me tonight, Els."

"Anytime," she jokes, offering an understanding smile as we stand and make our way out of the attic. "Just do me a favor;

when you publish your guidebook, don't include tonight's activities. My grandmother would kill me if she knew what I was up to."

"Okay, I promise." I offer her a gracious smile. She hugs me before making her departure into the night, now far less afraid of a witch attack.

Once Elsie disappears down the road my smile plummets. I had completely forgotten about the guidebook until Elsie mentioned it; my motivation to finish it almost nonexistent. I had been drawn to write the guidebook to help save a town that Finn loves so dearly because I love Finn. But now, I'll finish it for no reason other than because *I've* fallen in love with the small, rustic town I have called home over the last several months. Regardless of where Finn and I's relationship stands, I will go to Boston tomorrow morning to fulfill a duty to Havenwood and to fulfill a duty to Martha because *I* want to. Because saving her reputation and Havenwood is important to *me*. I sit down on my couch and fire up my laptop, retrieving the notebook full of Agnes' tales as I do.

The rest of the night is spent typing away, documenting the truths, fables, and hot spots of Havenwood, USA. I had been lured here under false pretenses and lied to repeatedly by the people I trusted for the small possibility that I could save Havenwood. As I sit with my laptop in my lap, writing about the most quaint and adorable coffee house staffed by a red-haired barista, I know I will do just that.

* * *

I wrote until the sun peaked in at me through the living room window and only then did I realize I'd worked on my guidebook the entire night through. I had been fueled by the unrelenting image of Finn's face that plagued me when I dared to close my eyes and oat milk chai lattes alone. When 6 a.m. rolled around, I decided it was time to start my road trip to the south side of the state; if I left now, then I could make it to Boston around 8 a.m., right when the state's Historical Conservancy Foundation was set to open. I had had all night to sit with my thoughts and emotions, so by the time I got into my car and headed towards Boston in silence, I felt next to nothing. I'd spent hours last night feeling every and any emotion possible, I'd phased through each stage of grief and was now left with emptiness, *numbness*. I was tired of hurting, tired of feeling betrayed, and tired of being used.

Each fiery orange sugar maple leaf reminded me of Finn, and I saw him in each cobblestone that made up Havenwood's historic roads; I wanted to leave. Go far away, somewhere without reminders of Finn Abernathy and the agony he had put me through. Deep down, I know no matter how far I run, the pain will persist, but putting distance between me and Havenwood is a good start to some sort of healing.

I had left California to escape men and their manipulation, only to cross the country and fall back into the same trap once again. It's time to remind myself that no one could truly love me; they could only use me for their own personal gain. And this time, I won't forget it.

When I arrive at the Massachusetts Conservancy Foundation, I give the petite blonde receptionist my name, and within minutes, I'm having my hand shaken by several gray-haired men, most of whom wear bulky glasses and suspenders. The bigwigs of the Conservancy Foundation, I quickly come to find out. They have been in conversation with Milo and know exactly who I am. After presenting them with Martha's letter, they each take turns trying to convince me to allow them to keep the letter at their foundation. I decline each time, citing that it belongs in Havenwood right beside Martha's bones, clearing her name for the rest of forever. I do, however, allow them to make copies for their records and I make certain that my name is listed as the person responsible for discovering it. I can already imagine the jealous shriek Milo will let out once he finds out and honestly, karma feels good.

After much more schmoozing on their end, the older men finally sit me down with the infamous document, the very thing that has been the cause of all my misery. I sign my name on the dotted line, allocating my ancestor's body to remain in Havenwood indefinitely. I expected to feel lighter, or maybe different, but as I watch the ink dry, I'm still left feeling empty.

The bigwigs spend an unnecessary amount of time chatting with me about "the miracle" it is that a descendant of Martha Brant's was discovered just in time to meet the October 31st deadline. *A true miracle, indeed.* I say my goodbyes and head back out to the main lobby, grateful to finally be leaving.

"Happy Halloween!" The blonde receptionist calls to me. I pause, my hand resting on the door handle. I didn't even notice that today is Halloween. What better way to mark my last day in Havenwood?

29

Hysteria

Finn

As I help Sheriff Cotton tape up the broken window, I can't help but relate to the pieces of glass scattered on the ground. I feel shattered and fragmented just like them, knowing I've hurt the only woman I've ever loved and ruined our relationship beyond repair.

The hangover didn't humble me the way I had expected but my lack of sleep certainly had. I had stayed up until the sun began to peak over the horizon, tossing, and turning and thinking. Thinking about Courtney, thinking about how terribly I feel for hurting her, thinking about how much of an asshole I am for betraying her trust. Truly, it was a world-class pity party and I can recognize that but I don't feel capable of doing much else. I don't know why I even agreed to be here today. Haven't I done enough for Havenwood? I could have taken today off from mayoral duties and no one would have noticed.

"Finn?" Dean repeats my name, his deep brown eyes regarding me with concern.

"Sorry, sheriff. Can you repeat that?" I advert my gaze from the glass on the ground to the stout man in front of me. I do my best to fix my melancholy expression and appear I'm listening.

"I was just saying it must've been some kids from a town or two over. The place is a mess, seems like they might've been looking for something but it doesn't look like anything is missing." He repeats, I don't offer him any response aside from a curt nod which earns a sigh. The sheriff folds his thick arms above his round belly before calling out my phlegmatic behavior.

"It's that girl, innit?"

"I messed up, Dean." I shake my head despite myself and dig my thumb painfully into my opposite palm. My eyes once again gravitate to the glass on the floor before me.

"I lied to her and used her to try to save Havenwood. This town is everything to me - or at least I thought it was - until I met her. Then it all changed, *I* changed, my priorities changed but I didn't come clean when I should have. Now," I take a shallow breath.

"Now I'm afraid I've lost her for good."

A light pressure on my shoulder calls my attention to the spot. I look to my left and find the source, Sheriff Cotton's burly hand is resting on me supportively. His face is full of soft sympathy, much different from his normal unfazed demeanor. The look causes my insides to tighten, knowing I don't deserve his empathy.

"Son, I don't mean to patronize you, or date myself," he huffs out a chuckle from below his thick black mustache.

"But I watched you grow up. I saw you smile when you won the election and I saw you cry when you lost your folks but

I've never seen you so full of regret. Go, talk to her, let her see this raw and genuine side of you. She probably doesn't even know it exists."

I give the sheriff's back a firm, appreciative pat but remain silent, not trusting my own voice. The old sheriff makes a valid point, Courtney had once told me she wanted a man with all good sides. We both know now that I can't be that man but maybe she would accept my flawed sides if she knew there were sides of me that were repentant and could learn from my mistakes. I clear my throat as we both walk back to our respective vehicles.

"Have fun tonight, sheriff," I call as I open my driver's side door.

"You might get to break up a fistfight or two at Starr and Soul's concert."

"That'd certainly be my action for the week," he huffs out another laugh. "I'm just hoping this little show doesn't bring a bunch of eyeliner-wearing hooligans into town."

It's my turn to laugh, feeling slightly lighter as I get into my car. I need to find Courtney.

Courtney

By noon there was no evidence that Courtney Berrycloth had ever inhabited 2213 Queens Avenue.

All my personal belongings, including clothes, laptop, and suitcases, are sloppily stuffed into the back seat of my car. Anything too big to take with me, like furniture, is covered with a makeshift dust jacket and will be dealt with later. When? I can't exactly say, considering I never planned to come back to this place.

I make my way up to the attic, my last bowl of strawberries

in hand. I look up into the rafters to see two reflective green eyes staring back at me from a tiny cloud of black.

"Look, Olive, goodbyes are hard for me. Back home, I'm famous for my 'Irish exits' - leaving when no one is watching so you don't have to say goodbye." I explain. I chew on my bottom lip, fighting the tears that threaten to overflow my waterline. "I'm going to miss you, you little rodent."

A high-pitched squeak comes back in response, letting me know I will be missed too. The edge of my lips curl into a small smile as I sniffle.

I set the ceremonial offering of strawberries on their usual altar and walk over to the small attic window, cracking it open and allowing the cold autumn breeze to flow into the small space. Olive might have wanted to stay when the house was lived in, and there was a transplanted servant around to bring her fruit, but once I was gone, she may want to occupy someone else's attic. The thought makes me slightly jealous as I envy the make-believe people who get to enjoy the attitude of the sassy little creature but I know it's what is best for her.

Olive glides down from her perch, taking up residence beside the fruit. Her round black eyes watch me knowingly as if understanding the meaning behind my words and wishing I wouldn't go.

"Maybe I'll see you again one day." I shrug, willing myself not to cry again for the seventh time today. I silently wonder what a fruit bat's life span is and whether I can see myself returning to Havenwood in that time. Not likely.

I peel my eyes off Olive and decide to take in a final 180 of the attic. I try to take a mental picture of the A-framed roof and its rafters, the horribly dated and faded purple wallpaper. I guide my gaze to the center of the room in search of the old trunk for one last look of appreciation but to my surprise, it's not here. I walk over to the exact spot where I had left it last night, and it is simply gone.

"What the hell.." I crease my brows in disbelief. No one has been in or out of the attic, my doors are locked and have remained that way before and after my outing to Boston earlier this morning. I scavenge around the empty attic, looking for any sign that the chest had been moved or that someone else had been up here but find no evidence.

I complete a thorough search and fold my arms across my chest, huffing in disbelief. The chest had simply vanished. After standing in beguilement for numerous beats, I give up and decide that this is simply one of Havenwood's many mysteries and clearly not one that I'm meant to solve.

A harsh rapping at the front door pushes my curiosity aside. I look over at the small fuzzy bat, happily munching away at her strawberries. A bittersweet smile forming on my face.

"Goodbye, Olive." I exit the attic, shutting the thin wooden door behind me for the last time. I hesitantly descend the stairs as another round of knocking sounds. I groan to myself, acknowledging the fact that the knocks don't sound very happy and that I do not have the mental stamina to deal with whoever the hell it is. I contemplate pretending like I'm not here and simply waiting out my uninvited visitor.

"I know you're in there, Courtney. Open up!" A familiar voice demands. A voice belonging to someone I *especially* do not want to talk to right now. A lightbulb illuminates over my head as I realize that right now will likely be my only chance to enjoy the smidgen of revenge I had chosen to take earlier today.

I hold my chin up high and stride over to the door, yanking

it open. Some of my confidence deflates as I'm met with Milo's angry hazel eyes, his hands are posed fiercely on his hips and the expression on his face tells me he's pissed.

"Why did I just get a call from the Massachusetts Historical Conservancy Foundation? What letter?!" His voice remains eerily calm until he mentions the letter. I can almost see his blood boiling below his skin and that satisfies me to a degree but victory doesn't feel as rewarding as I thought it would. His anger isn't fixing any of my pain and, honestly, I feel a bit guilty for snaking him the way I did. *After all the wrong Milo had done to me, I was still left feeling guilty, Jesus Christ.* The revelation annoys me so I give him a look that should tell him all he needs to know and attempt to shut the door on him. He jams an expensive-looking leather boot between the door and its frame, effectively halting me.

"Move. Your. Foot." I demand through clenched teeth, the sight of this traitor in front of me making me more angry by the second. I shouldn't have opened the damn door, no amount of petty revenge was worth the way seeing him made me feel. *Betrayed, lied to, naive, used, stupid.*

"I don't think I will," he retorts, crossing his arms and pushing out an authoritative hip. I've dealt with tons of aggravating people in Los Angeles but none of them were able to get under my skin quite like Milo and his sass do. I once considered Milo a friend and that's why his audacity to confront me over a letter, when he should be apologizing for using me, bothers me so badly. An annoyed growl involuntarily rumbles out of me as I tighten my grip on the door, my knuckles whitening from the force. Being the stubborn ass that I know Milo is, I also know he will not leave without answers.

252

"They're going to analyze it and then have it sent right back here. You'll have the damn letter within a week and can put it on display with a plaque that says *Discovered by Courtney Berrycloth, someone we lied to, manipulated, and deceived just to benefit ourselves.*"

"Get over yourself, Courtney." Milo rolls his eyes, the action sending red-hot fury piping through my veins.

"It's not all about you. Finn and I did what we had to to protect this town, you're the one choosing to end your relationship over it."

I scoff, tempted to try to slam the door on his smug face once again.

"My relationship was built on lies! He only dated me to make it easier to get me to sign off on those papers and I'm just supposed to accept that and move on?"

Milo's dark eyebrows knit together, a look of surprise overtaking his narrow face.

"Finn didn't date you to get you to sign the papers. Not everything was a deception, Courtney. I hope you can see that before it's too late."

I feel my throat constrict, a similar feeling to attempting to dry swallow a handful of chalky pills. I glare at the historian through blurry vision as stinging tears threaten my eyes. How do I know that what he is saying right now isn't another lie? It's not like he wasn't above manipulating me.

"What about Martha's remains?" Milo shakes his head at me with indignation, changing the topic.

"I signed them over to Havenwood at the same time as the letter. You win." I shrug, my hands slapping the sides of my legs as I do. Milo is silent for a beat, seemingly without something smart to say for the first time in his entire life. His light eyes move away from mine, a less intense expression overtaking his face before he speaks again.

"It's not easy to choose between your home and your happiness." He attempts to defend Finn once again. Weirdly, I admire Milo for not trying to justify his actions, for not groveling for my forgiveness. He stands by what he did and feels vindicated in why he did it, despite my disagreement. But his undying protection of Finn is what makes me commend him; at least, he is loyal to someone.

"He chose wrong." Is all I say. That's all I need to say. Milo's defense won't fix Finn and I's relationship. Nothing will. Milo turns his head towards the driveway, eyeing my car and taking note of my belongings stuffed miscellaneously in the backseat and trunk. "I'm sorry, Courtney. Safe travels."

He turns on his heel and walks down the driveway, heading back in the direction of the historic center. I watch him go, the feelings of betrayal and anger bubbling up again inside me as I watch a person I once called a friend walk out of my life. While losing Milo doesn't hurt nearly as much as losing his brother, I will miss Milo and I's friendship and our ability to connect on an academic level. Despite my admiration of his resolve, seeing him show such little remorse for his part in all of this felt like a huge slap in the face.

I slam the front door shut like I wish I could have ten minutes ago. I lean forward, allowing my forehead to meet the cool wood of the door as another cry rips from my throat. This time not from sadness but anger as I pound my fist against the sturdy wood, silently cursing myself for even answering the door. Each second spent in Havenwood is only causing me more and more turmoil. I need to leave.

I remove myself from the front door and march into the

kitchen, avoiding looking at the table as I bent over the sink and splashed cool water over my face. The biting sensation of the cold water helped to clear my head. I know I have to say my goodbyes before fleeing town but I also know that the more people I go to see the higher the probability is that I run into *he who shall not be named*.

I make a short mental list of people I absolutely can not leave without saying goodbye to, grab my coat, and leave my house on Queens Avenue for the last time.

30

Halloween

Courtney

I make my way to Elsie's coffee house without any upsetting sightings, without many sightings at all actually. It's a breezy Halloween evening and the sky holds the threat of pouring at any minute. Because of this many of Havenwood's residents are choosing to stay indoors, avoiding any unnecessary outings until trick-or-treating hours roll around, giving me the perfect opportunity to escape town unnoticed.

Regardless of the lack of locals, I still attempt to keep a low profile. The fewer people I have to interact with the better. I'm barely keeping myself together as it is, any questioning, no matter how innocent, will send me into another sobbing fit. Then I'll have to deal with being sad *and* embarrassed.

I'm wearing my thick autumn coat, muted Dodgers hat, and overly priced sunglasses that I bought from a Sunglass Hut one summer on the Santa Monica pier. A discrete combo that makes me completely unrecognizable, or so I think. I peer around the brick corner of the Mystic Brew and, upon seeing no one lingering out front, hastily make my entrance.

The little bell attached to the door dings as I clamor inside, alerting Elsie to my arrival. A happy smile stretches onto her freckled face as she recognizes me, *so much for my disguise*.

"It's 4 p.m. and cloudy," She graciously reminds me, motioning to my glasses. I chuckle and move them up to rest on the bill of my hat, disregarding any attempt at anonymity.

"Oat milk latte?" She questions, cleaning a spent espresso shot from the basket of her portafilter. I shake my head, angling my nervous gaze towards the floor.

"No, Els. Actually-"

"You're leaving." She cuts me off. Her tone is sad but understanding, I knew Elsie would empathize with my decision.

"I'm sorry," My voice cracks as I anxiously tuck a brown strand behind my ear.

"I just can't stay here."

Elsie rounds the counter, removing her coffee-stained apron before embracing me tightly. Her tiny frame squeezes my own so tightly I feel like I might burst.

"Don't be sorry, we both know you have to heal and you can't do it here. Havenwood will always be here," she shrugs casually before offering an encouraging smile.

"You made sure of that."

I smile back and, though it hurts like hell to say goodbye to the best friend I have made during my time here, I know I'll see Elsie Murphy again someday. Our friendship is not defined by the amount of time we have known one another and it won't be defined by the amount of time we spend apart either. Elsie releases me but quickly pins me with a concerned look.

"What about Courtney's Cover to Cover? It's ready to open,

are you just going to cancel your lease?"

I had had this very same thought earlier today and had come prepared. I pull out the small key landlord Gable had given me and press it into her reluctant palm.

"It's only a six-month lease, I'll continue to pay the rent on it. But here's the key in case you need a quiet reading spot. Maybe somewhere to hide from your dad and grandma?" My comment causes her to giggle, the look of mirth swirling in her brown irises giving me the perfect mental picture to remember her by and queuing me into making my exit.

"Bye, Els."

"Bye, Courtney. Don't forget to text me!" She calls as I push the front door of the coffee house open. I give her a nod through the front window before once again lowering my shades over my eyes and heading for my second and final destination.

Visiting Agnes at her bakery is a much more dangerous venture since the front of her shop is not comprised of giant window panes like Elsie's coffee house is. I'm essentially be going in blind, running the high risk of my visit overlapping with Finn's or Milo's. But it is a risk I'm willing to take, knowing I'd hate myself forever if I skipped town without saying goodbye to the sweet old baker.

I take a deep breath and yank the honey-colored door open, pleased to see the bakery vacant aside from Agnes and the wonderful scents wafting from the ovens. Her back is turned to me as she reaches for a can from a tall cabinet.

"Figured I'd be seeing you, at least I hoped you wouldn't leave without saying goodbye." I take a few hesitant steps into her shop, savoring the gooey smell of the dough she is currently baking. Agnes turns to look at me, her eyes warm and knowing as ever.

"Milo was here before you, he told me about the.. hubble bubble." Agnes hesitates as she steps out onto the floor in front of me. I laugh through a constricted throat as a tear slips past my lids, I palm it away with the sleeve of my shirt. It's at this moment I realize just how much I'm going to miss Agnes Booker.

Her presence had become a calming and reliable one through the insecurities of moving to a new town, navigating falling in love, and even now as I made the hardest decision of my life. Agnes had made Havenwood my home from day one, making it devastating to say goodbye now.

"Oh," Agnes clicks her tongue as she pulls me into a motherly hug, the softness of her body reminding me of the best kind of hugs you get from your grandma.

"I won't bore you with details," I say lightheartedly as I squeeze her back, enjoying the way she rubs my back as we embrace, intuitively knowing I need the comfort in this moment.

"Good," She teases, pulling back from our hug but still holding me close by my arms affectionately.

"Just remember that sometimes good things fall apart so that better things can fall into their place." She looks me over, studying me with kind eyes as she tosses one of my caramel strands over my shoulder.

"Sometimes people need to understand what they've lost to appreciate what they had." I give her a doubtful smile in return. I strongly doubt anything can come of Finn and I's relationship now, let alone something better, I still appreciate her blind optimism.

"Thank you for everything, Agnes. You truly are the heart

of Havenwood and I'm going to miss you." I reach into my pocket and pull out a folded piece of paper.

"I wrote down my number." Agnes gently shoos the paper away with a wrinkled hand.

"I'm not one for phone calls, child. Just promise me you'll come back and visit me sometime." I bite my lip in hesitation but a stern look from the baker coaxes an agreement out of me.

"You drive a tough bargain, Agnes." I joke, shaking my head with a small laugh.

"You'll be back. I know things are bleak right now but I also know you and Finn have something special. Time heals all things."

I chose not to respond to her comment about Finn and I, not wanting to even contemplate what the future might look like. Instead, we hug once again and say our final goodbyes.

As I push through the honey-colored door and into the final rays of sunshine emanating from the horizon line, I leave the bakery behind for the last time. As I put more distance between us I can't help but ruminate on Agnes' words and think about how wrong she is. *Time doesn't fix all things, actions do, growth does, and forgiveness does.* And for now, and for the foreseeable future, forgiveness is not happening on my end.

The crisp evening air nips at my cheeks as I trek back to Queens Avenue and my car full of belongings, Havenwood's way of biding me farewell. The sun has just set, plunging the world into darkness and gearing up for a particularly cold Halloween night. As I make my way across town I start to notice people and faces I don't recognize, the sight of them baffling me. I had stayed in Havenwood for months and had only seen a select few dozen rotations of locals and these people were not them.

As I look further up the cobblestone road I see groups and clusters of strangers, validating my theory that these aren't locals and sending me further into confusion. Most of them appear to be mid to early twenties with dyed hair, piercings, and thick lines of eyeliner smeared across their waterlines. Some are positioned against trees, others texting and some are smoking things that don't smell like cigarettes. Did I accidentally stumble into a My Chemical Romance audition? What are they all doing here?

"What the hell.." I mutter under my breath as I sidestep to avoid a particularly goth couple gagging on one another's tongues in the middle of my path. My long list of questions is quickly answered as I approach the park.

A makeshift stage has been assembled in the middle of the green grass, roaming stage lights help to illuminate the thickening sea of black clothes and nose rings that swarm in front of it. I put two and two together as I spot a pair of women dressed in skimpy devil costumes, tonight was Halloween and therefore the night of Soul and Starr's concert. To my dismay, it seems that Starr wasn't lying when she bragged about drawing a crowd, a pang of jealousy courses through me as I silently curse her success.

A group of five takes the stage and announces their band name over the blaring speakers, sending the crowd into an animated wave of cheers. Obnoxiously loud metal music follows as the openers begin their shitty set, the frenzy of the crowd only intensifying when they do. The motion of bodies jumping up and down temporarily prohibits my ability to navigate through the crowd that I have somehow found myself in the middle of. I do my best to persist, passing out *excuse me*'s in abundance as I shove through.

"Courtney!" A familiar voice cuts through the bustle of the music and the crowd. I turn around and instantly regret it when I see a handsome, pale face staring back at me from a few feet away.

I had done a great job at remaining low-key and avoiding Finn all day but in this crowd of black my light tan sweater stood out severely, making me all too easy to spot. At the sight of him, I feel the tears begin to summon themselves back to the surface, I turn away quickly and double my efforts to escape. *I can't talk to him, I just can't.* I repeat to myself as I shove past person after person, ignoring Finn as he continues to desperately call my name, somehow managing to keep pace with me.

I want to completely forget he exists, I want to pretend that Finn Abernathy was never real, just an amazing dream, and therefore his betrayal wouldn't been real either. But if I speak to him now it will only prove that he is real and he did hurt me and that will solidify the painful inferno blazing inside of me. Making it hard, immovable, and permanent like lava that has cooled over.

Just as I escape the sweaty crowd and the frigid air dances up my middle, signaling my freedom, a hand wraps around my bicep. Before I know it I'm being whipped around, forced to face Finn's blue eyes that are much icier than the night's breeze.

"Courtney, please." He begs, holding me to him. The desperation in his voice forces me to swallow all the colorful words that just died on my tongue. Before I can think of more to spew at him, he speaks again, this time much more gently.

"I messed up, baby. Very badly. I sent those emails, I plotted to get you here and I was dishonest. I wasn't fully truthful with you but I *never* meant to hurt you." He rambles as he attempts to find the right words. I stand there, stone-faced but listening. I'm not entirely sure why I do, maybe I want an explanation? Maybe I'm a masochist? Maybe I truly want to believe him when he says he never meant to hurt me...

Just as he seems decided on what he wants to convey to me in these stolen moments Starr and Soul come onto the stage and the crowd screams in adoration. The noise drowning out Finn's attempt to explain himself.

"HELLO, HAVENWOOD. LET'S PARTY!" Starr calls out, throwing up a *rock-on* hand signal, an action quickly mimicked by the overly hyper crowd. The two waste no time in beginning their concert, loud flurries of electric guitar bombard the speakers once again.

Finn keeps his attention on me, ignoring the loud music and enamored crowd behind him as he raises his voice to be heard over it all.

"When I emailed Agnes' rental house to Courtney Berrycloth I was hoping to lure a lonely, old woman to Havenwood and convince her to help me save my hometown and what I *thought* was my only connection to my parents. But instead, *you* came and lured *me* in, not only with your beauty and attitude but with your ambition and heart. I never, in a million years, could have expected you to be *you*. And I never expected to fall in love with you as hard and as fast as I did."

My breath catches in my throat. Hot tears now streaming down my cheeks as I stare into Finn's teary eyes, trying to keep my expression unreadable and failing miserably. Finn confessing his love for me was not something I was prepared to hear tonight and is definitely not something I wanted to hear, considering I was in love with him too.

"And by the time I realized how I felt about you, I had gotten myself too deep to be able to tell you the truth without ruining what we had between us or without hurting you but I still planned to tell you when the time was right because you deserve the truth. You deserve a relationship that isn't built on lies or deception, you deserve everything, Courtney. I was scared to lose Havenwood because I thought that was my last connection to my parents but I realize the love I have for you connects me to them in a way that doesn't need a physical location to be real or tangible. Loving you connects me to them, it connects me to you and it connects me to the parts of myself that I don't want to admit exist. But being with you makes me want to fix those sides, to be a better man for you."

I feel my heart break for the second time. This time not because of Finn but for him and the pain he so obviously carries from the loss of his parents. He releases his grip on my biceps and slides his hands down my arms, interlacing our fingers. The warmth of his palms against mine feels like solace as I begin to piece together the bigger picture.

"You once said all my sides were good. Now that we both see that that's not true, can you accept me and those sides that are learning to be better?"

"I-." The crowd goes wild over some particularly dark lyrics sung by Starr, causing me to look up at her on the stage.

A feeling of deeply seeded anger rises in me at the sight of her, causing me to realize that maybe not all of *my* sides are as perfect as I had initially thought. If I was feeling such intense jealousy over Finn's ex-hookup then I clearly need to work on bettering myself as well before even considering taking on a second chance with Finn. And, unfortunately, I know that growth couldn't happen here in Havenwood. I need space, a neutral environment, to sort out my feelings and try to be better.

I want to voice this revelation to Finn, to tell him that we need time apart to replace what was once good with something great. But I'm too emotional, far too deep in my own thoughts and feelings to communicate anything rationally. I've never felt so overstimulated in my life as I do at this moment. I desperately want to reach out and touch the stubble dusting his cheeks or force him to hold me safely in his strong arms but I don't allow myself to do so. I don't want my actions to represent an answer that I'm not ready to give yet.

I pull my hands from his and turn from him. I do my best to ignore the look of disappointed agony on his face as I run away. I literally run, my boots kicking up stray gravel from the cobblestone road.

I run all the way back to my car and this time Finn doesn't chase me. He doesn't call after me. He lets me go.

Upon reaching the house I immediately unlock my car, hop in, and throw it into drive, not even bothering with my seat belt until Havenwood is long gone from my rearview mirror. I drive away from my friends, from Olive, from my ancestor, and from the man I love. I drive back to Los Angeles where I can think clearly.

31

Repentance

Three Months Later
Finn

I stroll through downtown Havenwood, USA, bundled in my many layers, I can barely feel the winter frost that wraps our corner of the troposphere this time of year. As I walk along the slick new sidewalk that surrounds the park I notice a family playing in the newly fallen snow. A mom and a young daughter frolicking about, attempting to catch the small snowflakes that fall lazily from the sky while the dad makes snow angels with their older daughter. All four of them wave excitedly with mitten-clad hands as I pass by. I recognize them as the Cardenas family, recent transplants from California. I return their wave, a content smile on my face as I witness a new wave of families enjoying the many gifts Havenwood has to offer. But something is missing from my smile, it's been missing for a while.

Over these last few winter months, we've seen a considerable swell not only in tourism but also in transplants, along with dozens more parties interested in calling Havenwood home. Admittedly, the boost has nothing to do with Milo and I's scheming. Milo had put Martha's remains on display only days after Courtney left and, despite everything we sacrificed to keep the remains in Havenwood, hardly any tourists showed the slightest interest. It was a devastating blow that further proved the notion that there truly is no victory when lying is required to win. A sentiment I know all too well.

Havenwood had started to feel lost entirely. Many towns-folk saw the lackluster effect that our plan had had and began to take the final steps towards leaving Havenwood behind and I truly couldn't blame them. I had run out of motivational words and well-intentioned promises to keep them here, I was fully prepared to let them go. However, at what felt like the final hour, people started rolling in in flocks.

At first, I had no idea what had caused the uptick in the public's interest in Havenwood until Elsie interrupted my morning sulk over my oat milk latte, placing a small book into my hands. *Havenwood: New England's Nonpareil,* Courtney had published her guidebook. I scoffed out a laugh of disbelief and pleasure as I shifted my gaze between the barista and the book.

"She did it!" I had said, excitement and pride swimming inside my chest.

"She did it."

Courtney truly had saved Havenwood, not by signing over Martha's remains as we had expected, but instead by releasing her guidebook that had convinced dozens of younger people and families to give our small town a chance. The bump in younger people moving here helped not only our economy and relatability but also helped to balance out the population's age median. Courtney was the savior I knew she'd be just not in the way I'd expected, even if she'd never know it, I was eternally grateful for her and silently thanked her each time I said hello to a new face.

Six months ago I would've been content with our town's progress, thrilled even. Havenwood was thriving, I was just reelected, and the town was even on an uphill trend financially. Havenwood was saved, that was my goal all along. *Right? Then why did I feel so empty?* I already knew the answer.

I look down at my gloved palm as I walk on, remembering what her hand felt like in mine, the electric current that passed between us anytime our skin touched. I exhale deeply as I reminisce on the way she would cuddle her cheek into my palm affectionately, I want to feel her again. I had spent the last three months wallowing in self-pity and I'm tired of it, I'm ready to take action. I'm ready to be a man that is worthy of Courtney Berrycloth.

As I continue my walk I pass by the newly erected memorial that I had commissioned in honor of Martha Berrycloth-Brant. A silhouette standing beside the memorial catches my eye, pausing me midstep. The person's back is turned to me as they admire the marble obelisk and its matching placard that quotes Martha's famous letter, exonerating her of any wrongdoing. I can't see the admirer's face or discern who they are due to their layers of winter clothing so I assume they are a tourist. Despite my somber mood I decide to do my mayoral duty and say hello, maybe provide them some insight into Martha's story, and formally welcome them to Havenwood.

I take a few steps closer to the figure, as I do the fresh ice crunches below my boots. The noise startles the onlooker, causing them to whip around to face me. Deep chocolate eyes meet mine, and a surprised, tan face contrasts the white snow around her. Her hair is a few shades lighter since the last time I had seen her but there is no mistaking her.

"Courtney?"

Courtney

One week earlier

The second I had arrived in Los Angeles I put my guidebook in front of every publisher that gave me the chance. I wanted to put the guidebook in qualified hands and wash my own of all things Havenwood. I needed a fresh slate and a clear head so that I could think clearly about my next decisions, about myself and figure out what I really wanted. With a large publishing house handling the publication of the guidebook, I was free to do all those things.

In the meantime, I went back to screenwriting. The strike had ended days after I arrived back in California, something about the timing of it all seemed like too much of a coincidence, and with my newfound perspective on the supernatural, I knew I probably had a certain ancestor to thank.

I tried therapy for the first time and loved it, I worked on some big TV shows and a couple of movies but I didn't stop writing for myself. In fact, I was able to complete the first draft of my manuscript during my time of deliberation. I had written a chick-lit book about a resilient witch named Martha and her sassy black cat, Olive, who was able to find her own happily ever after despite many obstacles and a particularly brutal curse. I wanted to give Martha the happy ending she deserved in this life and through my writing I had done just that.

I thought back to my own *almost* happily ever after often in therapy, late at night when I stared up at my popcorn ceiling when I reached out in my sleep searching for Finn's warmth. Each time I was filled with regret.

Now, having been a few months removed from the situation and through several hours of therapy, I could see things a bit clearer. I know I should've communicated with Finn much more maturely on Halloween night, I should've told him I needed space to think. I should've told him I understood him but needed time to understand myself, time to improve myself to be the perfect person I thought I was. Instead, I ran and this time Finn didn't chase me. I hadn't had a single text or call from him since that night and I worried that I'd lost him forever.

"C'mon! We need to hurry up and get ready or we'll be late!" Kashvi urges me as I fish my keys from my purse. I chuckle at her impatience as I insert my key into the lock of my apartment door.

I had agreed to go out for the first time since being back in L.A. and only after incessant groveling and guilt-tripping from Kashvi on an almost professional level. My favorite coworker knew I had returned home in a slump, I told her about everything that had transpired in Massachusetts and she had done her best to keep me company and support me any way she could. I'm forever grateful for her.

Tonight is her twenty-seventh birthday and despite not feeling like partying I know I'd be a terrible friend if I missed it.

"I only turn 21 once!" Kashvi cheekily jokes as she pushes into my apartment before me. Her smile drops along with her jaw as she enters, her almost black irises landing on me in surprise.

"Oh em eff gee, Courtney! Who did this to your place?!" I feel my heart sink to my ass, *what's wrong with my apartment?! Had someone broken in and trashed it looking for valuables?* I pin her with a look of concern as I follow her in, taking in the sight of my apartment.

Every inch of every surface is covered with flowers. Roses, daisies, carnations, lilies, orchids, tulips, azaleas, marigolds. The entire 700-square-foot unit smells like a fresh, lush garden and is as colorful as the night sky on the fourth of July.

"Oh my god.." I breathe, taking in the sight in bewilderment.

"The mayor!" Kashvi exclaims excitedly, walking over to me, a small white card in her hand. I try to snatch it from her but she moves her hand away deftly, reading the scrawled message out loud.

"I was so caught up in trying to explain myself and justify my actions that I never told you what I truly needed to say. I am so sorry. Though words or flowers will never be enough I hope it's a start. AWE!" Kashvi exclaims, stomping her heels as she gushes over Finn's note. "You have to go get him, girl! Do it or I will." She teases, resting a perfectly manicured hand on her hip. I'm finally able to snatch the card from her and I reread the note for myself, the scent of florals dizzying me as I do. I can't help but attempt to hold back a smile as the decision I've been contemplating for days now finally solidifies inside of me.

"Let's get ready," I remind her, navigating around the flowers as I head for my closet.

"You're not hopping on a plane right this INSTANT?!" Kashvi calls after me in confusion. I just giggle as I throw my closet doors open, planning my outfit for dinner.

"No way, we have dinner plans. I can't miss my best friend's 21st birthday!" I shoot her a smirk. A small grin crawls onto Kashvi's plum-colored lips.

"Courtney's back!" She declares, giving me an approving look.

* * *

Our Uber driver drops us right out front of the golden doors of the high-end restaurant Kashvi had selected for her birthday dinner. The restaurant is located in WeHo, or West Hollywood as the tourists refer to it, so there were often celebrities and big names dining here. Reservations proved nearly impossible to get but somehow I had been able to snag them a few weeks ago just by mentioning my literary agent's name. If that isn't Hollywood politics I didn't know what is.

We are shown to our table by an extremely sterile yet professional waiter. Kashvi had insisted on being "fashionably late" as she called it, so we were the last two to arrive at our table of seven. We are greeted with excited applause from the other five guests as Kashvi steps into their view, we say our hello's and hug each attendee, most of which are coworkers we both know.

As we sit down and scan the cocktail menu I become aware of a blond demon watching me from a few tables away. I almost freeze up entirely when I see him approaching from the corner of my eye, he descends upon me swiftly giving me no time to prepare.

"Courtney," the voice is all too familiar as I lift my gaze to make eye contact with a gleaming Carter.

"Carter." I greet curtly, a tight-lipped smile is the best I can manage despite the work I'd done in therapy to forgive the wannabe Ken doll.

"Crazy to see you here, I heard your guidebook did really well and now you're signing with a big-name agent to release a fiction book? That's incredible, you're gonna be - like - famous." He finishes his sentence with a small, astonished chuckle. He's clearly done his research on me and now that I'm more renowned I'm magically deemed worthy of his attention once again.

"Yeah," I confirm, dropping my eyes back down to the list of alcoholic beverages before me.

"I heard the movie you starred in flopped. 18% on Rotten Tomatoes, right?" I inhale through my teeth, offering him a look of faux sympathy. He wets his lips, attempting to let my comment roll off his back.

"I'm glad you're back in town, I was thinking about you a lot while you were gone. I was thinking a lot about us. I'd love to buy you dinner sometime, we can reminisce on old times." He gives me a flirtatious wink, running a hand through his blond mane. At this point, Kashvi has tuned into the conversation and I can see the fire in her hitting a raging point.

"Who do you think-" I gently place a hand on top of Kashvi's, alerting my volatile friend that I have this situation handled. Although I appreciate her fierce defense of me, we're in a nice restaurant, and Kashvi likes to get heated very fast. Besides, I'd rather hit Carter where it really hurts, *his ego*. She slumps back in her chair, nostrils flaring as she watches the scene play out.

"Carter," I lean in closer to him, lowering my voice. He leans in closer to me, that arrogant grin still on his face.

"I can't date a *nobody*." I watch that smug smile melt off

his lips as I turn his own words against him. Red flusters his cheeks as he searches for something to say in response to save face.

"BOOM. OWNED!" Kashvi cries out in her obnoxiously perfect way, laughing mockingly. Though the rest of the table didn't hear Carter and I's conversation they still break out in a wave of mocking "*ooh's*", adding to Carter's embarrassment. He observes them all with blazing eyes then aims his red-hot gaze directly at me.

"You are an entitled and ornery little bitch with an attitude problem. No one is going to want you." His voice is uneven and low as he speaks through clenched teeth, his attempt at keeping a low profile as he insults me. I simply shrug, finally deciding on a lemon drop martini as I say.

"Carter? Go fuck yourself."

He gives me one more indignant huff before storming off, not to his table but out of the restaurant completely, leaving the group of men he was with confused. Kashvi grabs my arm and I turn to face her, a prideful grin evident on her round face.

"You are fucking phenomenal!" She belts out one of her hearty high-pitched laughs and pulls me close to her in a tight embrace. I return her hug, giggling in shock at myself and my ability to handle that situation.

Six months ago I would've caved and given Carter a second chance, I would've believed him when he told me no one would want me but I know better now. I know a handsome mayor back in Massachusetts who has shown me that no man is perfect but neither am I and that is okay—a man whom I'd been denying myself for far too long.

The rest of Kashvi's birthday dinner goes amazing. We

drink creatively crafted drinks and eat deliciously Instagramable food until we feel like we're going to burst. We catch up with our incredible coworkers, reminiscing on good times and listening to their plans for the future. And when it comes time to leave we all say our goodbyes and get into separate Ubers and Lifts, in true Los Angeles fashion.

Before I hop into my Uber, Kashvi pulls me into another tight hug, the alcohol she consumed making her even more affectionate than usual. I laugh and hug her back, enjoying the way her curly hair tickles my nose as I hold my friend close.

"I'll miss you," her words are muffled against my shoulder but I still make them out.

"Miss me?" I question, scrunching my brow at her in confusion. She nods, pulling back from our embrace.

"I know you'll be heading back to Havenwood soon, if not tonight." She chuckles, her valley girl accent extra strong thanks to that last mojito.

"You belong there, Coco. I'll come visit you. I heard really great things about it in this guidebook I read." She gives me a bittersweet smile. It's totally like Kashvi to know my next move before I've even thought of it myself. I laugh and hold her to me once again, her height of 5-foot-nothing making it convenient for me to rest my chin on top of her head. *Do I belong in Havenwood?*

"I know a single apothecarian who you'd love."

"I only date Sikhs," she teases, giving me a final squeeze.

"But for real, give him my number." She blows me a kiss before I duck inside my Uber. I wave to her as I drive down the street back to my apartment. I locate my phone from deep inside my handbag, my slightly blurry vision making the task more difficult than necessary but I manage to scroll through my contacts. Selecting the appropriate one, I hold the phone up to my ear.

"Hey Elsie, I need a favor."

32

Welcome Back

Courtney

I anxiously readjust my stance, tamping down the ice below my boots and staring back at the man I have simultaneously loved and hated through tiny dancing flurries. My mind races a million miles an hour and when the dust settles seconds later I'm left with the realization that Kashvi was wrong about me, I don't belong in Havenwood. I belong wherever Finn Abernathy is and that answer rings out like truth in my ears. Seeing him again reaffirms every feeling I have for him and sends my heart into a tailspin, my tongue practically ties itself as I decide what to say to him.

"Courtney?" His icy blues are wide as I watch his entire body lock up at the sight of me. *Is that a bad thing? Did I come in vain?* I take a beat to calm my landsliding thoughts, running through deep breathing exercises I learned in therapy.

I offer a timid smile as my response. I had had dreams and nightmares about this exact moment, about the day I would see Finn again. In my dreams, he had been happy to see me and in my nightmares had rejected me completely, still scathed from me running away on Halloween night. This time it's real and I'm terrified, knowing I can't wake up if I don't like his response.

"It's great," I offer, testing my voice. I tick my head behind me at the four-foot obelisk of marble.

"The memorial for Martha, it's beautiful." We both take a few subconscious steps closer to one another. We can try to argue that it's to hear one another better but we both know it's the magnetic pole between us, each of our magnets singing to one another, pulling us to each other.

"I.." He shakes his head slowly in disbelief, keeping his sights on me as if afraid that I'm a mirage that will disappear if he dares to blink.

"I never thought I'd see you again. At least not here in Havenwood." He adds on.

"What does that mean?" I ask, still unable to fully gauge his reaction.

He reaches into the left pocket of his trench coat and retrieves a rectangular slip of paper, a boarding pass. The sight of the physical boarding pass causes me to giggle, proof that the mayor is as stuck in his old-fashioned ways as ever. He extends the flimsy piece of paper towards me and I accept it, making extra sure I don't accidentally brush his fingers with my own as I do.

I look over the slip, a grin creeping onto my face as I read the flight details.

"Logan International to LAX. For tomorrow." I laugh despite myself, covering my persistent smile with a gloved hand.

"You were coming to see me?"

"I had to make sure my flowers got delivered." He jokes

softly. Finn looks like he might be on the verge of tears, his nerves are as evident as mine.

"I don't know where we stand," he begins, his expressively beautiful eyes pouring his thoughts and feelings straight into mine. I can feel the raw emotion behind them, I see his desire to reach out and hold me, and the same feelings are reflected just below my own surface.

"What I do know is that these past few months without you have made me realize that I will do everything and anything I can to win you back because without you I'm incomplete." My eyes fill as he voices every sentiment I've felt since departing from Havenwood and spending those lonely and reflective three months in LA.

He takes a step into me, his large hand cupping my frigid cheek. Finn's face is so close to mine as I reach up and trace his strong features—the high bridge of his nose, the sharp cliffs of his cheekbones, his full lips. I nuzzle into the warmth of his palm, his touch feeling so right. It feels perfect.

"Havenwood might hold my past but you are my future and I promise to prioritize you, like I should have from the beginning, until forever." I barely hold back my hot tears as my head swims in his sweet, unadulterated words.

"Forever is a long time, I'm sure I can learn to forgive you by then." My voice trembles as I form the words through my constricted throat. I had forgiven Finn weeks ago—before I had even crossed Havenwood's border. But now I had sufficiently worked through my own traumas and unrealistic standards and nothing can keep me from being with Mayor Finn Abernathy. Not even myself.

"I will grovel at your feet every day until you do." With that promise he draws my face close and presses his lips to mine, the familiarity of his mouth welcoming me back as if I'd never left. I'd almost forgotten how perfectly his bottom lip fit between mine, the subtle mintiness on his tongue, his mustache brushing against my skin, all the things I'd fantasized about experiencing once again.

I wrap my arms around his neck, pulling him in closer as I tip my head back, deepening our kiss. I let out a quiet moan as Finn grips me tighter, my thoughts dipping out of innocence as I rack my brain trying to think of the closest possible spot I can get him naked.

My less-than-pure thoughts are interrupted by a deep voice clearing their throat. Finn and I peel apart, both of us rosey-cheeked from the embarrassment of getting so carried away in public. I look over and see that the person who has caught us is Milo.

He stands a few feet from us, looking stoic in his long, lavender winter coat and extremely fashionable boots. His long, handsome face is devoid of any telltale expression that might cue me into how he is feeling about seeing me again.

"You're back." Is all he says, his voice just as inexpressive as his body language. I offer him a curt nod. Through my healing journey, I'd learned to forgive Milo for his role in my deception. Though, unlike Finn, Milo never asked for my forgiveness.

Milo takes two big steps forward, closing the distance between us. His face finally conveys a glimpse of readable emotion as he wraps his long arms over my shoulders. I pause for a beat in confusion, had Milo *missed* me? I don't stop to question him now, instead, I wrap my arms around his slim middle, accepting his silent apology.

"Good," Milo smiles his bright, white smile, reverting to his normal eccentric character.

"The redhead said we had somewhere to be right about now." He looks to his brother who in turn looks to me in confusion.

"We do?" Finn raises a raven eyebrow at me. I offer him a playful grin and take his hand in mine, grabbing Milo's with my other freehand.

"Let's go, boys," I instruct guiding them in the proper direction down the frozen cobblestone streets, extremely eager to show them the surprise I have in store.

Finn and I use the short walk as an opportunity to catch up on the last couple of months and what we have missed in each other's lives, each of us taking turns talking and listening. Our topics range from the tourism boom in Havenwood, the new transplant population, signing my book deal, Agnes having to hire an entire crew to help her manage the new demand for her pastries, and even my encounter with Mr. Sweatpants. Milo was extremely proud of me for my witty comebacks.

Milo only chimes into the conversation occasionally when he feels Finn like has forgotten any details or to fill me in on his recent dating conquests. I laugh as we go, feeling whole again with the two of them at my side.

As we near our destination, I squeeze Finn's hand a little tighter, working up the courage to talk about what is coming next for me.

"I think I'm going to make my presence in Havenwood a little more.. permanent."

Before he can respond, the three of us round the corner of the red brick building and are greeted by a small group crowding outside of *Courtney's Cover to Cover*. Finn's eyes widen as his jaw falls limp, he stares at the new professional sign hanging over the shop as he trips over his words.

"What-? How-? What is this?" He sputters out a disbelieving laugh, beaming down at me with a happily confused expression on his handsome face.

"*This* is Cover to Cover's grand opening." I admire the crowd of familiar faces who have shown up to support me. From where I stand I can spot Landlord Gable and his wife, Fred, Cathleen, Micah, and Agnes. I'm so eternally grateful for each of them being here today.

"I called in a favor," I inform Finn as I drag him to the front of the crowd with me. The doors to the shop are at our backs as I prepare to address the group. Finn stands dutifully beside me, still in a state of shock but supportive nonetheless. He's still grinning down at me as prideful admiration reflects in his icy eyes.

A familiar freckled face breaks through the crowd, making a B line for me. Elsie throws her arms around me, almost toppling us over as she pounces. I can't help but laugh and squeeze her back as we rock together in a tight embrace, I had missed my barista dearly.

"Welcome home," she greets, pushing a cool piece of metal into my palm. The key to my bookstore.

"We have A LOT to catch up on." She raises her eyebrows to emphasize her point but finishes with a smile, letting me know the gossip can wait.

"We sure do," I giggle, thanking her before she rejoins the small sea of people. I take a deep breath, knowing now is the time to make my grand opening speech. With Finn's hand in my own and the supportive faces in the crowd, I know I've got this.

"Thank you all for being here and thank you, Elsie, for

making this possible. When I decided to rent this space and turn it into the bookstore of my dreams I knew its grand opening had to be just as perfect as it was. I wanted to open the store when the time was just right and I could be surrounded by family and friends.

"It took traveling to California and back to realize that every face I see in front of me right now has become my best friend and honorary family over the past six months. And now, that the timing is in fact just right, it's my pleasure to welcome you all to Courtney's Cover to Cover!"

I insert the key into the door, disengaging the lock and allowing the cheering mob to enter my perfectly renovated shop. The gorgeous shades of moody green and accents of gold dazzle them all, a complete turnaround from the dusty brown color that used to fill the space before. I notice Finn peeking in, attempting to catch a glimpse over the heads of the crowd.

"Go," I encourage, shooing him inside.

"Go see it!"

"I'll be right back," he promises excitedly, kissing the top of my hand and following the others inside. I wait by the front door, greeting new and familiar faces alike and accepting congratulations when a tight grip on my bicep forces me to turn.

Standing in the doorway is a familiar rain cloud with juniper green eyes bearing into me, Starr. *Oh no*, I internally groan, I'm not prepared to deal with a confrontation on a day that is supposed to be filled with positivity and I'm really not prepared for *this* confrontation in particular.

"Welcome back, Hollywood." Her words seem almost genuine.

I stare at the pale woman in disbelief, completely stunned into silence. I watch as part of Starr's hard outer shell melts away in front of me, revealing a small portion of her soft center. She must sense my hesitation because she exhales through her nose, her green eyes focusing anywhere but on me.

"He was completely ruined when you left." Her gaze tracks through the open doors and lands on Finn. I follow her line of sight, watching the mayor interact diligently with his townspeople. The thought of Finn being hurt and alone sends a lightning bolt of guilt through me, knowing I was the cause.

"I can see how much you mean to him, Courtney. I will always *always* wish that was me, there's no point in lying about that but he loves you and I want him to be happy. Even if it's not with me." She blinks away forming tears before they can begin to threaten her thick eyeliner.

"And it seems like you're not going anywhere anytime soon," Starr motions to the newly installed sign above the shop.

"So, truce?"

She extends a hand tipped with black nail polish. I ignore it and instead pull her into a hug. I can see how much Finn means to her and even though I'm never going to give him up - and I mean *ever* - there is comfort in knowing that there is someone else who cares about him as much as I do. She stands as stiff as a corpse under my embrace but awkwardly pats my back.

"You know, Starr, you're not so bad. Almost sweet even."

"Don't go around telling people that," she separates herself from me by pushing gently on my shoulder.

"It's bad for my punk rock image." And for the first time ever, I see Starr smile. Her canines are filed into sharp fangs and are almost as white as her skin but it is still a pleasant look on her.

"See you, Hollywood." She gives me a nod before walking off into the weather. Only now do I notice that she is wearing ripped jeans in thirty-five-degree weather, causing me to chuckle at her dedication.

"Ready to go in?" A silky voice calls from behind me, enjoyable little goosebumps rising all over my skin in response. I turn and find Finn leaning against the open doorway, looking as delicious as humanly possible. Once again I find myself wishing we were alone. I look past him momentarily at all the happy faces inside the store, the sight of people picking books off the shelves and admiring the decor earning me a warm feeling of pride.

"Before we do I need to tell you something," I say, taking a few steps into Finn so that we are close enough for our breaths to mingle, practically breathing in the same air. I look up at his soft face as he gently swipes a stray strand from my forehead.

"Anything."

"You once told me that I amazed you because I saw potential in a beat-up, old flower shop in a dying town. You asked me if I could do the same for a person and at the time I didn't know what you meant but I do now.

"After my breakup with Carter, I convinced myself that I could only love someone who was 'perfect', a man with no flaws and all good sides. But then I met you and I realized you're perfect because of your flaws. Finn, I love you."

A smile slowly spread across his face and before I knew it I was being lifted in the air and spun in a short circle before my boots touched the ground again. Laughter flies out of me as

Finn's lips crash onto mine, I run my hands into his raven hair and savor this moment the best I can, wanting to remember it forever.

"Come on," he coaxes as he pulls back from our kiss.

"Let's go enjoy this opening and celebrate you."

"I can think of a couple of ways we can celebrate later." I wink at him as he holds the shop door open for me, the two of us giggling as we enter, hand in hand. I turn to comment Finn when a familiar face in the crowd catches my eye.

A woman in a gray dress stands across the room, her caramel brown hair is topped with a linen cap and her forest green eyes are watching me. A proud smile is stretched across her plump lips as she offers me a slight bow of her head, I stare at her for a beat, confused as to how no one else has noticed her presence. I return her nod just as Finn turns to see what I'm staring at but the woman is gone. Vanished into thin air.

I smile at the spot where Martha had just stood, satisfied in knowing that I'm not the only Berrycloth woman who was able to rewrite her story. Standing here now with the man I love, surrounded by my friends and my future shining brightly ahead of me is a gift I never could have predicted; it is more beautiful and fulfilling than anything I could have written myself.

This was my piece of paradise and it was right here in Havenwood, USA.

THE END

Epilogue

Finn

Courtney, Agnes, Milo, Micah, Elsie, and I sit around Agnes' old dining table swapping scary stories and enjoying a wonderful Halloween dinner of cabbage soup, affectionately nicknamed "witches brew". The six of us were beginning to wrap up our meal, knowing that with sunset approaching we'd have little trick-or-treaters at our door within the hour. The table erupts into laughter over one of Milo's infamous dirty jokes, earning him a scowl from Agnes, who is attempting to stifle her own laughter.

"How is it being the owner of the coffee house, Els?" Courtney changes the conversation, spooning another forkful of Agnes' famous pumpkin pie. Elsie's grandmother had passed away while Courtney was in California nine months ago, leaving Elsie and her dad in a vicious court battle over ownership of the family business. Elsie earned soul ownership last week when she was able to prove through CCTV footage that she had been running the business all by herself since she was fourteen. Once the coffee house was officially in her name Elsie rebranded, changing the shop's name to Cove Cup Coffee and officially adding oat milk chai lattes to the menu in honor of her best friend.

"It's amazing," Elsie admits, relief washing over her soft features.

"My dad never cared about the coffee house, having his hand out of the pot really just makes it easier to run the business efficiently. But I can barely supply enough oat milk to these hipsters you brought from California!" The barista jokes, shooting Courtney a playful glare as she cuts her own slice of pie.

"Well get ready for one more," Courtney giggles, the dazzling sound like music to my ears.

"Because my girlfriend Kashvi is coming to visit next week and she is the *biggest* oat milk coffee connoisseur you will ever meet."

"Is she hot?" Micah questions through a mouthful of pie.

"Oh boy." Elsie rolls her eyes, earning her a laugh from Milo.

"Courtney, tell your hot, gay, California friends to come visit every once in a while," Milo complains, folding his arms across his chest in a faux pout.

"I'll work on that," Courtney answers noncommittally. I nervously palm the little box hidden in my pants pocket.

"Hey Courtney, can I take you for a walk before the trick-or-treaters arrive?" I keep my voice as level as possible so as to not cue her into my nervousness. She smiles at me, tucking a strand of caramel behind her ear.

"Yeah sounds fun, let me just help clear these plates-"

"I've got it!" Agnes and Elsie both declare in unison, earning them each a look from me.

"Go on, darling." Agnes encourages.

"We've got this," Micah reassures, nodding his head too many times.

"Go on, now." Milo waves her off fervently. Leave it to my family to make the biggest, most awkward scene before I propose to the girl of my dreams.

"Um. Alright," Courtney creases her brow, looking to me for an answer to everyone's weird behavior but I keep my face blank as I extend my hand for her to take. Once she does we head out the door.

We walk together in comfortable silence, huddled close together to combat the brisk October air. I lead as we stray from the pavement and climb a small, grassy hill to our final destination.

"What a beautiful sunset," Courtney remarks as we ascend the hill, her warm chocolate eyes trained on the horizon. I stand behind her, pressing my front to her back and sharing my warmth as I wrap my arms around her protectively. I admire the view too, noting the passionate oranges and vibrant yellows that make up this particular sunset. The autumn leaves that sprinkle the grass below us must have taken inspiration from the same hues.

"I love our life." Courtney hums as she pulls me in closer to her. Courtney's Cover To Cover is doing well but her books are doing even better, I'm enjoying my mayoral duties more than ever now that I have a healthy town to run and we spend each free moment surrounded by our closest friends.

"I do too, baby," I answer honestly, kissing the top of her head.

"Which is why I was thinking.." I feel my heart begin to drum loudly against my rib cage, Courtney must feel it too because she turns to check on me. I take the opportunity and fish the dainty ring box from my pocket and bend at the knee. Her hand flies automatically to her mouth, covering her dropped jaw.

"Courtney Berrycloth, would you do me the honor of-?"

"Yes!"

Before I can even finish the iconic line we are both down on the ground, surrounded by the fiery leaves, giggling and exchanging excited kisses. I can tell by the look on Courtney's beautiful face that she wants this just as much as I do, the sentiment warms from the inside out as we continue to drown one another in affection.

"Can I show you the ring now?" I chuckle, pulling it from its snug cushion inside the box and gliding it onto Courtney's delicate finger. She admires the thin gold band and delicate cushion-shaped diamond.

"Wow, Finn, it's perfect." She remarks in awe, watching as the stone collects the bright orange rays of the setting sun.

"It was my mother's," I smile at her reminiscently. That ring was one of the only items that had survived the fire that took my parent's lives and I had always wondered if there was a reason why. Now I knew it was destined for Courtney.

"Now it's a family heirloom." She spares me a look of admiration before once again pinning me to the grass and attacking me with kisses.

Visions of Courtney as a beautiful autumn bride run rampant in my head as we eagerly jog side by side back to the house on Queens Avenue. Courtney had insisted on living in Agnes' rental even though I owned my own house, citing that there were too many memories there she didn't want to lose and I agreed. As soon as we are within the door frame Courtney's mouth is on mine and we are busy ripping at each other's clothes. A distant squeak from Olive welcomes us home as I chase Courtney up the stairs.

Milo, Agnes, Micah, and Elsie will have to manage passing out candy alone this year because Courtney and I will be confined to her bedroom, celebrating our engagement.